FERRY TAILS

A Whidbey Island Thriller

Ted Mulcahey

For Patte and Emma

One

My name is Roger Wilkie. Whidbey Island, my home for less than eight years, is a peculiar landmass at the north end of Puget Sound. It's a place where half the residents proudly display a decal of the island's shape on their vehicles, a symbol often misunderstood by mainlanders as a splat from a passing gull.

The tranquil landscape, dotted by small farms and ranches on the south end, recalls the countryside depicted in many of the shows aired on Britbox. The U.S. Naval Air Station dominates the north half of the island.

Thankfully, my patch on the south end, with a population of around sixteen thousand, has been pleasantly uneventful for almost six months. I'm grateful for this respite, as the strange events of the previous year were enough to last a lifetime for any deputy.

We operate out of the Freeland office, where my second-in-command and best friend, Wally Turpin, keeps track of the routine crimes and misdemeanors, freeing me to focus on any significant infractions, should they arise. Bruce Strickland handles the dispatch desk when he can tear himself away from his phone. If not for his volunteer status, I'd ask him to retire.

I arrived at the usual time—seven a.m.—and began wading through the pile of paperwork accumulated over the weekend. Because it was a Monday, Wally and Bruce didn't show up until eight, and I wouldn't be disturbed for the next hour.

The two deputies working the weekend had been busy, albeit with only minor disturbances and traffic violations, so I had plenty to process.

When Bruce wasn't around, or the station was empty, the dispatch chores were handled by the Sheriff's Office in Coupeville, the Island County seat. I was surprised when the phone rang a few minutes before eight, but I still had a few things to get through, so I let it get forwarded. After three rings, it stopped, and then five seconds later, it started up again. This happened four times rapidly and seemed to warrant my attention, so I finally answered it.

"Wilkie here."

"Rog, it's Danny Collins on the *Tokitae*; we're five minutes from Clinton."

"Okay…" Danny was a ferry captain who now worked the *Tokitae*, the Olympic-class vessel used on the Mukilteo/Clinton route. When he wasn't overseeing the operation of over nine million pounds of steel, in gusts frequently reaching 60 mph across the Saratoga Passage, he played golf with my buddy Kevin at the Mutiny Bay Club.

"Rog, we had an issue on the lower car deck and need you at the dock when we land."

"Um…what kind of issue would that be, Danny?" He was a quiet but often humorous fellow in his mid-fifties—a few years older than me—and there were times when it was necessary to pry the words from his lips.

"One of the deckhands was passing a Toyota and noticed the driver's window was spidered and had a hole in it. When he checked on the woman inside, he noticed she had the same kind of hole in her head."

I expected ferry captains to be much the same as airline pilots, and every event was relayed with a matter-of-fact delivery, no matter how serious.

"Someone was *murdered…on the ferry*?"

"It seems that way. Could you meet us at the dock? I suppose we'll need to wait to disembark until you've done whatever you need to do."

"I'm on the way. Don't let anyone off the boat." If I used the lights and siren, I'd get there when they landed.

I rushed out the door just as Wally was parking his pickup. "C'mon, Wally, we've got work to do."

He knew better than to ask anything until we were rolling, which was only one reason he was a great cop.

***

We covered the nine miles to the Clinton ferry dock in less than six minutes. The traffic was light for a Monday—it *was* Whidbey Island, after all—and even though we were obviously on official business, it didn't stop some of the folks in the ferry line from casting disapproving glances our way. Few transgressions were worse than line-cutters when it came to island life.

We managed to weave through the holding lot and pulled up to the boom gate just in time to see the deckhands wrapping the giant mooring lines to the dock cleats. Danny, dressed in his captain's garb—navy slacks and long-sleeved white shirt—stood at the front of the lower car deck. He was a shade over five and a half feet and probably twenty pounds heavier than he wished. I guessed golf was less about physical fitness than camaraderie, but then that was O'Malley's bailiwick.

"Roger, Wally...looks like it's gonna be a beautiful day, huh?" Captain Collins' voice could barely be heard over the thrumming of the 6,000 HP diesel engines.

It *was* sunny and April, so technically, he was right. When the usual mid-spring overcast skies were interrupted by a day of sunshine, it was an occasion to be celebrated. That he was able to do so even when confronted with a possible murder spoke to the man's even-keeled disposition.

"Show me what you've got, Danny," I thought it best to get to business lest we have a hundred and fifty angry commuters to deal with if we kept them on the boat for too long.

While Wally stayed on the dock to ensure no one left or boarded the ferry, we made our way to the mid-point of the cavernous lower car deck.

Before we reached the crime scene, we passed a flatbed loaded with building materials and three UPS vans impatient to make their island deliveries. Three deckhands surrounded the relatively new Camry, making it clear the car was off-limits. To their credit, while I was sure the folks in their cars were curious, most were content to rubberneck from their vehicles rather than risk a stern look from one of the ferry workers.

The car was in the left lane, which meant the damaged window was only a few feet from the side bulkhead. A Ford pickup and two other vehicles were lined up behind the victim while an older Econoline van was in the center lane, just to the right of the Camry.

I'd been on too many crime scenes to remember, but this was a first...and a royal clusterfuck. While the deckhands and Danny backed away, I carefully opened the door and confirmed the victim was, indeed, dead. The woman appeared to be in her late thirties, was stylishly dressed, and had a hole the size of a nickel in the middle of her forehead. Very carefully, after snapping on a pair of latex gloves, I reached into the open purse on the console and retrieved a wallet with a driver's license showing through a plastic window. It was a California license displaying the woman's picture and the name "Hannah Stucki." I placed it back, then closed the door gently, trying not to dislodge the brittle, cracked window, and turned to the captain.

"We'll need to get the techs here, Danny, and it's gonna take some time."

"What about the passengers? We can't keep 'em here all day."

He was right. The problem was the murderer was probably one of them...*or* one of the deckhands *or* one of the crew.

"Did anyone say anything or hear the shot?"

"Nobody said anything. Terry—the big guy behind you—was the one who noticed it and told me. We've gotta get these folks off the boat, Rog."

I sidestepped his concerns and asked, "What about CCTV cameras? You've got them on the boat, right?"

"We do, but the cameras on the lower decks have been out of commission for over a month. We've submitted a maintenance request, but nothing has happened."

"Shit...of course, they wouldn't be working." *That would have made things way too easy.*

"Okay. Let's do this. It'll take a little time, but it's better than having everyone sit here all day. We let the walk-ons and the vehicles off one at a time after they show their IDs and give their contact info to Wally. I'll get a couple more deputies here to speed things up. I assume you have that info for the crew and the deckhands, right?"

"Yes. Does this mean the *Tokitae* will be out of service?"

"Sorry, but yes...maybe even for the rest of the day."

"Oh boy... that means only one boat service until we find another one. You realize what this will do?"

I did, but it was unavoidable. When the island's south end had limited ferry service, there was hell to pay. Residents couldn't get to doctors' appointments or to work without making the two-hour detour over the Deception Pass bridge. There was nothing worse for the ferry system's reputation.

"Sorry, Danny. We'll get it done as fast as possible. Can you use the north terminal for the rest of the day?"

He'd already started back toward the forward end of the boat but raised his thumb in acknowledgment. It was going to be a long and tedious day.

Two

The Washington State Ferry System is the largest in the United States and second in the world to only the BC Ferries. It is an integral part of the Puget Sound transportation network, with ten routes, twenty-one vessels, and over eighteen million riders annually.

Because a state patrol canine unit often patrols the ferry holding lots, there is rarely any serious crime on the water. The vessels' captive nature makes escape when docking virtually impossible, and the rapid effects of hypothermia from jumping into fifty-degree water were lethal.

With the arrival of two more deputies, emptying the *Tokitae* was completed in less than two hours. All that remained was for the crime scene unit and the coroner to finish their work. The ferry would return to work as soon as the vehicle was removed to be examined by the techs at a remote location.

In addition to the twelve-person crew, we compiled a list of 141 people in 110 vehicles and thirty-three walk-ons. Unless someone had managed to find some other means of escape, our killer would be one of these 186 people. All we had to do was figure out which one.

We completed a final search of the *Tokitae* with Captain Collins, then headed back to Freeland to begin the tedious work of eliminating most of the possible suspects. However, investigating the life of Hannah Stucki would be first on our list.

The Camry turned out to be a rental. Ms. Stucki had picked it up four days ago from the Hertz lot at SeaTac Airport and was expected to return it later this afternoon. The address on her license showed Dana Point, California, as her home. I'd been there once or twice during my stint in LA and recalled it as the quintessential charming SoCal beach community. I contacted the local police department and told them she had been shot and relayed whatever details we had. It would be their job to notify the next of kin, which was never easy. They promised to get back to us with any information they discovered that would help with our investigation.

Serious crime is rare on South Whidbey, so when a search warrant for a murder investigation is requested, it is granted without undue delay. We were able to track the victim's travels by viewing her American Express credit card purchases from the time she picked up her rental until she met her death on the lower deck of the *Tokitae*.

After landing Thursday afternoon at six o'clock on an Alaska Airlines flight from John Wayne Airport in Orange County, Hannah Stucki checked into a room at the Bellevue Club Hotel. The pricey hotel was located just outside the city center and was frequented by wealthy patrons who preferred anonymity. She took her meals there and checked out early this morning. We wouldn't know much more until we interviewed the people at the hotel and got reports back from the police in Dana Point.

"I guess I'll head to Bellevue in the morning, Wally; one of us needs to talk to the employees at the hotel."

"Okay...what do you want me to do?"

"We should hear from the cops in SoCal soon, so maybe deal with them. How are we doing on eliminating the passengers and crew from the boat?"

"The crew all live on the island, and only one has less than a year in service. She's Danny's kid, so I think she's safe."

"And the passengers?"

"I'm still working on it. Most were delivery folks and part-timers coming over for the week. I'm guessing if they've had homes here for a while, they're probably not murderers—at least, not likely. A few were coming home from the weekend shift at Boeing, too, but I can't see any suspects there. You know how strict they are with vetting their employees."

"How many left to check out?"

"Five or six individuals who said they were just visiting. We're working on checking out their backgrounds and addresses on the mainland."

"Gut feeling?"

"I don't know, Rog. None of them strike me as hit men or women, but I suppose if they were pros, they wouldn't."

"Pros?"

"Well, she *was* shot in the center of her forehead, and nobody saw or heard anything. Seems like a professional hit to me."

"Yeah...what I thought too. Who's checking on them—the visitors?"

"We've got calls into the cops whose jurisdictions they live in. We've asked them to check them out. We should hear back in the morning."

"Sounds like we've got most of the bases covered; let's call it a day. I'll take the seven in the morning, and you can pull together everything here. How's Ms. Mahoney?"

Wally had moved to a farmhouse in Greenbank with his girlfriend, Kate Mahoney. Kate was a detective with the Bellingham Police Department, and the events of six months ago had forged a lasting bond between them. He was happy, and I was happy for both of them.

"She's great. I can't wait to fill her in on our day."

"I'm sure she has her own stuff to deal with. Make sure she doesn't get involved."

Mahoney was a brilliant and dogged investigator, and I'd love to have her on our team. However, she was valued likewise at the BPD, and I didn't want any conflict to arise.

"No worries, Boss, she knows better. See ya."

"Yes...I'm sure," I muttered as he left the building.

It was only a ten-minute drive to my restored farmhouse on the west side of Lone Lake. It was a Monday, so my wife, the world-famous microbiologist Dr. Andie Saunders, would be home cooking something scrumptious...hopefully.

I pulled into the gravel courtyard just after six. It would be almost another hour before sunset, and the temperature was nearly sixty. It wasn't California, but it *was* home, and I'd rather be here than anywhere. When Andie didn't step on the porch to greet me, I assumed she was either in the kitchen or in her office back by the barn.

Once inside, the place smelled like cumin, and I could see a pot full of quinoa on the range top. It looked like the makings of our favorite Mexican dish, and my mouth watered. I called her name but got no reply. I took the hallway off the kitchen to the back door, which led to the barn and her lab, and checked it first. Still, there was no Andie.

Then I heard them...meh-he-he...meh-he-he. I walked into the barn where my lovely wife was feeding her three pygmy goats. She still hadn't noticed my quiet approach, but seeing her administering to her three pals inherited from a previous perilous adventure was worth it. Her thick, brown ponytail sticking out from the back of her Mariners ballcap swished from side to side as she spoke softly to her charges, but then the goats gave me away. The little guys' bleats became faster and higher pitched when they were as excited as now.

"That you, Roger?" she asked without looking.

"How did you know?"

"I can tell how they react when they see you."

"I could have been a robber or murderer."

"Right...you *do* know where we live, yes?"

She stood and gave me a welcome-home hug as she said this. Although we'd been together for less than three years, it seemed like we'd known each other our entire lives. The intelligence and humor in her ice-blue eyes could be off-putting if necessary, which was likely how she'd risen to head the entire scientific staff at UDub when most at her level were of the male persuasion.

"You might think differently if you knew how I spent my day."

"Let's go inside, and you can fill me in. I've got to finish dinner."

As I suspected, Andie was stunned at the murder on the *Tokitae*.

"Nobody heard anything?"

"Nope."

"And the lady is from California?"

"Yup."

"Do we know why she was coming to Whidbey?"

"No, *we* do not."

If she noticed my use of the plural pronoun, she ignored me.

"If you could figure that out, you'd know who the killer was."

"Gosh, this is helpful, Darling. How about joining us in the Sheriff's Department."

"Is that sarcasm I hear? I would think if my husband expects any dessert—and by that, I mean *after* we hit the sack—he would behave himself."

"On second thought, Andie, you make an excellent point. Wally and I will focus on that Tomorrow.".

"Much better, Dear. I'm glad you took my advice."

Three

B ecause I was with law enforcement, negotiating the lines at the Clinton ferry terminal wasn't necessary. I left the house at 6:45 and had a minute to spare when I passed through the toll booth. I nodded at the deckhand as he pointed to where he wanted me. The Mukilteo/Clinton route was continuously operated by two boats, usually the *Tokitae* and *Issaquah*, although maintenance issues and staffing problems frequently meant substitute vessels. When one ferry was leaving the island, the other was returning. The trip usually took twenty minutes, weather dependent.

Today was drizzly and overcast, with temperatures expected to be in the high fifties. It was spring in the Northwest. Because my good friend Kevin O'Malley had become embroiled in several noteworthy cases in and around Bellevue, which somehow spilled over to Whidbey Island, I was acquainted with Bill Owens, the chief of detectives for the city's police department. Bill was O'Malley's best friend and another golfing buddy.

After sorting through the heavy traffic on I-405, I finally reached the affluent city just east of Seattle, where Bill's office was my first stop.

"Hey Rog, good to see you. How's my buddy Kevin doing these days?"

We shook hands and sat in a small conference room with four chairs, a round plastic table, and nothing else. Owens was a solidly built man with a curmudgeon-like personality that diverted attention from his skilled approach to crime-solving and genuine desire to help. When he and O'Malley got together, the ball-busting was nonstop.

"You'll be glad to know he's staying out of trouble...not that he isn't trying. He was peripherally involved in a recent case involving a coven of witches, but we did a good job keeping him away from the action."

"Witches?"

"Yeah...more bizarre than you can imagine, but that's maybe for another day. Right now, we need to find out about this woman who was murdered on the ferry yesterday."

"Hannah Stucki, you said in the email, right?"

"Yup. She stayed at the Bellevue Club Hotel from Thursday until Monday morning, when she took the ferry to Whidbey Island. Her return flight was scheduled for late Monday afternoon, so whatever business she had on Whidbey would be brief."

"I'll send Detective Houser with you to talk to the hotel staff. Julie's usually pretty good at getting folks to open up. I take it you haven't had any luck with any of the ferry passengers."

"Still narrowing it down, but it doesn't look like anything will pan out. The crew looks solid, too."

"Seems like you've got your work cut out for you on this one. Let me know what we can do to help."

As he said this, he stood, signaling the end of our meeting. I appreciated his help, aware that his daily crime-fighting battles were far greater than mine.

Houser and I took separate cars to the hotel and met at the front desk. She'd called ahead to tell them what to expect, and while the two receptionists looked nervous, they seemed eager to help.

The agent who checked her in when she arrived reported that Stucki had little to say. "She booked one of our Fountain Suites and seemed anxious to get to her room."

"Was the suite expensive?" Houser asked, but I couldn't see why.

"Well...it *is* 1100 square feet," the agent answered defensively.

"Yes, I understand. How much did the room cost?" The Bellevue detective was like a dog with a bone.

"Our rate is eight hundred a night."

"Dollars? You're shitting me."

Julie Houser's preoccupation with the cost of the room, while not endearing herself to the hotel staff, did tell us our victim was used to expensive trappings. I thought it best if I stepped in lest my associate piss them off even more.

"Do you remember anything particular about Ms. Stucki?" The admitting agent seemed relieved to be talking to a more reasonable person.

"I remember she wore a Hermes scarf around her neck and oversized sunglasses." She made circles with her thumb and forefinger and put them over her eyes. "I thought it was odd that she wore these expensive things and had on a cheap Padres baseball cap."

"Do you think she was trying not to be seen?"

"I don't know, but if you asked me to describe her, I couldn't."

Hannah Stucki was turning out to be a bit enigmatic, and I wasn't sure we would get much more from the hotel staff. In parting, I asked the receptionist who hadn't spoken if there was anything *she* could tell us.

She looked down at the desk, then reluctantly looked up and spoke, "I thought it was strange that this woman would stay at this lovely hotel in an expensive suite and not leave her room. We often have guests from around the country and even the world staying here, but they either have meetings, or visit expensive stores, or use the spa services here. This guest stayed in her room, ordered room service, and instructed the server to leave it at the door. She didn't leave the hotel until the day she checked out. It was just unusual, that's all."

She seemed surprised that she had revealed this much about a guest and received a disapproving look from her associate. We took the opportunity to say our thanks and then left the posh hotel. If nothing else, we discovered our victim wished not to be noticed or remembered.

I left Detective Houser in the hotel parking lot and thanked her for her help. Other than the two front desk attendants, it appeared there was no one else to interview. I returned to the ferry dock in Mukilteo and called Wally when I got to the holding lot.

"Anything back yet from Dana Point or the techs going over the car?"

"Still nothing from our pals down South, but an interesting development from the team working on the Camry. They found a post-it note that had fallen between the seats and had a name on it."

"Don't keep me in suspense."

"It said Francis Early, followed by Whidbey Island. I guess that means she was coming here to see someone by that name. Should we start looking for him?"

I was quiet for a moment, trying to grasp the ramifications of this development.

"Boss...you there?"

"Yeah...I am Wally. Don't bother looking; I know Francis Early. I'll stop by and see him as soon as we land."

"You sound as if this is maybe gonna get complicated."

"Yeah...well, maybe it is, maybe not. Francis is a unique individual with a heart of gold, but he has sort of a checkered past. That and, of course, he's a buddy of O'Malley's."

"Oh, no."

"Oh, yes... hey, meet me at the Early residence. It's time you met this guy anyway. I'll text you the address after I make sure he's home. See you in thirty minutes."

Four

I turned onto Goss Lake Road and, two hundred yards later, pulled into the gravel courtyard of the rambling log ranch home where the Early brothers lived. Before I could open the car door, Wally's cruiser crunched up beside me.

"Nice place," he said as we both exited our vehicles.

"Yup, it belongs to Jake, Francis's brother."

"Isn't he one of the county commissioners?"

"He is. Got elected a couple of years ago, just before all that nasty shit with Harry Hogan." Every time I thought back to Hogan's attempt to poison the people I was responsible for, it gave me the chills.

"It's just the two of them?"

"Yup. Jake has been in a wheelchair since Vietnam and, until a few years ago, was an agoraphobe. When Francis got out of McNeil—he's almost fifteen years younger--he came here to live with his brother and help him out. When Hugo Navarro, the drug kingpin, was killed here—that was Francis's doing also—it was cathartic enough to entice Jake out into the real world. He thought giving something back to the community was a good idea, so he ran and was elected commissioner."

"I was on Camano then, but I remember hearing about all that stuff. Did you say Francis was in McNeil? Isn't that where they housed the sexual predators?"

I chuckled because every time someone heard Francis was a prisoner at the notorious prison, their alert bells began clanging. "Yes, but he and a few others ended up there on minor drug charges because of overcrowding. They kept them in a separate building, away from the general population. There was an occasional dust-up, but Francis can be intimidating."

As we walked up to the formidable front door, I noticed Wally seemed to be processing the background information I'd given him. Otherwise, he wouldn't have almost tripped over the edge of the wheelchair ramp that sloped off to the side of the entrance.

"Whoops, sorry about that, Rog; just picturing what life must have been like in that hellhole."

"Yeah...did you know Charles Manson and, before him, Stroud—the 'Bird-man'—were residents there back in the day?"

"No, but that doesn't..."

Before he could finish, the door swung inward, and Jake Early greeted us warmly.

"Roger, it's great to see you. And this must be the famous Wally Turpin, who was involved with that little astronaut on Lone Lake Road," he said as he shook the deputy's hand with more vigor than I could ever muster. The "astronaut" he referred to was what we called the little warlock named Buzz Aldrin, who was at the center of the Lone Lake Road incidents.

Rather than dwell on past events, I suggested we get down to the reason for our visit. Jake backed his wheelchair up and invited us into his spacious foyer. The concrete floors and hand-hewn logs of the interior reminded me of a five-star lodge I'd once been a guest at.

As we moved into the great room, he asked, "You didn't say much on the phone, Roger, so what's up? Something to do with Francis?"

"We're not sure about that yet. You said he was here? If he joins us, we'll tell you all we know."

"Sounds a little mysterious. Anything to do with that murder on the ferry?"

I shook my head, smiled, and said, "I've forgotten how fast word travels on the island. Yes, it does; how about getting your brother here."

Jake hit a button on his cell, and we heard Francis's gruff voice on the speaker, "Yo, what up?"

"Roger Wilkie's here and wants to talk with you."

"What about?"

"He won't say until you get here."

"Does he know I'm in the middle of a group chat with Mick and the guys?"

Jake looked at us and rolled his eyes before he answered, "Um, no, Francis, although I guess he does now. Can you connect with them later?"

"Okay, okay, I suppose. Anything for our island protector."

Wally looked a little concerned about the conversation. Because I knew Francis, I was familiar with his brand of sarcasm, which could sometimes be mistaken for surliness. The more I got to know him, though, the more I appreciated his uniqueness.

"It'll take him a couple of minutes; he's in his computer room in the basement. Francis has a weekly Zoom session with his former associates from McNeil," Jake said.

I explained the situation to Wally, who still seemed unsure: "While Francis was in prison, he became friends with a few other inmates on similar charges. They taught themselves more about computers and the Internet than most of the folks at Microsoft know. That's how Navarro eventually met his demise."

We heard the thumps of his footfalls several seconds before he rounded the corner. If Wally were uncomfortable already, meeting Francis for the first time would be an experience.

The younger Early approached, dressed in an old camo fatigue shirt and tattered messenger shorts and wearing ancient, unlaced Corcoran Jump boots. A shaved head, thick lips, and heavily lidded eyes did nothing to disguise the tattoed teardrops one of his prison pals installed. At a shade over six feet, his seriously muscled body tipped the scales north of 250 pounds. If there were such a contest, the man would have been voted the least desirable human to meet in a dark alley. His angry countenance disintegrated as he approached me, breaking into a wide grin and giving me a crushing hug.

"Whoa, easy there, big fella, you're gonna break something."

"Nah, I'm being gentle with you. And who's this guy you brought with you? He's not the one who was with you up at Ebey's, is he?"

"Yup. Francis, meet Wally Turpin, my good friend and right-hand man."

Wally extended his hand only to have it swallowed up by Francis's massive paw.

"I can't believe that shit you guys went through last year. What was it like way back then?"

Of course, he was referring to the Lone Lake Road incident, but we needed to get back on track. "Much as we'd like to relive the good old days, Francis, we're here about something else."

His face now took on a serious look, which he used when focusing his attention, which meant he was prepared to input data.

"Talk to me."

"The woman who was murdered on the boat was named Hannah Stucki. Does that ring any bells?"

He closed his eyes, probably scouring his immense database. "Nope. I got nothing. Why are you asking?"

"That's the odd thing. She was from Southern California, was in town, in Bellevue, for a couple of days, then boarded the ferry for Whidbey Island. And...we found a piece of paper in her rental with your name. It seems she was coming here to see you."

His blue-gray tears scrunched up as he tried to understand the situation. I'd seen too many people underestimate Francis based only on his physical appearance. That intimidating head of his housed a remarkable brain that was often many steps ahead of others when presented with the same set of circumstances

"Geez, I don't know why that would be, Rog. I don't know or can't recall the name, and nobody's contacted me."

"Shit, I was hoping you might know her. Do you think she's someone from before...when you were doing the drug thing?"

If my question offended him, he showed no signs of it.

"Nah...sure, I did a bunch of drugs, but I was never that fucked up. They got me for sharing the stuff with my buddies and called me a dealer, hah. Anyway, no. Never heard the name."

I considered this momentarily, and then Francis said, "Tell you what, Rog, let me reach out to my former prison mates. Those guys have a much wider network than me, and maybe they'll find something."

"I'd appreciate that."

"No problem; I'm on it right away. Oh, and email me a shot of her driver's license."

He turned and walked away as soon as the words left his mouth, but then he said, "Hey Wally, good to meet you. Say hi to Kate for me.

My partner looked at me, his eyes wide in disbelief.

Jake must have picked up on it. He said, "Francis pretends he doesn't know much, but he gets around, Wally. I'm betting he knows someone who knows someone who knows your girlfriend. It's not like she hasn't been in the news recently. If something enters the public domain, Francis knows about it. Never underestimate my brother."

We thanked Jake and made our way to our vehicles. Wally was still overwhelmed by the experience, and I said, "He has that effect on people. You should have seen Andie when she first met him."

Five

W hen we returned to the office, two messages were waiting for me. One was from the coroner's office, the other from the Dana Point Police. I handed off the California connection to Wally and returned the coroner's call myself.

During Harry Hogan's reign of terror, Maggie Ryan, the chief medical examiner for the coroner, distinguished herself with her diligence and professionalism. I was glad she was on the job for this one. She had been the ME for the county for almost fifteen years, and although many municipalities had tried to lure her away, she still chose to live and work on Whidbey Island. It was to our benefit.

"It's not enough that I have to deal with all the locals, huh Roger; no, you gotta import bodies from Southern California."

I should have mentioned Maggie grew up on the East Coast and still had that edge of cynicism that endeared her to me and others, while some thought her a bit abrupt.

"I heard you were getting bored with the island stuff, Mags, so I thought we should send you something to get the juices flowing."

"Good one, Rog, I'm honored. Now...Hannah Stucki...according to her license, she was thirty-eight years old when she died. As you probably deduced—the clever detective that you are—she died of a gunshot to the head. The slug we dug out of her brain was a .22 caliber. Once it got in there, along with some glass shards from the window, it rattled around and messed her up pretty well. Course, she was dead by then. I'm guessing a Walther or Taurus. A small gun like that would barely be heard over those big diesels on the ferry. But, hey, don't let me do *all* your work for you."

I loved this woman's energy, even if she used it to needle me every chance she got. "What else did..."

"Wait, wait...I'm not done."

I knew she wasn't done; that's why I was asking a follow-up. Sheesh!

"Sure thing, Mags...please continue."

"I don't know who this woman was, but I *can* tell you she was either very wealthy or lived with someone who was. Her skin, hair, and nails... showed expensive maintenance and frequent attention. Her clothes were expensive too."

"Okay, well..."

"But wait...there's more."

"Tell me, please, Maggie."

"She led an awful life."

"You know this, how?"

"She had bruises on her arms and legs, and her facial bones showed signs of previous fractures. Whoever she lived with or went with beat the shit out of her, and it happened over a long time. This guy—I'm assuming it was a guy—has got to be a real asshole. When you catch him, be careful...and, please...hurt him."

It was rare for Maggie to associate her feelings with her clients, so something about Stucki must have struck a nerve. I only knew her professionally, so I assumed there was a connection somewhere in her past.

I gave her a few seconds to reel in her emotions, then said, "We'll do our best, Maggie. We'll get him."

We said our goodbyes, then I hung up and took a deep breath. I walked over to Wally's workstation, where he was still on the phone but held up a finger to let me know he was almost finished. The yellow legal pad in front of him was covered with words and scrawls and other things I couldn't make out.

He said thanks and disconnected, then turned to me with a look of high anxiety.

"We've got issues, Rog."

"What?"

"The reason it's taken so long for the locals—they use the Orange County Sheriff's Department, by the way—to get back to us is because her only address is a post office box; the one on the license is bogus. After some legwork, they found she was living at the Monarch Beach Resort. She stayed in a penthouse that ran over three thousand a night."

"What?"

"Yeah…I know. Anyway, they've found no next of kin and no friends. It's like she's a ghost."

"Did they interview the folks at the resort?"

"Yup. Everyone said she kept a low profile and was rarely seen. When she was, she always had big sunglasses on and wore a silk scarf even when it was hot."

"Sounds exactly like the report I got at the Bellevue Club Hotel. She wanted—or needed—to stay anonymous. Damn…this isn't getting us anywhere. How long was she there?"

"They said only about a week. They said she used the spa treatments almost daily, but in her room where she could stay out of sight."

This new information only raised more questions about our victim. We spent the rest of the day weeding out the last of those on the ferry passenger list. A couple had records, but both were DUIs, and neither appeared to be a murderer. We decided visiting them would be a waste of time. We agreed to meet first thing in the morning, both of us hoping for an overnight inspiration or revelation or something to get us going in the right direction.

***

We were at our desks sipping coffee when I heard the door to the station house open. I turned to see Francis Early's shiny bald head as he stomped into the room.

Bruce, abruptly jarred from his phone scrolling, almost fell backward at the frightening visage before him.

"ROGER," he screamed.

Francis paid him a cursory glance—he was used to such reactions—as he approached Wally and me. "Hey, you two, I got some information."

Now that he saw the invader was acquainted with us, Bruce tried to regroup, but he appeared still rattled. I suggested we go into the small conference room, eliminating the possibility that our guest might upset any other potential visitors.

The three of us pulled up chairs to the round table, the room feeling slightly claustrophobic with the addition of Francis Early.

"I told Micky about the murder and gave him the woman's name. He recruited Otis and Sparks, and they spent the last twenty-four hours researching her."

Francis's pals were graduates of McNeil Island, and all had been behind bars on similar convictions. When they weren't gaming with each other and their buddies, they spent their time hacking into databases with multi-level security just for fun. If not for them, the episode with Navarro and his murderous bodyguard might have taken a much darker turn.

"They couldn't find much, but then they started searching images based on her license photo. With all this new AI shit, you can't believe what we can do. Anyway…we found some pictures from six or seven years ago. Mick says he thinks most of 'em are from Utah or Nevada."

Once Francis got going, I knew he needed to deliver his report at his own pace. I'd learned earlier that an interruption only delayed the process, so I bit the inside of my cheek and waited.

"In many of these photos, she was with the same guy. Take a look at these copies."

He'd printed the images on regular copy paper, so they were a little grainy, but it was a younger-looking Hannah Stucki. She was standing next to a fellow who resembled the Seinfeld character, George Costanza, with thicker glasses. In every instance, the woman wasn't smiling; if she was, it seemed forced. The short, pudgy man seemed to constantly have physical contact with Hannah in the photos as if she were a possession or something to keep track of.

"Got a name to go with this guy, Francis?"

"I do. It's Joseph Driggs."

I had never heard of the name, so I told Francis and asked if he knew the man.

"Nah…but Sparks is from that part of the country, and Mick says *he's* heard of the guy."

Francis was a wonderful guy, loyal, and trustworthy to the end. But getting the whole picture from the man was like pulling teeth.

"Can you tell us everything Sparks or Mickey or Otis or anyone knows about Driggs?"

He looked surprised at my apparent impatience but then disregarded it and continued with what his friends had told him.

"He was raised in this big Latter-day Saints family and went to Brigham Young. He was one of those guys that always wanted, or maybe needed, to protest something. By the time he'd been there two years, he was well-known as a BAOC."

"Um, Francis...what's a BAOC?"

"Big asshole on campus...geez, don't you know *anything*?"

"Anyway...by the time he gets kicked out, he's only got a few friends, and they leave with him. He stops communicating with his family, and he and his pals find some land near Colorado City. He gets kicked out of the Church, too."

"That's gotta be in Colorado, right? And why'd he get kicked out?" Wally asked.

Francis looked at my deputy like he would a small child struggling to grasp a calculus equation.

"It's in Northwest Arizona, Wally. They kicked him out because he was *too* conservative for them. He wanted to go back the way it was when Joseph Smith was the head dude...you know, multiple wives, that whole scene."

Still trying to get the complete picture, I asked, "How long has it been since he left BYU?"

"Mick—or I guess Sparks—says it was around twenty-five years ago."

"And these pictures are at least six years ago?"

"That's what he says."

"So, we know she was with Driggs then, but she was living in Southern California recently."

It dawned on me that Sparks, Francis's buddy, probably had more information than we were getting secondhand.

"Hey, Francis...how did she get your name?"

"I don't know...um, didn't think about that."

"Could or would Sparks have given it to her? Did he know her?"

He wiped his meaty paw across his head as he contemplated the question.

"I guess...maybe he did...yeah, it makes sense."

"Where does Sparks live?"

"He moves around some. I'm pretty sure he's been in Vegas for at least the last few years."

"Will he talk to me?"

Francis seemed to consider the request for a few seconds, then answered, "I think if I told him you were cool, he'd go for it...yeah."

Since the Island County Sheriff's Department budget wouldn't allow me to jet off to Las Vegas, Francis helped me set up a Zoom session with his prison mate from McNeil Island later in the afternoon.

He'd coordinated things with Sparks, a man with an understandable aversion to law enforcement types, ahead of time, and five minutes before the call, I thought to ask, "Hey Francis, what's this guy's real name?"

"He doesn't like to use it much."

"I won't use it. Just tell me what it is."

"It's uh...Edgar...Edgar St. Germain."

"Edgar? Really? How did it get to 'Sparks'"?

"He was always fooling around with the electricity at McNeil. It started when he shorted out the receptacle in our dorm. It ended up shutting down the whole prison. Boy, were they pissed."

I had learned that the few inmates on the island convicted of less serious crimes were housed in a dormitory, away from the dangerous sex offenders and murderers that comprised the bulk of the population.

"I can imagine they were," I said

"Yeah...anyway, he figured out what went wrong—the joint had this old knob-and-tube stuff in a lot of places—and he fixed it. After a while, they used him to fix things whenever they had a problem. They started calling him Sparks, and it stuck."

It made sense to me, I thought, as the screen on my computer changed from a solid blue to a lime-green room somewhere in Nevada. A short, slightly built man entered the picture and sat down, his face almost filling the monitor. He had a wispy white mustache and wore thick glasses displaying tiny reflections on his computer screen. A sweat-stained Red Sox ballcap covered his head. His expression was uncomfortable, and I was glad Francis agreed to stay with me during the session.

Francis took the lead: "This is Roger Wilkie, Sparks. He's the guy I told you about. It's about that Stucki woman...like I told you."

He nodded his head. I knew the microphone was working because I heard a blower humming somewhere near his location, although he had yet to speak. I thought I should move things along, so I said, "Hi, Sparks. Okay, if I ask you a few questions?"

"Okay."

"Did you know Hannah Stucki?"

"Yes."

"How? Was she a friend?"

"Uh...no, she was my sister's daughter."

"So, your niece?"

"I always thought of her that way, but she was adopted, so I guess, technically, she maybe wasn't."

Francis's expression told me he, too, was surprised at this revelation. His initial explanation was that they had to do a deep dive to determine who the victim was, but if she was Spark's niece, he knew her identity as soon as he saw the license photo. I ignored the subterfuge and plodded ahead.

"Well...I'm sorry about what happened to her. What can you tell me about her? What was she up to? And how did she get Francis's name? Did you give it to her?"

The face on the screen disappeared as Sparks covered it with his hands. We could hear him take a deep breath, then remove his hands and look upward as he pictured the events he was about to relate.

"I'm sorry I pretended not to know who she was, Francis. It's just she had some tough times, and when I tried to help her ...well, it seems things didn't turn out too good."

Francis's demeanor changed from one of anger to concern for his friend. "Tell us about her, Sparks."

"Holly—that's my sister—used to come and visit me at McNeil, and when she did, she sometimes brought Hannah."

"I knew you saw your sister once in a while, but I didn't know she brought her kid," Francis said.

"Yeah...well, I never mentioned it at the time. She was just a kid and always looked scared of the place."

While he continued, I tried to imagine what I might have thought of the notorious prison as a youngster.

"Anyway, when I got out, I lived with them until I got back on my feet, so I got to know the kid a little better. She was serious most of the time, but we ended up shooting baskets together, and she started to open up. She was a hell of an athlete. When I moved out of state, we wrote to each other occasionally, but after a while, the letters stopped.

"By this time, she was off to college—remember, this was twenty-some years ago—and my sister lost track of her for months. She got into this fundamentalist group, and Holly thought she got brainwashed. Her grades tanked, and after another semester, she just dropped out and moved in with this Driggs character.

"Holly asked me if I could find her and bring her home, so I tried. I found out where their little commune, or whatever they called it, was and paid them a visit. They had this gate across the only road leading into the property and two guys with guns guarding it. When I told them I was there to visit Hannah, they said they were told not to let any visitors in. I told 'em I wasn't leaving until I saw her.

"One of them left and went to tell Driggs, I guess, because, after about twenty minutes, he comes back with Hannah and this short bald guy. He tells me his name and says Hannah is now one of his wives. He says she's happy there and wants me to leave her alone. All this time, Hannah is just standing there with a blank look, and the guy is holding her hand. I tried to talk to her, but she wouldn't even look up at me and finally she says, 'Leave me alone, Sparks. I'm staying here.'

"There wasn't much I could do then, so I called Holly and told her what happened. She wouldn't let it go, so she called the cops. They told her they knew about Driggs, but he wasn't breaking any laws, so there wasn't much they could do. They told her there were a bunch of other women there, too, and even though they'd gotten some complaints from the families, the women said they were happy when they were asked."

It seemed a little far-fetched, but I'd heard of cults like this before, so I didn't discount Sparks's story.

"How, or why, did Francis become involved?" I asked.

"Holly kept pestering the local cops, but nothing ever came of it. She didn't hear from Hannah again until about a year ago. Over the years, this Driggs character became more and more abusive to his wives, and a couple of them cooked up a plan to leave.

"Driggs funded his commune by offering temporary asylum for some of the big drug dealers, and he suggested his wives would be available to them for a price. Last week, the FBI finally got wind of what he was doing and raided the place. They rescued about a dozen women, but Driggs was in the wind.

"Shortly before the raid, Hannah and this other gal—I think her name was Becca or something—stole a pile of money from one of their guests and took off. The guy was pissed and made Driggs pony up the dough. Driggs was livid and sent his bodyguard to handle the situation.

"Hannah and her friend managed to get to Vegas, and she called me. She said someone was after them and asked for help." Sparks stopped his narrative momentarily and gulped from a glass of water.

"I put them up in a motel just off the strip and put the room in my name. I figured if Driggs sent someone after them and the nearest big city was Vegas, then he'd get here soon enough. I was right, but he got here before I expected it.

"Only two days after they got here, a guy named Shane Mullins came calling on them. Don't ask me how he knew where they were—maybe someone's cell phone or something—but he did. He busted into their room and beat the shit out of both of them. Hannah got away, but her friend wasn't so lucky. He hit her so hard she ended up dying on the way to the hospital."

Sparks recited the saga almost as if he was in a trance. I hesitated to interrupt, but I did, "How did you find out who it was?"

"Since the room was in my name, the manager called to tell me I needed to pay for the damage. I was worried as hell, especially when that Becca woman died, but I didn't hear from Hannah until the day after the break-in. She called me and told me she was hurt but okay. She was in LA. I asked her if she needed money, and she said she had plenty. She asked me to get her some ID if I could. I knew a guy who could do it fast. He did, and I overnighted it to where she was staying."

"How did you know it was Mullins who did this?" Sparks still hadn't told me how Francis fit into the picture, but I supposed he'd get there when he was ready.

"The motel had cameras, and I told them I'd pay for everything right away if they let me look at the footage. There was a clear picture of him. I'd heard about him from some guys I know; a real nasty fucker."

"You're certain it was him?"

"Oh, yeah. I'll send you a picture. He was always an enforcer for hire until he hooked up with Driggs, and then that became his steady gig. It seems Driggs had to make good with the dealer on the money the women stole, and he sent Mullins to recover it.

"I didn't know what I could do or how I could help, so I told her if she was in real danger to call the only guy I knew who would be tough enough to handle Mullins. That was you, Francis. You watched out for us in McNeil, and you were the only person I could think of who could help her if she needed it."

Francis hadn't said a word during Sparks's story, and now he looked away as if embarrassed by the situation. He turned back and said, "And she never made it here."

It was quiet for a few seconds; I could still hear the faint sounds of the blower. Then he continued, "I didn't hear from her again until a week ago. She said she'd had a couple of close calls with Mullins, but she got away. She thought he had finally given up. Said she was staying in some fancy place in Dana Point, treating herself now that she'd gotten away. I guess she was wrong."

Sparks looked miserable, exhausted by the ordeal. I told him to please let us know if he thought of anything else and that we'd fill him in if we made any progress. Then, the blue Zoom Workspace screen appeared, and we were done.

Six

I t was approaching dinner time when Sparks signed off, and Francis, Wally, and I sat around the small conference table, my laptop the only item on it. Knowing the background story and who the likely killer was, was helpful, but we still needed to do some sleuthing. Wally began to ask a question when my computer chirped, signaling an incoming message. I'd forgotten Sparks was sending the picture of Mullins.

"Holy shit!" Wally said as the three of us studied what Sparks had sent. The poor lighting did little to obscure the figure of Shane Mullins. Even though the camera's angle might have diminished the man's height, he had to be well over six and a half feet. And he was beanpole thin. The short brim of his scally cap did little to distract from the cruel twist of his thin lips and an angular nose that appeared to have been broken with regularity. The enforcer had to be in his mid-fifties, but his weathered, ruddy face suggested he was at least a decade older. His features were memorable, and one physical trait stood out. The camera had captured only his right arm and the attached hand, which held what appeared to be a short-handled, three-pound sledgehammer. I said appeared because the size of the man's hand swallowed almost all of the wooden handle. If the left one were as formidable, I shuddered to think what damage his fist could inflict on a human being.

"Yeah, interesting-looking fellow," I added. "Wally, first thing Tomorrow, let's find out about this guy. Check with the Feds, the locals in Utah, Nevada, Arizona, and maybe Interpol. A guy that looks like this and likes beating up women has to have left a trail. Francis, I hate to ask, but will you see what you can find out, too? You know, from some of your contacts?"

Wally nodded while Francis seemed preoccupied and turned to look away.

"Francis?"

He turned back. The look on his face was one I hadn't seen before and hinted at what probably deterred the nastiest of the bunch at McNeil from giving his friends any trouble.

He spoke quietly, but there was no mistaking his fury, "Roger...rest assured that I *will* find out about this guy. If Sparks gave his niece my name for me to watch out for her, and this asshole murdered her...well...then it's *my* job to take care of things."

I didn't want Francis doing things on his own.

"I said, "Remember how you ended up in the hospital when you went after Hogan?"

He stared at me, perhaps recalling his confrontation with the deceased murderer, but didn't answer, so I pressed the point, "Francis, I appreciate your help and welcome your support, but this has to be done my way. Will you be a team player on this?"

It took him a few seconds, but he answered the way I figured he would: "I will."

It remained to be seen whether he would, but at least he knew what I expected. I knew how single-minded he could be; it was a double-edged sword.

"Can you check with your sources by noon Tomorrow?"

"I'll be on it all night; my people don't keep banker's hours. Yeah...noon's easy. See you then."

The big man rose and left the room without a sound.

"Kinda glad he's on our side, Rog."

"Me too, Wally...me too. See what you can dig up on Mullins by Tomorrow, and the three of us will get together then. I'm gonna see if I can find out anything more about Driggs. He has to have left a trail somewhere."

***

I slept fitfully, images of Mullins and his huge fists standing over a helpless Hannah Stucki flashing through my mind, and I finally gave up shortly before five. Andie was still asleep when I left for the station, so I texted her with hearts and smiley faces. She'd spent the previous day on campus at several staff meetings, and the trip into town, through traffic, and then back to Whidbey always left her exhausted. I was glad she could sleep in for a change.

I immediately began sending emails to any law enforcement agencies I thought might have heard something about Driggs or his whereabouts. He appeared to feel that obeying laws and society's norms was beneath him. With such an attitude, it would be difficult to hide from the authorities indefinitely.

Wally showed up at seven and began following up on Mullins. By the time Francis brought his imposing self into the station at noon, we were ready to share. Bruce had provided sandwiches and soft drinks—at my direction—but made himself scarce before Mr. Early's arrival.

Wally was munching on something, and even though Francis appeared to be chomping at the bit, I began with my findings.

"The FBI and the Arizona, Utah, and Nevada state police all have warrants out for Driggs. Most agencies looked the other way when he was hunkered down on his little commune with his gaggle of wives. Because no one complained, and it appeared the women were there of their own accord, they left him alone. It was when he started acting like the place was a VRBO for drug cartel members on the run that the FBI and the others started to take notice."

"How long had he been doing that?" Wally asked, wiping mustard from the corner of his mouth.

"The agent I spoke with from the FBI wasn't sure, but he thought it had been going on for a few years. From interviews with the women and some of the folks who delivered provisions to the place, it appears Driggs was able to stash a substantial amount of money away. Except for what Hannah and her friend took—and they think it was plenty—they figured he had somewhere in the millions."

"Wouldn't that be a pain in the ass to hide or store?" Francis was always looking at the logistics of things.

"You're right. It would. But, a good portion was in diamonds, and the rest in cash or drugs. When they raided the place, they found evidence of all of it. There was even a loose diamond or two lying around."

"So, except for what the women took, Driggs made off with the rest?"

"That's what they're assuming."

"What happened to the women who were left there?" Wally wanted to know.

"A few are still there—there are a bunch of kids there, too—and the rest went back to whatever families they have. The LDS Church is doing its best to bring them back into the fold."

"Any leads on where Driggs is?" Asked Francis.

"There have been reports of sightings all over the place. One in St. George, a few in Vegas, one or two in Flagstaff, and one as far south as Tucson. He can buy his way out of sight with as much money as he's got. The last one was in Phoenix, which was a few months ago. The Fibbies say he's a vindictive son of a bitch, and he uses Mullins to do his dirty work. It's also how he kept the drug dealers in line when they were holed up at his place in Colorado City.

"I checked with the Vegas cops, too. They didn't have much on Driggs, but they issued an arrest warrant for Mullins for the murder of Rebecca Thomas. They identified him from the camera shots at the motel."

Wally swallowed the last of his ham and cheese as I completed my report and asked the question that had been troubling me, "So, we're sure it was Mullins who killed the Thomas woman, and we know he also attacked Hannah Stucki. But how could he have shot Stucki if he wasn't on the ferry?"

"Yeah, well...that's what we need to figure out. If he did it, then how? And if it wasn't him, then who? How about telling us what you've found on Mullins, and then Francis can tell us what he's got."

He pulled out a yellow legal pad with bullet points, doodles, and exclamation marks scattered over the page. "What I found out is Mullins is one nasty dude.

"As a youngster, he'd been in and out of prison a half-dozen times. All of them were either assault or street fighting mixed in with the frequent destruction of property. It seems he loves that hammer he had with him in the camera shot, and he uses it to destroy stuff. By stuff, I mean both property and humans. Whenever dealers wanted to send a message, they sent Mullins to deliver it. He developed such a reputation that even the bad guys were afraid of him.

"He was born in Belfast, always wears that cap, and the folks I talked to say he still has that Irish accent. There are still open warrants on the guy, but nobody can find him."

"Sounds like a peach," I said. "How about it, Francis? What did you find out?"

"Mostly the same as Wally," he said, looking at both of us with piercing eyes. "But the guys I talked to said Mullins, besides being an enforcer, likes to hurt people just for fun, especially women who can't defend themselves. When he was in Colorado City with Driggs, he sent a couple of the sister-wives to the hospital because they wouldn't succumb to his wishes."

Francis always surprised me with his insights and his vocabulary. His appearance and background suggested an ex-con with limited tools for the civilized world, but being underestimated was his secret weapon. More than a few poor souls could attest to that.

"What else?"

"I talked to a guy who was with him in Monroe a few years ago. Said Mullins was going back to work solely for Driggs when he got out. He said there were plenty of women and money, too."

"This guy have any idea where he might go if he was hiding out?"

"Nah, but he seemed to think he and Driggs were joined at the hip. Said if we found Driggs, Mullins would be close by. He also told me Mullins got in a fight with one of the other inmates and that it wasn't much of a fight. He said Mullins hit him once in the face with one of those giant fists and broke his nose, both cheekbones and an eye socket. The guy almost died, and from what I hear, he doesn't have much of a life anymore. He said if I found him, to be careful."

When Francis finished, the three of us sat there quietly for a few minutes. I considered our next moves and was sure my associates were doing the same.

Wally was the first to break the silence, "Whether it was Mullins or someone else who shot Stucki, if we find Driggs, we'll know the answer. Right?"

"Probably, "I said. "If Mullins did it, then how could he have disappeared? It makes more sense to have hired someone else. In any case, though, it must have been Driggs calling the shots. And what about this money Hannah stole? Where is it? According to the cops in California, she checked out of that fancy place she was staying. I doubt if it was in the car with her or if she even carried it on the plane."

"Mullins is the hit man, and according to my sources, he loves his work, especially if a woman is involved. I don't know how he pulled it off, but my money is still on him." Francis seemed convinced.

Authorities in three states were already on the lookout, so it didn't seem like a couple of Island County deputies would tip the scales. The best we could do for now was focus on how Hannah Stucki was murdered on the *Tokitae*.

I cautioned Francis again to keep me informed if he found out anything. He nodded, then left the room, leaving Wally and me alone.

"What's our next move, Rog?"

"Where are we on the passengers we haven't cleared?"

"Only a few left. There's a couple from Woodinville who said they just wanted to get away for the day and took a road trip to Whidbey Island. There's also a guy—a walk-on—who parked on the Mukilteo side. He said he was taking a boat ride to clear his head. Said he was going through a divorce or something."

"Why are we still looking at them?"

"The local cops in Woodinville haven't been able to interview the couple yet. The ID and address we got when they left the ferry check out, but it looks like they haven't been home since the murder."

"Did we get their cell phones?"

"We did. But no answer from them either."

It wasn't unusual for folks to take the ferry from Mukilteo, visit the island, and then drive north through Deception Pass to return to the mainland. What was worrying was the inability of anyone to contact them.

"Did they check out their backgrounds, relatives, the full meal deal?"

"I'm not sure. I just read what they sent over."

Most cops, whether county sheriff's departments or city police, were conscientious about following up on appeals from other law officers outside their jurisdictions. Still, with the demands on police these days, it was understandable that local crime fighting took precedence over outside requests.

"Call them and tell them what we're up against—the whole Driggs scenario—and ask them if they can dig a little deeper into those folks. I'll follow up with the walk-on."

FERRY TAILS

Seven

It was late afternoon before I could track down Gary Maynard from Edmonds. The city police there had been unable to reach him since he left Whidbey Island on the day of the murder. I took the liberty of calling his cell, and he picked up on the first ring.

"Gary Maynard?"

"Yes?" The voice was quiet, almost weary sounding.

I told him who I was and why I was calling and asked why we couldn't reach him.

"Um...sorry. I haven't been answering my phone. Four days ago, my wife told me she wanted a divorce. It was our fifth anniversary. It seems like she ran into someone at the office she liked a little better. I took the ferry to try to clear my head, but it seemed to make things worse. All I could do was think about her, you know?

"When I got back to Mukilteo, I turned my phone off, got in the car, and drove until I was almost empty. I didn't care where; I ended up in Moses Lake. I turned around and drove back to Edmonds, got shitfaced, and stayed in bed for two days. I just turned my phone on ten minutes ago. Why did you want to talk to me?"

It didn't seem like this guy was someone we needed to be concerned about, so I told him we were clearing all those on the ferry, and now that I'd talked to him, we could cross him off the list. He sounded like he was in his early thirties and was seriously depressed. I wished him well and thought about life's curves for a few minutes. Whoever said, "Man plans and God laughs," hit it on the nose.

Unless whoever killed Stucki managed to get off the boat before it docked, the only folks we had yet to exclude were the couple from Woodinville. I walked over to Wally's workstation to see if he'd had any luck.

"What'd you find out about that couple, Wally?"

"The Gleasons, Randy and Marianne. Still no contact."

"We knew that. What else?"

"The sheriff's station responsible for the location of their residence—it's out in the woods, by the way—sent someone to their house after I told them it was important. They had a dog tied up in the back that looked like he hadn't eaten in days; the deputy took him to the Humane Society, where at least he'll be taken care of."

"What about relatives, previous addresses, jobs?"

"That's what's weird. They were renting the house. The woman who owns it said she rented it to them because she got a referral from one of her friends from church and never bothered to have them fill out any paperwork."

"So, we don't know anything? Did they even have jobs?"

I knew Wally could sense my growing frustration because he didn't even attempt a joke or a wisecrack.

"They had no close neighbors and no relatives they could find."

"How about this church lady and the person who referred the Gleasons?"

"The deputy hasn't interviewed her. He said they were swamped and, if we wanted to have a go at her, to be his guest."

The last thing I wanted to do was travel off the island to interview someone who probably didn't know anything anyway, but there were few other strings to pull.

"Okay, Wally. Set something up for tomorrow, and we'll pay...what's this person's name?"

"Cheryl Haddow."

"Right...we'll pay Ms. Haddow a visit."

***

The following day, we took the eight o'clock boat, which, coincidentally, was the *Tokitae*. We'd picked up a coffee at the Whidbey Coffee drive-through on the way to the dock and sat in our cruiser sipping it during the fifteen-minute crossing to Mukilteo. Starbucks had yet to invade the island's south end, and if the locals had their way, they never would. Danny was probably on duty, but he had enough to do without us pestering him. Sitting inside was an easy decision since the weather was overcast and chilly anyway.

The church lady lived in Cottage Lake, a rural area east of Woodinville, and she was expecting us at nine-thirty. The address led us to a tidy little neighborhood south of the lake—Cottage Lake, of course.

We pulled into the driveway of a modest bungalow sporting a late-model Honda under its carport and made our way to the front door. Ms. Haddow answered on the first ring.

"Please come in, officers. I'm not sure if I can help, but I'm happy to do whatever I can."

The house reminded me of visiting my grandmother's home when I was ten years old. Everything was neat and orderly, and there had to be hundreds of framed photographs of what I presumed were family members. *There were just so many of them.* She invited us to sit at the small kitchen table and offered us water, which we declined.

"We're deputies, ma'am, from Island County. I'm Roger, and this is Wally; he's the one you spoke to yesterday. We had a few questions about those folks who rented your property."

"Well, certainly, anything I can do."

The woman had to be in her early sixties, medium height, and probably thirty pounds overweight. I could see where she might have been attractive as a youngster, but now, with her gray hair pulled up in a tight bun on top of her head, she resembled Aunt Bee from the ancient Andy Griffith Show.

"You sure have lots of pictures, Ms. Haddow. Are all these photographs of your family?" Wally had his own method for icebreaking.

"Why yes, they are, Deputy. My husband—he's the man smiling in those pictures on the mantle—passed away a few years ago. We had six wonderful children, and now they're all married and have lots of children, too. I have eighteen grandchildren."

She beamed as she told us of her progeny, proud of them and their achievements. I was sidetracked for a moment, trying to do the math to figure out how this person's six children could *all* be married and popping out offspring left and right. Fortunately, Wally took the reins and cleared things up.

"Yikes, Ma'am, how could someone as young as you have six children who are all married?"

"You're very kind, Deputy," she said as she reached over and patted his hand. "Ralph—he's...or he *was* my husband—and I were married as soon as I turned sixteen. All of my girls—there are four of them—were married before they were twenty, and my two boys were twenty-one when they took wives."

I stole a glance at Wally and recognized both surprise and a look of confusion in his expression. I thought we should get back on track, so I asked, "On the phone, you said you rented your property to the Gleasons because of a referral from your church?"

"Yes, that's right. George Alberg—he's the bishop of our ward—told me they were friends of his from Provo. He knew I was looking for renters for our place in Woodinville, and he said they were new to our church but good people. I didn't bother checking any references because I trusted George."

"How long did they live there?"

"It's been almost four months. They're very prompt about paying their rent, too."

Cheryl Haddow didn't give us any more information on the Gleasons than we already had. I told her we were looking for her tenants because of an incident on Whidbey Island and that we were having trouble locating them. Would she mind if we took a look at their home?

"Gee, I'm not sure. They're entitled to their privacy, aren't they?"

"Of course. But if they are missing or something's happened to them, you'd like us to find out, wouldn't you?"

"When you put it like that, then, well...I guess so."

Still unsure, she gave us a key to the Gleason's place, and we promised to return it.

The rental had a Woodinville address, and it, too, was located in the Cottage Lake area. Only four miles from the Haddow residence, the A-frame cottage was considerably more isolated. We turned off Mink Road onto a gravel drive that meandered through tall firs and cedars for a third of a mile. At the end of the drive, in a small clearing, sat the now deserted house.

The drizzle had abated, but the low clouds hung on, adding a layer of insulation to the surrounding forest. It was as if we were wearing noise-canceling headphones as we crossed the porch to the front door. Even our footsteps on the cedar plank decking were muted.

Upon entering, a musty odor with hints of charred wood from a corner stove greeted us. With the heat turned off, it was as chilly inside as it was out. The floor plan was simple: one big room, including the kitchen, a bedroom, and a bathroom off to the side. The bed was unmade, and whoever did the housekeeping needed retraining. The place was a mess.

"Rog...over here." Wally seemed to have found the only thing that might help us: a laptop partially covered by throw pillows on the sofa.

After he handed it off I hit the power button, but no soap. "Damn thing's out of juice. We're taking it with us."

We spent a few more minutes searching for something to shed some light on who the Gleasons were but were unsuccessful. We locked the place back up, drove back to the Haddow home place to return the key, and then made our way back to Mukilteo to catch the next ferry back to Whidbey Island.

No matter how often—or infrequently—I left the island, coming back always filled me with a sense of comfort. The pace, the people, the water, and the beauty wherever I looked made me very happy this was my home.

Eight

We probably should have visited George Alberg while on the mainland, but I thought it better to glean as much as possible from Gleason's laptop before tackling that interview.

I handed it off to Bruce—our IT specialist—and told him to get the damn thing working as fast as he could. We busied ourselves with the mundane duties of keeping our constituents safe from murder and mayhem until we could again focus on the mystery of who killed Hannah Stucki and how they did it.

In the next five minutes, our investigation took a turn.

"Roger," Bruce shouted from across the workstations. "Pick up the phone."

Usually, he would have just transferred the call, so I assumed this one was special.

"Rog, it's Tom Davis."

Davis was the Sheriff of Island County and my boss. He was undoubtedly a political animal, but he was also an excellent administrator, boss, and friend. If he was calling, it was important.

"I know you've got your hands full on this ferry murder, but I think this has something to do with it."

"What is it?" *Forget the preamble; just tell me why you're calling.*

"Couple of hikers in Whidbey State Park found a vehicle with two dead people in it. It happened this morning. I sent a team there to investigate, and when they ID'd the bodies, they saw it was Randy and Marianne Gleason. Weren't those the two you were trying to clear for the ferry murder?"

"Shit…yeah, they were. How did they die?"

"The guy was shot in the head, and it looks like the woman had her head bashed in with something. The two women who found them will be having nightmares for a while. The car was a Honda Civic, pushed into the brush off the trailhead parking area. It looks like they've been there for a couple of days."

"And they were just found today?"

"Weather's been shitty, so not too many hikers. That and the car was green and pretty well hidden. Anyway…I got a couple of deputies there protecting the scene until you and Maggie clear it. I called her already."

With only an hour or two of daylight left, I needed to hustle. I said goodbye, told Wally to get in the car, and we bolted for the seven-mile drive to the park. By the time we arrived, I'd filled my second-in-command in on the details. Maggie was already doing her thing.

The deputies had cleared enough of the brush away for us to investigate and for Maggie to have room to do what she needed to do. When we approached, she was peering inside on the car's passenger side.

"Hey Mags, long time no talk, eh?" She stood and faced us, her ever-present smirk tugging at the corners of her mouth. She was all of five feet tall, wore square-rimmed glasses under a Tacoma Raniers ballcap, and had the look of someone possessing extreme confidence. I'd never seen her without jeans and Hokas; today was no exception. Although she had to be in her late forties, she appeared ten years younger and could run a ten K without breaking a sweat.

"What's the deal, Rog? Every time I get a chance to take a day off, you're turning up bodies again."

"Don't look at me. Your buddy Tom Davis dumped this in my lap."

"Looks to me like it's in your jurisdiction, no?"

She had me there, and I knew better than to get into a sparring match with someone of superior intellect, so I resorted to getting down to business. "What's the verdict?"

"Two dead people."

"Maggie…?"

"Oh, you mean what *happened* here?"

I chose the high road and kept my mouth shut.

"Giving up, eh? Okay...these two have been here for a couple of days. I'm surprised no one found them sooner." She tilted her head toward them and continued, "I'll know better when I get them back to the lab. The guy was shot in the face with a small caliber round similar to that woman from the ferry. The woman...ugh, what a mess...she was clubbed in the face. Whatever was used on her was enough to break through the skull and scatter brain matter all over the seats. What I can't figure out is how two dead people managed to get their car into this pile of brush, but hey, that's your department."

I had already considered that but figured finding who did this was a higher priority than worrying about *how* it was done. "When will you know if the slug is the same?"

"Since there's no exit wound, it's safe to say it's still there. If we can get these two back to the lab soon, I should have an answer by mid-morning. If we're lucky, maybe there will be some trace material from whatever was used to kill the woman. The techs should be here any time; maybe they'll find some prints somewhere that we can ID. You know I work on the island because I love it, and there's little violent crime. But since you've moved here, we've had our share of interesting cases."

"Hey, don't blame the messenger. I'm just a poor county deputy doing the best I can."

She let out an infectious guffaw, and I had to raise my hands in surrender.

Then she turned serious, "We're lucky you're here, Roger. We *have* had some strange cases lately, but I can't imagine anyone better to handle things."

Wally had been searching the perimeter for clues and had approached unnoticed during our conversation.

"How about me? Am I special, too?"

I looked at Maggie, and we shook our heads without saying anything.

"No... really...am I?"

"He's all yours, Rog; leave me alone and do what you gotta do," Maggie turned to continue her inspection.

"C'mon Wally, let's see if we can find anything."

He gave a loud "Humph" and joined me in scouring the surrounding area. I didn't expect to find anything, but we needed to check all the boxes. Whatever clues had been there were long gone, thanks to the folks who had stumbled upon the victims, so we left Maggie and the other deputies and returned to Freeland. It appeared the demise of Hannah Stucki wasn't all we were dealing with.

Nine

I woke up the next day both tired and lonely. Andie had spent the night in Seattle; something about a reception at UDub for all the important people, of which she was one.

I was up into the morning's wee hours searching for anything on Randy and Marianne Gleason and had come up empty. I finished feeding the pygmy goats and caught myself in the mirror as I walked through the hallway leading from the barn to the house.

What I saw was a fifty-one-year-old guy who looked sixty. Gray hair, red-rimmed hazel eyes, and a bit of a tummy that seemed to have developed out of nowhere looked back at me. The muscles in my arms and shoulders were still there, but the weathered Scottish face, etched from years in law enforcement, seemed weary. I'm not sure what Andie saw in me, but whatever it was, I hoped it was something other than the guy who was staring back at me. *Screw it,* I finally relented; *it's just the people dying around you—they're bringing you down.*

I abandoned the pity party and resolved to remedy the blues by diving into the investigation as soon as I hit the office. Maybe Francis or Wally found something that would cheer me up.

***

"Gotta be Mullins, right?"

Wally assaulted me before I even had a chance to grab a coffee.

"Huh?"

"The murders from yesterday. My money's on Mullins."

He was probably right, but I knew waiting until we had further evidence to declare success in solving the crime was prudent.

"It seems like that's a good possibility, but let's see what Maggie comes up with. Even if the slugs match, that doesn't prove anything. I suppose there's a scenario where the Gleasons take out Stucki, and then Mullins does away with them, but what's the connection? Why would the Gleasons kill someone they didn't know?"

Looking like I'd just doused him with cold water, he said, "Yeah...I know all that, but I still like Mullins for it."

Maggie called an hour later and confirmed that the bullet taken from Randy Gleason's head did indeed come from the same gun as the one that killed Hannah Stucki. This news confirmed the two killings were connected, but I wondered how Geason could have been killed with the same gun he used for Stucki. There were still so many questions. She said the crime scene techs had pulled several prints from the vehicle's rear fender and were running them through AFIS.

"Hey, Boss, guess who got that laptop working and who found the password to get into it," Bruce was proud as a peacock.

"I gotta believe it was you. Right, Bruce?" Wally was ahead of me.

"Yup...here you go. Check out the emails. Oh, just so you know...the password was *password*. You'd be surprised how many times that works." Our specialist strutted off after placing the computer on my desk.

The emails started over five months ago and were between Marianne Gleason and someone named Jennifer Hansen. According to their conversations, it seemed they had both been swept off their feet by Joseph Driggs's charisma and fervor while they were still in college, but after too many years as sister wives, they became disillusioned.

Driggs wouldn't let them have a computer, but they were able to smuggle one in with the assistance of a Randy Hughes. From what we could deduce, he was a mid-level drug dealer who occasionally took advantage of Driggs's offer of carnal activities with some of his wives. He became enamored with Gleason and brought her the laptop on one of his visits.

They hatched a plan to leave the compound together after Hughes convinced her he had a contact in Washington who could help find them a place to hide. She tried to persuade Hansen to come with them, but she was afraid to leave the nest. Marianne left the laptop with her friend and told her she would continue to correspond.

Once they set up house in Woodinville with Alberg's help, they both used the name Gleason, and she kept her promise to stay in touch with her friend. Two weeks ago, Marianne learned of Stucki and Becca's escape, and Jennifer told her how incensed Driggs was that he had been robbed. She told her about Mullins and what a prick he was and that he would stop at nothing to take care of those who had screwed over Driggs.

One of Jennifer's last messages was a warning to be alert for Mullins. He was on a scorched earth campaign to make examples of those who had wronged Driggs, whether the offense was imagined or real.

The emails helped us understand the acrimony between Driggs and his followers. Still, we had yet to come up with a plausible scenario for the murder on the *Tokitae*.

"Sounds like it wasn't the utopia promised in Driggsville, eh Boss?" Wally broke the silence with the same thoughts I was having.

"Yeah…it still amazes me that folks can be brainwashed by someone pretending to have all the answers. Maybe those who capitulate are looking for something or someone to latch onto, to assuage an emptiness in their lives."

"Yup, and then they end up with an asshole like Driggs who uses and abuses them. Then, if they cross him, he sends his enforcer to straighten things out. What a dick!"

I still thought it had to be the Gleasons who did Stucki on the ferry, and then Mullins cleaned up afterward, but I needed more corroboration. I thought I knew of someone who might shed some light on these questions.

"Hey, Wally, you up for another trip to America?"

"Sure. What are you thinking?"

"I'm thinking we should pay a visit to George Alberg. I suspect he can shed a little more light on this investigation."

***

We took the eight o'clock boat the following day and returned to Woodinville.

We discovered that Alberg was a supervisor for a company that manufactured exercise equipment. Not knowing what we'd run into, we chose to show up at his workplace unannounced.

When we pulled up to the visitor's parking area, I was surprised at the size of the facility. I guessed if they were shipping treadmills and exercise bicycles worldwide, they'd need a giant factory.

The lobby was smaller than I expected. It looked like a dentist's office, with a half-dozen chairs and a young man sitting at a desk behind a glass partition. I asked him if we could speak to George Alberg about our investigation. We wore our uniforms whenever we were off-island during work hours, so I didn't think telling the fellow who we were was necessary.

"I think he's in a production meeting right now. Those things sometimes last a while."

Being pushy wasn't my style, but we weren't about to cool our heels until the damn meeting was over. "This is a murder investigation. If you don't fetch Mr. Alberg, we'll have to interrupt the meeting."

If I hadn't had the receptionist's complete attention, I did now. He immediately stood, pushing his task chair against the wall and bobbing his head.

"I'll get him right away, sir."

It was fifteen minutes before Alberg joined us in the lobby. Either the meeting was at the other end of the building, or he decided to take his time. The man looked in his fifties and was seriously out of shape. It was apparent he never used any of the products he was in charge of manufacturing.

Laymen served as bishops in the Latter-day Saints Church but were not paid for their services., hence the need for secular employment to support their families. With thinning hair and a sallow complexion that suggested the sun was not his friend, the worried look on his face gave me the impression George Alberg would rather not talk to us.

"What questions do you have?" he asked as we settled into a small conference room beside the lobby.

"Did you tell Cheryl Haddow the Gleasons would be good renters for her?" I asked.

"Yes."

"Did you know them well?"

He hesitated for a few seconds, seeming unsure how much information he should offer, but finally surrendered, "No. I told Cheryl they were good people because I was told to."

"By whom?"

"I worked for the church for a long time when we lived in Provo. We moved here to Washington only a couple of years ago. All of my time there was spent in the recruiting office at BYU. There was a guy there years ago named Joseph Driggs...you've heard of him?"

I looked at Wally, who seemed unfazed, then nodded in acknowledgment and asked him to continue.

"If you've heard of him, then you know his story. What you can't understand is this guy's power over everyone he met. Even as a college kid, he was a force of nature. He seemed to have a way of looking into your soul. Like everyone else he encountered, I was a true believer for a time.

"He was expelled from the University and went on his mission. When he left, I realized what a dupe I had been. Because of it, I was embarrassed, and I developed a loathing for the man. I heard he set up that commune in Colorado City and how he rented out the place to drug dealers and felons.

"The Gleasons; what about the Gleasons?"

"I'm getting there. The reason we had to move here was because I got hooked on drugs. First, it was painkillers for a knee operation I had. I couldn't get off them, and that led to stronger stuff. I started getting what I needed from dealers who hung around the school. When my superiors found out, they forced me to go into rehab at a place in Salt Lake City. They said if I didn't clean up my act, I'd be excommunicated from the Church. I couldn't let that happen.

"Once I finished at First Step—that's the name of the place--they told me I needed to leave the University, and if I stayed clean, there was a place for me in Woodinville. I've been able to help some folks here, and we like the town. Then, a few months ago, I got a call from Randy Hughes—the dealer I used to get my stuff from. He told me unless I found a way to find him a place to live, he'd tell my story to the entire congregation here.

"So, I told Cheryl I knew them, and they'd be good renters. And they were."

"This guy, Hughes, was he a violent man?"

"Well...he *was* a drug dealer, and I think he was pretty high up in the organization, so yeah, I would say he probably was."

I was starting to picture how this whole scenario was tied together. And it began and ended with Driggs.

Before I could ask the next logical question, Wally jumped in: " Have you ever heard of a guy named Mullins? Shane Mullins?"

"Um...no, doesn't ring any bells."

"How about Driggs?" I asked, "Have you had any contact with him lately?"

The disgusted look on his face answered me even before he said, "If I never see him again, it'll be too soon. After he left BYU, I had nothing to do with him. I knew Hughes had some connection there, which was even more reason to make sure he left me alone."

I didn't think we would get much more from Alberg, so we thanked him and returned to the cruiser to head back to Whidbey. As soon as we were inside, Wally asked, "You think he was telling the truth about not knowing Mullins?'

"I do. He seemed to be giving us the straight scoop on Gleason or Hughes, and I don't think he had anything to gain by lying about Mullins."

"So let me see if I've got this straight: This guy Randy Hughes hooks up with Marianne Gleason, who wants to leave Driggs's groupies. A few months back, with Alberg's forced help, they move to Woodinville to escape. More recently, Hannah Stucki and her friend, Becca, steal a bunch of money and diamonds from Driggs and skip to Vegas, where Mullins attacks them. Hannah talks to Sparks, who gives her Francis's name, and after a side trip to California, she comes to Whidbey Island to find him.

"The way I figure it, Mullins contacts Hughes, who's now Gleason, tells him to be on the lookout for Hannah, and he'll pay to have her eliminated. He tracks her down somehow. Maybe the guy Sparks knew who did the ID for her had loose lips. Mullins probably kept his eye on Hughes for Driggs until he needed him for something.

"Anyway...they follow Hannah until she gets on the ferry, where they kill her."

I mainly agreed with what Wally was reciting but still had questions.

"Why kill Hannah until she gives up the money she stole? And how does Mullins kill Hughes with the gun Hughes used to do Hannah? And where are the diamonds?"

"All good questions, Boss. Another one is why Marianne Gleason would go along with all this, and what do we do next?"

"Maybe she didn't have a choice. Remember, she was under Driggs's thumb for years. That's gotta have scrambled her brain."

The murders of the Gleasons could simply have been Mullins cleaning up loose ends. How he managed to get the gun from them was curious but not necessarily meaningful. Maybe he met with them after they got off the ferry to pay them and took care of them then.

"We know for sure—at least pretty sure—that Mullins is involved, which means Driggs is too. We can't do much about Driggs, but as long as Mullins is in our neighborhood, he's fair game. I don't think he'll leave Washington until he comes up with whatever Hannah Stucki took. Let's focus on that for now."

"What about Francis?"

"What about him?"

"Do we know what he's doing?"

"No...but I'm afraid to ask."

As we boarded the ferry in Mukilteo, my phone buzzed. It was Maggie.

"Hey, Mags, what's up?"

"The prints from the Gleason murders; they're Mullins's. No doubt he's the perp."

Ten

Francis Early had been out of jail for over twenty years. Still in his mid-fifties, he was happy living with his brother and assuming the role of property manager for the five-thousand-square-foot log home built from the profits of Jake's investing acumen.

Now that his brother was more independent, Francis spent his free time gaming with his former inmates and researching anything that piqued his interest. Being an ex-con living on an island and spending most of his time helping Jake left little time for romantic entanglements. There had been a few short-term relationships—very short—over the years, but ultimately, he'd given up on the idea of any long-term female companionship.

He was under no illusions that his appearance could somehow be attractive to members of the opposite sex. Shoppers in the local grocery store, unless they knew him, especially women, were quick to avoid him, even going so far as to cover their children's eyes. He did his best to smile and nod, but even his genuine attempt at affability backfired more often than not. He supposed he could have his prison tears lasered away, but when he looked in the mirror, he was reminded of those days at McNeil and the hurdles he'd overcome. They were part of him, and so be it if others found them offensive. He wasn't convinced it was just the tears, either; his physical appearance, even minus the tears, might have had something to do with it.

He considered the irony of his involvement in the *Tokitae* murder of Hannah Stucki. Years ago, he'd accosted Kevin O'Malley on the vehicle deck of the *Sug-*

uamish ferry on a cold, rainy night. That meeting led to a series of events culminating in a shootout at the house. Now, after over four years, he was involved in another altercation on another ferry. Only this one was a woman who was murdered while looking to him for help.

The more he dug up about Driggs and Mullins, the more effort he needed to control his simmering rage. He firmly believed in the "live and let live" philosophy, but when people chose to impose their will on others, he took exception to them. And this one was personal because he hadn't been able to prevent Hannah's death. He knew the Island County deputies were good, but they had limits on what they could accomplish; they had jurisdictions to worry about, too. He did not.

His brother was off-island for the day for a meeting somewhere, leaving him alone to ponder his next moves. Sparks had been helpful, but Francis was a "hands-on" kinda guy, so he did the most logical thing—at least to him. He booked a flight from Paine Field to Las Vegas. He'd be there before dinner.

***

Colorado City was a two-and-a-half-hour drive from Vegas, so Francis decided it was best to drive north to St. George, Utah, and spend the night; then, he'd have less than an hour drive the following day.

While still springtime in the Northwest, Southern Utah seemed well into summer with temperatures in the upper eighties. He drove from Sin City to Littlefield on I-15 in his rented Chevy Silverado, then took Highway 91 for the final sprint to St. George. The journey mesmerized Francis, who'd never spent time in the Southwest.

Miles and miles of Joshua Trees led to the ragged, twisting hills of the Paiute Indian Reservation, followed by the stunning entrance into St. George. With the majestic, rust-colored mountains surrounding the city now ablaze from the setting sun, it was a vista that touched the soul of the former McNeil Island inmate. Although he didn't understand how someone could be duped into following a cult leader like Driggs, if Colorado City looked anything like St. George, he could see how the raw beauty of the place might conjure up feelings of inadequacy.

He spent much of the night researching the towns of Colorado City and Hildale at a Best Western on St. George Blvd and was back on the road by 9 a.m.. State Highway 59 S took him past the towering El Capitan red mountain—no relation to El Capitan of Yosemite—and into the center of Short Creek. Colorado City, Arizona, and Hildale, Utah, both towns skirting the border, are known as the Short Creek Community, even though they have separate local governments and services.

The Fundamentalist Church of Jesus Christ of Latter-Day Saints (FLDS) began arriving at the Short Creek Community in the late 1930s. The Church of Jesus Christ of Latter-Day Saints outlawed polygamy in 1890, much to the dismay of some of its followers. Led by John Barlow, the splinter group chose the location because of its inaccessibility, allowing them to have multiple wives, which they believed was a central part of their religion.

The cult-like following of the FLDS went through some turbulent times under the more recent leadership of Warren Jeffs, who served as president of the religious faction. Rumors of child marriages, sexual abuse, and child abandonment surrounded Jeffs, who was eventually convicted of child sexual assault and is now serving a life sentence in Texas. Some FLDS members still consider him their prophet despite his incarceration.

Now that he knew the backstory of Short Creek, Francis had no difficulty understanding how a man like Driggs could establish his own subset of the runaway religious sect. If some of the followers were upset at the demise of Jeffs, it made sense they'd look to someone else to deliver them to the gates of Heaven. Even though his romantic entanglements had been few and of short duration, Francis could only begin to imagine the complications of having multiple wives or girlfriends simultaneously. *If it ever happens*, he thought, *one would be plenty.*

His first stop was the Hildale Police Department. He chose Hildale because he'd read where they had elected a non-FLDS woman as mayor, and he figured they would be a little more forthcoming than the more conservative city government in Colorado City. It felt odd that even though Short Creek was a singular community, it was still two municipalities in two separate states.

As often happened when his imposing appearance graced a room, everyone stopped what they were doing. The desk sergeant bolted upright and rested his hand on the butt of his holstered sidearm. Used to such reactions, Francis raised his hands in a peaceful gesture and announced his intentions.

"Hi, folks. My name is Francis Early, and I'm here to get some information."

"Some ID on you, sir?" asked the sergeant.

As Francis moved to get his wallet, the young policeman's hand nudged closer to his gun's grip. When his visitor removed his wallet, he relaxed a little.

"I'm consulting with the Island County Sheriff's Department on Whidbey Island in Washington State." It wasn't the truth, but he hoped it would allay the locals' fears and maybe even get them to help.

He took Francis's license; then the cop looked up and asked if someone could vouch for him.

"Um...sure. Call Deputy Roger Wilkie at the Sheriff's Department. Here's his number." He knew Roger would be pissed off at his undertaking; he trusted that his friend would do the right thing.

Eleven

"Hey, Rog, some cop from Utah calling for you."

We had just walked through the door when Bruce informed me of a call. Wally retreated to his workstation while I did the same and immediately picked up the phone.

"Wilkie here."

"Deputy Wilkie, this is Officer Thomas from Hildale, Utah. There's a man here who says he's consulting with you on a case. I wanted to verify his capacity before we spoke with him."

I figured it *had* to be Francis. Once he got his teeth into something, there was no stopping him.

"Um...he wouldn't be a very large man with tear tattoos, would he?"

"Yessir...that's right, sir; that's him."

"Francis Early...correct?"

"Correct, sir."

"Yes...he's uh...he's working with us on a case. Any help you can give him would be appreciated...and officer?

"Yes?"

"May I have a word with him?"

"You bet. I'm handing him over."

In the few seconds that passed, I imagined the look on the faces of those in the small department when Francis entered their domain. It made me smile.

"Hey Rog, how's things?"

"Francis...do you remember when I said to keep me in the loop?"

"Um...yes, yes I do."

"Did you tell me you were taking a trip?"

"No...ah...no, I didn't."

I was upset, but only mildly. Francis hadn't done anything wacky yet, and maybe he could find something we couldn't access.

"We can talk about procedure later, but do me a favor and don't get into trouble...wherever the hell you are."

"You bet, Roger. I'll take care of that for you. I'm sure these folks will be very helpful. Talk to you later."

Wally had meandered over during my phone conversation and already had the gist of the interaction.

"Francis doing Francis things, eh Boss?"

"Yup. He's in Hildale, the sister town to Colorado City. Probably trying to get a handle on where Driggs is. The locals there wanted to verify that he's consulting with us."

"Consulting?"

"That's what he told them, and I confirmed. *We* have no business being there, but maybe he can turn something up. He has a knack for shit-stirring, and as long as it's on their patch, I'm okay with it."

As Wally started to return to his desk, I had a sudden thought, "Hey Wally, if it was Mullins who ordered the hit on Hannah Stucki, why did he do it?"

"Cuz Driggs told him to?"

"Yeah...I got that...but if she took a bunch of diamonds with her and Driggs wanted them back, why kill her unless he got them first?"

"You thinking maybe he's got them?"

"If that were the case, why kill the Gleasons? I think it's more likely Mullins told Randy Hughes/Gleason to make the hit and recover the diamonds. Maybe when he caught up with them after the ferry incident, he saw they didn't have the stones, and he lost it and killed them."

Wally considered this scenario briefly before coming up with a different one: "Or they did get them, Mullins took them and killed them for the fun of it?"

I didn't know the man, but his reputation as a brutal instrument of misery and violence seemed to allow for either of those possibilities. I came to a decision: "If he's got them, he's gone. If not, he's probably still trying to figure out where they are. I want the CCTV footage from the Clinton terminal sent to us daily. Have Bruce go through the video and tell him to keep his eyes peeled for a tall, thin man wearing an Irish cap. We get all kinds of visitors to the island, but Mullins is sure to stick out among the passengers."

Twelve

Shane Mullins was sick of the Northwest. It reminded him too much of Northern Ireland. After bouncing from one foster home to another and a few stints in youth detention, he left the country for good when he was nineteen. Since coming to America, he'd spent most of his years in the West and Southwest, preferring the warm, dry heat to the overcast drizzle that seemed to be a constant in the Puget Sound region. He'd been in the area almost a week and had seen the sun only one day. It reminded him of the six months he had spent at the correctional facility in Monroe after he'd been caught assaulting one of the women he tracked to Tacoma.

It was supposed to be a slam-dunk deal. Driggs wanted to teach his followers a lesson while getting his ill-gotten funds back. Mullins was supposed to hurt them badly but leave them alive to set an example for others who might think of deserting his flock. Now it was a shitshow.

He found the two runaways in Vegas. They told him they didn't steal anything. When he punched one of them in the face, he was sure the other would give up and tell him where it was. She didn't, so he did the same to her, but harder. She collapsed like a puppet, suddenly losing its strings, and hit the floor. As he bent over to check her pulse, the Stucki broad whacked him over the head with a bedside lamp, grabbed her backpack, and ran out the door. Stunned, a little by the blow but more by the audacity of the bitch, his sluggishness to react allowed her to escape.

Breaking the news to Driggs was difficult. Mullins had lived a life riddled with inflicting pain on others. He'd done it for so long it didn't bother him. He enjoyed it. It wasn't personal, and he was paid well by those in the drug trade for it. He hadn't intended to work solely for the charismatic polygamist, but something about the man was mesmerizing and, at times, downright creepy. It was as if he knew things that were about to happen, or maybe he caused them to happen. Either way, it was enough so that Mullins wanted, no, needed, to be in his good graces. And, of course, the man paid very well.

He knew his failure to secure the pilfered diamonds would be met with quiet disappointment, which would be enough punishment. He was glad he was doing it over the phone and not in person; at least he would avoid the look of disapproval from those piercing eyes.

All his life, he had been the aggressor, the tough guy. He never gave two shits about his employer; such was his love for his craft. The money was good, but he would have hurt people for nothing if he were honest. His relationship with Joseph Driggs, though, was something he couldn't explain. And it was unsettling.

Years ago, he had been evening scores for one of the dealers taking advantage of Driggs's offer of asylum. When he came to the encampment, either to collect his fee or to receive another assignment, he caught glimpses of Driggs surrounded by a dozen of his wives. He thought the whole thing was bizarre, but that was it. He was only in town for a night or two, and women were available.

One morning back then, while gathering his things to set out from Colorado City, he received a knock on the door of his shanty-like guest cottage. The woman who had shared his bed the night before was already gone, but he figured she'd forgotten something and was back for it. When he opened the door, he was surprised to see Joseph Driggs standing there.

"You're Shane Mullins?"

He felt discomfort facing the self-proclaimed prophet, almost like when he was a kid caught stealing.

"Yeah, that's me."

"From what I've seen, you are very good at what you do and take your assignments seriously."

Standing at the door facing the innocuous-looking portly fellow with thinning hair, Mullins wasn't sure what to say, so he said nothing.

"I have a situation that needs someone with your skills."

"I already have a job I need to take care of," Mullins wasn't sure where this was going.

"I've spoken with the man who was employing you. He'll get another person to handle it. You're free to help me."

Mullins was used to being in control and didn't like the conversation's direction. He said, "You had no right to interfere with my business. I'll be the one who decides what I do and don't do."

"I'm sorry; I didn't mean to offend you. It's just...well, I've seen you around, and all the visitors here who know of you say you are dependable and discreet. It would mean a lot to me if you would consider the job. It pays twenty-five grand, by the way."

Twenty-five grand was more than twice his usual fee. Driggs was strange, but it was enough money to make him put his concerns aside and take the gig. He was to locate a woman—according to Driggs, one of his wives—teach her that running away from her husband came with consequences and bring her back.

Using the information supplied by Driggs, he located the escaped wife by the following afternoon. She had been alone, staying at her cousin's weekend retreat in Cedar City. Mullins drove up to the isolated cabin, kicked the door in, startling the already frightened twenty-year-old, and landed a massive fist square in her face. He pulled the blow slightly so as not to kill the young woman but ended up knocking her out.

He tossed her unconscious body into his pickup and made the drive to Colorado City in a little over an hour. As he drove, he could hear her struggling to breathe through her now bloodied and broken nose. *She wasn't a beauty to begin with,* he thought, *but now the Miss America Pageant was surely out of the question.*

After he arrived at the compound, he threw her over his shoulder, walked to Driggs's house, and pounded on the door.

"Is this what you're looking for?" He asked when Driggs opened the door. Then he dropped her on the stoop, turned, and walked away.

Mullins spent the night in a fleabag motel in Hildale and planned to visit Driggs the next morning to collect his money. He was surprised when the fundamentalist leader knocked on his door soon after he awakened.

"Here's your money," said the round little man as he opened the door.

Mullins had intended to take the bag of cash and be done with this strange fellow, but the guy's vibe created some uncertainty. He took the bag, said "Okay," and stood there, unsure of himself.

Driggs, seeming to sense his discomfort, said nothing and looked up at him with a smile as subtle as the Mona Lisa's.

"What?" Mullins asked.

"I think you enjoyed yourself performing my request."

"Whatever..."

"What if I could provide you with work that you enjoy and pay you well? Would you consider an exclusive arrangement? Just between you and me?"

Mullins, his head only inches under the doorframe, didn't know how to answer. The guy was weird, but there was something magnetic about him. Whatever it was, it scared him, and nobody *ever* did that.

"Shane...may I call you Shane?"

"Um...sure."

"Let's do this, Shane. I have another assignment for you. It pays the same. When you've completed this one, then maybe you'll be prepared to agree to work for me exclusively."

Mullins thought it was an easy way to resolve his concerns or at least delay the decision, so he agreed. That was long ago. In the intervening years, Driggs had made him rich, but truth be told, he enjoyed the hell out of the work. His relationship with his employer was difficult to put into words. He thought he was conniving and ruthless, but he'd always been straightforward with Mullins. There was respect and, if he were being honest, a somewhat irrational fear he didn't understand. He couldn't wait to get away when they were together, yet when they weren't, he craved the attachment he felt toward Driggs. More than anything, though, he dreaded disappointing him.

***

"I'm sorry, Joseph, I still haven't located the diamonds." The words sounded hurried and ashamed, even as he uttered them.

"What about Stucki?"

"She's dead. The guy I hired to recover the diamonds killed her when he saw she didn't have them with her."

"Why would you hire someone incompetent?"

Mullins didn't have a good answer. Hughes was the only contact he had in this godforsaken place. He should have handled things himself, but he would have been easily noticed in the confines of the ferry, and he couldn't risk being spotted.

"It was a mistake, but I've handled it." He found it better to be upfront with Driggs; the guy's bullshit detector was uncanny.

"You're sure this person didn't get the diamonds from Stucki and keep them for himself?"

"Very. If he had, I'm certain he would have told me." Mullins flashed back to the damage he'd done to the Gleason woman's face as a threat to Hughes. No, he was sure.

"What now? What are you planning to do?"

He knew he should have come up with a plan before the call. He had to wing it: "I'm gonna retrace her steps from when she got here. She must have hidden them somewhere."

"Shane?"

"Yes?"

"Do not fuck this up. We are talking about a great deal of money, and now that the government is after me, I need to move about quickly. I need it."

It was rare that Driggs used profanity, and it revealed his anxiety. He had never spoken so sternly to Mullins before.

"I'll get them, Joseph. I'll call you when I have them."

He disconnected the call and devised a plan to recover what had caused his boss such worry.

Thirteen

W e could do little until we knew where Mullins was. There was a chance he had left the area and was back with Driggs, but the Gleason murders smacked of frustration, which led me to believe he was still looking for Driggs's treasure.

After reviewing the terminal's CCTV footage for three days, we finally got lucky. Or rather, Bruce did.

"Hey Boss, check this guy out. He's not wearing that Irish cap, just a ballcap, but he's pretty tall, and there's a glimpse from the side that shows he's got a honker on him." Bruce had a way with words.

Wally and I walked over to look at Bruce's monitor. From the mugshots we'd seen and the pictures Sparks sent, I was sure this was Mullins, and Wally agreed. "It's him, Rog; gotta be."

"When did this happen, Bruce?"

"These are from yesterday, the nine o'clock from Clinton."

"From? You mean he was leaving the island?"

"Yup. Looks like they caught him when he was walking on the *Tokitae*."

Shit, that meant he was on the mainland and could be anywhere by now.

"If he's walking on, that means he's gotta have a car on the other side."

"You're right, Wally, but how did he get around while he was here on the island?"

"You mean when he wasn't killing the Gleasons? Hell, probably took the bus."

I hadn't thought about that, but it *was* possible. Island Transit has been around since 1987 and is one of the actual perks of island life. Its routes cover Whidbey and Camano Islands and are free to all passengers.

"Bruce?"

"Yeah, I know...get the CCTV from Island Transit. But why? If we're sure this is him..."

"We're mostly sure. Bruce, but get it anyway. Maybe they'll have a better look."

We left our IT specialist and went to the conference room to spitball things. Wally spoke first, "What now? "

"We've been chasing our tails ever since the murder on the ferry. Let's send everything we have on Mullins to the local and state cops; maybe they'll spot him. Then, let's look at every place Stucki has been. The place she stayed in California was spendy, so we know she had some cash or fenced some diamonds there. The same goes for that Bellevue hotel. They've gotta be somewhere, and I'd rather we find them before Mullins or Driggs does.

"Tomorrow is Saturday. Why don't you and Kate spend tonight at the Bellevue Club Hotel and see what you can find out? I think I'll get together with Danny; they've gotta have other cameras on those boats, and maybe we'll see something that'll help."

"Uh, Boss...that place isn't cheap. I don't think I can afford it."

"You chip in a couple hundred bucks, and the county will pick up the rest plus your meals. Deal?"

"Hell, yes. Wait until Kate hears about this."

"Uh...Wally?"

"Yes?"

"Please keep your wife out of this. I know she's a great detective, but it's not her jurisdiction, and...well, you know what happens when she gets a whiff of something."

I wasn't telling Wally anything he didn't know. His wife *was* a great detective, but the last time she got involved, she ended up being locked up alongside a warlock, and things went downhill from there.

"Don't worry, Rog, I'll keep her on a tight leash."

"Huh, Wally?"

"Sorry, bad choice of words. I meant to say I'll make sure she knows the rules...sorta."

"Yes...I'm sure you will. Just make sure you both stay out of trouble and see if you can find out anything. Otherwise, you two enjoy yourselves. You deserve it."

***

Wally took off, and I called Danny Collins. He answered his cell, which meant he wasn't on duty.

"To what do I owe the pleasure, Roger?" Danny fancied himself quite the proper individual, but we both knew better.

"Cut the shit, Danny. You're off, right?"

"For the next three days. Tell me you're not gonna screw it up. I've got golf to play with your good buddy O'Malley."

"Perish the thought, Sir, I'll not be taking much of your time." He wasn't the only one who could feign a European accent.

"What's up?"

"You've got cameras on the ferry, right?"

"Yeah, but remember? The ones on the car deck weren't working."

"Yes, I recall you saying that, but what about the others on the boat? Do they work?"

"Most of 'em."

"How long do you keep the footage?"

"The requirements are a little vague, but usually, it's stored online for not less than thirty days. After that, unless it's flagged for some reason, it's archived."

"So, anything that's happened over the last week is still available?"

"Supposed to be, but I've never had any reason to check them out."

"I need to see all you've got from the day of the Stucki murder. Maybe we'll get lucky and see something that will help."

"The whole day?"

"Let's start with the sailing she was on and go from there."

"Let me make some calls. This will have to be cleared through the Port Captain, but because of the murder, it shouldn't be a problem."

"How long will this take?"

"Not very, I hope. I've got a tee time with O'Malley in an hour."

"Danny..."

"Just kidding, sheesh. Let me call Rogers and get it done. If you don't hear back from me, you'll get a link to the footage in an email from WSDOT within the next half hour."

I was surprised that things could happen so quickly, but I knew better than to ask how it was possible. "Thanks, Danny. I appreciate it and give my best to O'Malley."

"Hey, why don't you join us sometime?"

"Um...that would be a no. Can't see the sense in chasing a little ball for four hours."

Fourteen

They arrived at the stylish boutique hotel a little after six. The ferry traffic was the usual Friday slog, but the county police vehicle was allowed to the head of the queue. The journey southbound on I-405 was slow but not nearly as bad as the northbound lanes where the commuters were headed home for the weekend.

Wally and Kate had been so focused on their cases that it took the better part of the trip to realize they were off the clock—mostly—and could start to enjoy themselves. They made an interesting couple as they pulled up to the valet and strode into the small but elegant lobby. In her mid-thirties, Kate was never mistaken for anything other than Irish. With short auburn hair highlighting a splash of tiny freckles across her cheeks, her emerald green eyes twinkling above her prominent cheekbones often led to poor judgment by those she encountered seeking to deceive her. Her slender physique hid well the hours she spent in the gym to ensure she was more than capable of defending herself should the need arise.

On the other hand, Wally Turpin was a smidge taller than Kate's five-foot seven-inch frame but infinitely thicker. His bushy, sandy hair topped a smiling, ruddy-complexioned face. Broad-chested, with Popeye-like arms, he was considered everyone's best friend. They made for an unlikely couple but were soulmates and deeply in love.

"I think I'm gonna hit the gym before dinner," Wally announced after they'd checked in.

"Huh...what did you say?" Kate's surprise was evident since the gym wasn't Wally's favorite place.

"You spend an hour and a half every day there when we're home. Since they have this fabulous club here, I thought I'd try to start a regimen."

"We get a free holiday at this cool place and you're going to start a *regimen*?"

"Yeah...you know...something you do over and over again."

Grinning from ear to ear, she shook her head and said, "Go ahead, numbnuts, just don't hurt yourself...you know...in case later, maybe there might be hotel sex available."

Wally was quiet for a few seconds, then looked back to Kate from the entrance to the club and quietly said, "Maybe I should start the regimen another time."

"Too late...you go ahead. I'll relax, then get ready for dinner. If you're lucky and don't do anything stupid, you can still make a reservation for that other thing we discussed."

"Promise?"

"Go...get outta here. I'll see you in the room when you're done."

As Wally trudged off to the gym, Kate turned toward the elevator. She stood facing the richly paneled door until it opened, then stepped into the dimly lit cab. As she turned and faced outward to the distant reception desk, the door began to shut. Then she reached out across the closing opening, forcing the sliding door to abruptly stop and return to the fully open position.

She had been enjoying their friendly banter so much she forgot why they were there. Yes, she was assigned to the Bellingham Police Department, but Wally was her guy, and she would do whatever she could to help his investigation.

She walked back to the reception desk, showed her detective's badge, and told the blue-blazered woman behind it why she was there.

"We spoke with two of your people about Ms. Stucki last week," the nervous woman said.

"Yes, I know that. We're here to take some time off, but honestly, we need some help trying to find the guy who murdered Hanah Stucki. Is there anything you remember about her that maybe slipped your mind when you were questioned last week?"

The more reserved of the two women from the Wilkie and Houser interview scrunched up her nose, trying to recall any detail about their now-deceased former guest. She turned her back to Kate and seemed to gaze off into a side office.

"There's nothing else about her that I can remember, but a package arrived by mail for her before she checked in, and I remember giving it to her when she arrived."

Kate asked, "How big was it, and was it light or heavy?"

"It was pretty small, maybe a three-inch square box. It was wrapped in brown paper, like from a grocery bag, and it was very light. When I took it from the safe, I remembered a pill, pebble, or something rattling around inside. Many of our guests have things sent here before their arrival, so I didn't think much of it until now."

"Thank you, you've been very helpful."

Kate strode back to the elevator. Based upon what Wally had shared with her about Mullins, Driggs, and the Stucki murder, she had a damn good idea what was in the little box that Hannah Stucki had sent to herself.

***

When I returned to the station, I found an email from Bruce with an attachment from the CCTV for Island Transit. It was a clear-cropped headshot of Shane Mullins. The cruel eyes and mangled nose were unmistakable. The son of a bitch had been right in front of us.

There was also an email from the Washington State Department of Transportation. It was from someone named R. Berner, who said: *Danny Collins requested I send you this link to the camera footage from the Tokitae. Let me know if you have any questions.*

I clicked on the link, and a screen popped open with a list of numbers and times opposite them. The times were all within a twenty-minute window, and from the looks of them, it had to be the *Tokitae* sailing when Stucki was killed.

Upon closer inspection, the numbers were accompanied by a small emoji-looking object that appeared to be a tiny camera. At least twenty cameras were present, which was no surprise since the Olympic Class boat had a million nooks and crannies.

I began cautiously clicking on one camera at a time until I found the one on the deck where Stucki's car was parked. It was a still shot of an empty boat. This was the one that wasn't working, and it showed the last shot when it went down.

When I was comfortable navigating the videos on the site and watching passengers walk to and from the upper decks, I noticed it was no longer light outside. Andie had said she'd be back from the University early, was planning a surprise for dinner, and that I shouldn't be late. I hurriedly closed down the computer and locked up the office. As I made my way to the cruiser, I wondered how Wally and Kate were doing on their almost-free night of vacation.

I drove up the gravel drive to our home on the western shore of Lone Lake and saw Jake Early's van parked in front of the house. When I entered, he was sitting with Andie, both sipping something red from a wine glass, and it looked as though they were having a serious conversation.

"We were just talking about you," Jake said, looking up from his wheelchair.

"Nothing disparaging, I hope."

Andie walked over and hugged me, and I immediately felt better.

"Of course not, Dear. I bumped into Jake on the ferry earlier and invited him for dinner. I told him to bring Francis, too, but he told me he was still somewhere trying to track down this Driggs character. Something about him working with you on it."

I looked at Jake and saw the beginnings of an "*I told you so*" smirk at the corners of his mouth.

I shrugged and said, "Yes...it looks like he is. He took it upon himself to visit the old stomping grounds of Driggs and Mullins. There are still some remnants of the FLDS in Short Creek." I explained the twin towns on the Utah/Arizona border to Andie.

"It sounds like an interesting place," she said with a smile. What are the chances Francis will stir something up?"

Both Jake and I said "Excellent" at the same time.

I continued, "When he's committed and personally invested like he is now, nothing will stop him. He's relentless. He will turn over every stone, break through any barrier, and will never, ever take no for an answer."

"That's my Bro," Jake said, his grin spreading.

"And you're letting him do this by himself?" Andie asked.

"Andie, you do know who we're talking about, right? Francis is his own dog and knows how to take care of himself," I said.

"There's that," Jake chimed in, "Plus, the only way to stop him would be to lock him up. He'll be fine; we just need to keep our fingers crossed that he doesn't piss off the cops or the folks living there."

Over dinner, we continued discussing the odds of Francis upsetting the remaining members of the ultra-conservative FLDS, and we all finally agreed it was only a matter of time.

Fifteen

For two days, Francis had been wandering the twin towns of Colorado City and Hildale, trying everything to get an inkling of where Joseph Driggs had gone.

The local police were less than helpful even though they knew he was loosely affiliated with a sheriff's office on some island somewhere. They confirmed Driggs was the former leader of the FLDS and that once the feds cracked down on his harboring of drug dealers and other miscreants, he left the area. He was met with headshakes and disinterest when he asked if they had any leads on his current location.

Francis was not surprised by the lack of assistance, especially from those in law enforcement. His threatening appearance was one thing, but when they checked to see if he had a record—and they always did—the door closed loudly.

When he attempted to strike up a conversation at one of the local eateries, the patrons either ignored him or turned and fled, hurrying their children along in front of them. He thought the place gave off a strange vibe but decided to spend the night anyway and give things another try the following day.

With few lodging options, he selected a place called Zion Country Cabins. There were two of them, and they were both available. Since Short Creek's existence was primarily as a refuge for the FLDS, there was little need for *any* overnight accommodation, much less even the smallest of hotel chains.

The smell of mold with subtle overtones of roach spray assaulted his olfactory senses as he entered the one-room shack. At almost five thousand feet of elevation, the early spring nights, still occasionally dipping below freezing, required more heat than the little wall heater could provide. He could see his breath as he flicked the switch and turned on the bedside lamp. The double bed looked adequate, and the thick quilt at its foot appeared suitable for offsetting the lack of heat. At the rear of the room, a tiny corner stall shower sat opposite a toilet and wall sink. The so-called bathroom was separated from the main area by a shower curtain. There was no TV.

Tired from the trip and the day's lack of progress, he collapsed on the bed, clothes and all, and pulled up the fluffy quilt. He promised himself he'd make better progress tomorrow.

He awoke before sunrise, and after attending quickly to personal hygiene requirements—one of the benefits of a shaved head, *no combing*—he headed back to the diner he had visited the previous day.

He sat at a counter reminiscent of the Woolworth's staple of three generations ago. After his night in the stuffy cabin, the smell of frying bacon and brewing coffee reminded him of how hungry he was.

"Hey, Stranger...an early bird, eh?"

He saw a uniformed waitress sporting a beehive hairdo and wearing red, horn-rimmed glasses who appeared somewhere in her fifties. Her nametag said Darlene, and she stood holding a green order pad, her pencil in hand and a broad smile on her heavily lipsticked lips.

"What'll it be?"

The fact that she didn't even blink when he faced her with his prison-tatted face surprised him and, for a few seconds, left him speechless.

"Cat got your tongue, Mister? Take your time. It's not like there's anyone else here for me to wait on."

"Um...uh...sorry. You're the only person in town who hasn't ignored me or run away when I've approached."

"If you've seen the crap I've had to put up with in this shithole of a town, nothing would surprise you."

Instinctively, Francis glanced around and confirmed he was the only patron in the restaurant.

"How come you're still here if you don't like it?"

"Oh…just because it's a shithole doesn't mean I'd live anywhere else. My parents were born here, and so were theirs. It was a sleepy little town before Rulon Jeffs and those FLDS knuckleheads began showing up. Then Driggs came along and started his own little fan club and began letting those drug dealers hide out. I'm happy the little shit is gone."

Finally, Francis thought, *a person I can relate to.*

"I'm here looking for Driggs. He's involved in a murder back in Washington."

"You want the number two or three?"

"Huh?"

"Breakfast, Dearie, if you're gonna sit here and bullshit, at least order some food so I can earn a living."

"Oh…yeah, sorry. I'll take number three."

She scribbled something on her pad, tore off the sheet, and slipped it under a clip on a carousel, which she then turned around so whoever the cook was could get things started.

She turned back to Francis and said, "A murder, huh…doesn't surprise me. Never liked that little asshole; couldn't understand how he suckered all those wives into marrying him."

"Any idea where he took off to?"

"Nope, and I hope he never comes back. Little by little, things are getting better here, and I'm afraid he'll just fuck up the works if he returns."

He appreciated her colorful language, and her feelings for the cult leader were crystal clear.

His breakfast arrived much faster than he thought possible, and he ate ravenously. Darlene busied herself refilling the Bunn coffee maker, then poured him another cup.

As he finished mopping up the remains of his eggs with a slice of toast, she moved closer to him, still on the opposite side of the counter.

"If you're trying to find him, you might wanna check with one of the Lost Boys. A couple of 'em live in Kanab. I think they're still working at that Best Friends place."

"Best Friends…Lost Boys…huh?"

"Damn, Honey, you just fall off the turnip truck? Best Friends is that ginormous ranch where they take homeless animals. It's the biggest in the country, and they have over a thousand acres. If you want a dog to adopt, that's where you go.

"Anyways...that's where a couple of the Lost Boys work. They know Driggs cuz he's the one set 'em free."

"Um...Darlene, I'm afraid you'll have to tell me what the Lost Boys are. Is it like a club?"

"Oh, it's a club, alright. You know how the FLDS practices polygamy, right?"

"Ah...yes. Yes, I do."

"Well, if a man has three or ten wives, don't you think they'd run out of women eventually?"

"Well, yeah, I guess so."

"So the way they manage it is they take away some of the young men to reduce the competition for the ladies."

"What do you mean...take away?"

"Just what I said. They round up some of the less physically gifted boys and dump 'em on the freeway miles from here."

"You're shitting me...sorry for the language."

"Fuck...don't be sorry. These folks are fucking nuts. I'm glad their numbers are dwindling. Maybe in a few years, we'll have our town back."

Francis was still trying to grasp the callous disregard for life harbored by a religious sect supposedly living according to God's teachings.

He took a minute, then gathered himself and asked, "Do these boys, or I guess men, have a name? Maybe I can find them, and they might know where Driggs would go."

"Ask for the Barlows. They're different families but have the same names...go figure. Hell, the way these folks procreate, I'm sure they're all *closely* related... if you know what I mean."

Francis was pretty sure he knew what she meant. He thanked her for everything—especially the information—left her a generous tip and headed back to his truck to begin the forty-mile trip to Kanab.

***

Driving through Kanab, following the instructions from the navigation lady on his phone, he proceeded five miles north of town on Highway 89 until he reached the Welcome Center for the Best Friends Sanctuary.

The modern ranch-style building was tucked at the base of a mountain of deep red rock walls. Even though it was early in the day, the hustle and bustle of the employees engendered a sense of purpose and direction in the place. He took the three steps up to the open entry doors and stopped a twenty-something woman walking across the lobby with a German Shepherd glued to her left leg.

As Francis stepped into her path, she halted while her companion bristled with concern. She barked something in German, and the dog immediately sat, although his attention was still zeroed in on Francis.

"It's never a good idea to step in front of someone walking a dog whose purpose in life is to protect. You're lucky Henry here is well-trained."

Francis was seldom concerned or afraid for his well-being, but something about this dog's intensity caused him to back up. "I'm sorry. I was just trying to find someone here to ask about some employees. This dog of yours seems very attentive."

The woman was deeply tanned, wore ebony hair in a short bob, and was a foot shorter than Francis. She smiled at his discomfort and said, "That's cuz he *is*. I'm Terri Millar, and this beautiful creature is a purebred GSD. A couple of years ago, the previous owner went to Germany to get him; then, six months ago, he suddenly died. His kids wanted nothing to do with the dog, so he ended up here. It's taken that long to get him to bond with me."

"So, he's yours?"

"Well...no. I'm one of the managers here, and I help acclimate the animals. Henry is a special case. Early on, he was very difficult, and now...well, now he's my buddy."

While conversing, Francis noticed the dog relaxed somewhat but kept his eyes glued to him.

"How many dogs are here?"

"It varies. Right now, I'd guess close to eight hundred."

"Eight HUNDRED?"

"Yup. We're the largest in the country by far and a no-kill sanctuary. Even if an animal is old or injured, we care for them until they die. We have a fully staffed veterinary hospital, and we're spread over three thousand acres. We lease another thirty thousand from the Federal Government."

"Holy shit…uh, sorry. I'm just surprised at the scope of this place."

As Francis spoke, Henry stood, walked over to him, and started licking his hand. The simple gesture startled him, and he was reluctant to pull away.

"Yikes…I've never seen him do that to anyone but me. Do you have food in that hand?"

"Uh…no, nothing." As he spoke, the shepherd lay down at his feet. "Um, why is he doing that?"

"I don't know. Maybe there is something in your smell, but he likely senses something about you. These animals are incredibly intuitive, and they can pick up fear or aggression, or even kindness. I'd trust Henry's judgment long before another human's."

The conversation almost made him forget the purpose of his visit. With Henry's paw still on his left foot, he asked, "Do you know if two men are working here by the name of Barlow?"

With Henry seeming to approve of the visitor, Terri appeared less confrontational. "And who wants to know?"

"I apologize. Let me start over. My name is Francis Early, and I'm from Washington State. There was an unfortunate murder recently, and the woman—whom I don't know and I've never met—had my name on her. I'm working with the Sheriff's Department from Island County, trying to track down some leads, and it's taken me here."

"And these Barlow fellows, are they suspects or in trouble?" She appeared wary once again.

"No, no…not at all. I was told by someone from Colorado City that they might have information that could help me locate the suspect. I'm pretty sure he's an asshole and was abusive to these two. Uh…sorry about the language."

"Hah… what, do you think we're saints here? Feel free to speak your mind. Your information is correct; they work here and have been for almost a couple of years."

"Can I talk to them?"

"Well, you could if they were here. They went up to Provo to collect some abused pups. Animal control rescued them, but they're too crowded to keep them. We'll take them here, get them healthy, and maybe someone will adopt them. It bothers the shit out of me when people treat animals like that."

"Do you know when they'll be back?"

"They'll spend the night there and be back before noon tomorrow."

He took a deep breath, noticed Henry stir a little, and said, "I'm kind of at a dead end. I'd sure like to talk to them."

Terri seemed to have arrived at a decision: "How about this? We have cabins over in Dogtown. Take Henry with you and spend the night getting to know each other. You can talk to the boys when they get here in the morning."

"The cabin sounds great, but why Henry?"

"He likes you, Francis. Remember… sometimes the animals have the best judgment."

"But I've never had a dog, and I don't want one."

"Spend the night together. If you feel that way tomorrow, talk to the Barlows and leave. No pressure."

Francis had a feeling things were getting seriously out of control.

"Dogtown?"

"Oh, yeah. It's down the road, about a mile; you can't miss it. Ask for Bobbie; I'll call her and let her know Henry's bunking with you."

Henry jumped to his feet as she handed him the leash and stood at attention. When Francis walked to the door, his new companion moved to his left side, maintained an even pace, and kept his eyes on the new human in his life. He stopped before he went outside and called after her, "Terri…why Henry? It seems kind of an odd name for a dog."

She laughed loudly and replied, "It's a hell of a lot better than Sir Heinrich, which is his real name. We thought Henry was more appropriate."

Francis nodded in understanding and approval, then turned with Henry at his side and left the building. The large human and the young GSD headed for Dogtown.

Sixteen

With Francis stirring the pot in Short Creek or wherever he was, we could do little on Whidbey Island but review the daily CCTV from the ferries and monitor any information from the other law enforcement agencies involved.

The Gleason murders still had the locals on edge even though we did our best to convey the likelihood that it was a one-off event. There were no eyewitnesses, but there was little doubt that Mullins was the guilty party. The gun could be tied to the Stucki murder, and the prints on the Gleason vehicle confirmed it.

If he had retrieved the diamonds, he'd be in the wind, but I was guessing he hadn't, and Hannah Stucki had hidden them somewhere.

The previous evening with Jake was a pleasant retreat from the Driggs/Mullins/Stucki/Gleason case, but I needed something to provide some momentum in finding these guys. I was surprised when I arrived at the station and saw Bruce's car in the lot.

Before I closed the door, he shouted from his little cubby hole in the back room, "BOSS...that you?"

I approached his station and asked, "Why here so early, Bruce?"

"You know how those cameras on the car deck were out on the *Tokitae*, right?"

"Yeah?"

"And you had Danny get you all the video from the other cameras, right?"

"Yup...still right."

Well...I started looking at all the other, you know, to see if Stucki might have gotten out of the car before she was killed, and, well...take a look at this."

He had a shot of the vacant upper car deck on his screen. "This camera is just forward of the door access to the stairway that goes up to the lounge and down to the main car deck."

"Okay...looks pretty empty to me."

"Yes...yes it is, but watch as I put it in motion. Remember, this was an early sailing, and only the lower decks were full."

I watched the empty screen for a few seconds, and then a woman's back appeared; she had to have come up the stairs from the main deck.

"Look at her jacket...same one that Stucki was wearing, right?"

I nodded, still glued to the image of this person who was no longer with us.

"Right?"

"Yes, Bruce...same jacket."

"Okay, now watch this."

The woman strode quickly to the outboard side, where a large orange life preserver was mounted to the railing. She looked from side to side and quickly stuffed a small item underneath the bracket holding the flotation device. When she appeared satisfied it was tucked away, she turned, faced the camera, and hurried back to the access door. It was Stucki, her hair stuffed under her ballcap and still wearing oversized sunglasses.

"Holy shit."

"Yup...that's what I said. She must have done this just before she was shot. You think maybe they're still there?"

I wasn't sure what to think about the diamonds; I was still thinking how scared this woman had to have been.

"Why do you think she hid them, Bruce?"

"Hid what?" Wally, sensing something when he entered the station, burst into the small space.

"Watch," I said.

We replayed the recording, and when it was over, he gave us his theory: "I think I got this. Hannah Stucki was with Driggs for some time, right? At Colorado City, right?"

"Yes."

"Well, if she was, then she knew the Gleason gal and also probably knew the guy...Hughes or Gleason or whatever."

I saw where he was headed and finished the thought for him, "So somehow, she spotted them, got a bad feeling about what might happen, and hid the diamonds."

Wally confirmed my thinking; even Bruce appeared to be on board.

"Good work, Bruce, keep this on the low down, eh?"

"Wally...when's the *Tokitae* at the Clinton dock?"

He pulled up the WSDOT app from his phone, checked it, and said, "Just left, Rog, should be back here in an hour."

We had plenty of time to get there and let the captain know we needed to search the location shown in the video. The loading might have to be delayed for a few minutes, but I didn't expect anything significant. Either the diamonds were there, or they weren't.

We arrived at the Clinton dock five minutes before the ferry's arrival. I'd already called Danny Collins and confirmed that he was the captain on duty. We waded through the walk-ons and stood beside the dock hands as they prepared to receive the giant vessel.

The *Tokitae* eased up to the loading ramp, its reverse engines roiling the chilly Puget Sound waters into a frothing blue-green mass. The diminutive Danny Collins stood at the front of the car deck once again, ready to greet us. We boarded the ferry as soon as the lashing straps were shuffled to the side and the deck lines were fastened.

"What is it this time, Roger?"

"Hi Danny, It's good to see you, too. We need to check something out on the upper car deck. You can unload the lower deck, but wait until we finish with the upper."

"Care to enlighten me about what you're doing?"

"We think that woman who was murdered might have hidden something, and we need to check it out. This shouldn't take long."

"Have at it then, but please hurry. We *do* have a schedule to keep."

I was sensitive to my friend's plight. Hell hath no greater fury than a hundred and fifty pissed-off ferry riders who can't get where they're going on time.

We made our way quickly to the second-level car deck. After weaving through several pickups and SUVs, we arrived at the orange lifesaver. I reached under the mounting bracket but only encountered a mess of spider webs and insect detritus.

"Shit...nothing."

"Maybe the boat's vibration jarred it loose, and it fell off," Wally offered.

"Damn, I thought we'd finally gotten lucky with this. Let's tell Danny he can let these folks off."

Getting inquiring glances and stares from the passenger vehicles, we returned down the ramp to where Danny was still standing.

"Success? What were you looking for, by the way?"

"We saw some video where the victim looked as though she was trying to hide something under the life preserver mounting bracket, but nada."

Danny considered this momentarily, then said, "How did you know it was on that side?"

I wasn't sure about the question and said, "What do you mean?"

"You *do* know this is a ferry, don't you?"

"What do you mean? Of course."

"So, you also know that the port and starboard sides are mirror images, and depending on our direction, the sides reverse."

I finally understood what he was saying. If somehow the *Tokitae* was now in the reverse position of when Stucki was murdered, then we might have searched the wrong side of the boat.

"Thank you, Danny; we'll be right back. C'mon, Wally, there's one more place we need to look."

We took the ramp up to the second deck, but this time on the port side. Sure enough, there was another life preserver station towards the aft end of the ferry. It, too, was just beyond the door to another stairway, and it, too, had a camera mounted high up on the structure.

We ignored the family in the Volvo parked next to the large orange donut, and I reached under the second steel bracket of the day. This time, there was no sticky mass of spider webs. My fingers felt only a moldy paper-covered box. The days of being wedged away on a sea-going vessel had provided enough moisture to cause its wrapper to disintegrate. After my fingers slipped several times, I finally got enough of a grasp to pull it free from its hiding place.

"Got it, Wally."

His eyes grew large at the import of our discovery while the Volvo family was now occupied with other activities. We took the ramp to the main car deck, told Danny to turn the passengers loose, and thanked him for his help.

"Not gonna tell me what you found?"

"I will, as soon as we figure out what comes next. Thanks for the tip."

He tipped his cap, turned to his deckhands to release the vehicles, and returned to the pilothouse. He shouted over his shoulder as he left, "Hey, Rog, see if you can leave us alone for a little while. Every time you show up, our schedule takes a beating."

I raised my hand in acknowledgment and headed to the cruiser to see what was in the mushed-up brown box I had tucked in my pocket.

We waited until we returned to the station and the two of us were seated in the small conference room. We had Bruce standing by to document things with his phone camera. I'd learned long ago that a verified video of the proceedings was essential if the shit hit the fan and we ended up in the ass-covering phase of an investigation.

The brown paper wrapping was in tatters, revealing the square cream-colored cardboard box underneath. I removed the remaining paper and sliced the scotch tape holding the top. There were no markings, and it appeared to be something a jeweler or gift shop might use.

Carefully separating the cover from the body, the interior revealed a purple felt bag secured in place with cotton stuffing. When I pulled the squashed little bag from its resting place, a single diamond the size of a pea lay underneath.

"Holy shit." This from Bruce.

"Keep recording, Bruce, and make sure you get a close-up of the box and what happens next." I loosened the tiny drawstring, securing the bag, and gingerly poured the contents onto the table.

"Jesus...there's gotta be close to a hundred of these things," Wally was mesmerized.

"Yeah, and they're fucking huge. Gotta be at least three carats each, I'd say."

We both looked at Bruce, and Wally asked, "How would you know this?"

"My buddy was a jeweler. Before he died, he used to let me look at stones with his little eye thingy and told me what to look for. I remember this chart he had showing the sizes and colors of diamonds. I got a hell of a deal on something for the little woman."

The more I was around our office mate, the more I was surprised at the tidbits of knowledge he possessed.

"Would you hazard a guess as to how much these are worth, Bruce?"

"Well...if they're good quality, each of these stones could be worth anywhere between fifty and a hundred and fifty thou."

"You're saying there's eight or nine million bucks here?" Wally asked.

"Yup. 'Course, you'd have to verify the quality and find someone to fence them. You'd probably only end up with four or five million."

"That's *all*?"

"No wonder Mullins and Driggs are after these," I said, "They could get lost real fast with this kind of money."

I told Bruce he could stop recording, and we sat there for a few minutes, wondering what would happen next.

"I got an idea, Boss."

"Go ahead, Wally. Let's hear it."

"Let's make sure the paper runs a story about what we've found and how it could have something to do with the Stucki and the Gleason murders. If Mullins is so wrapped up in getting his hands on these things, maybe he'll make a play for them. We'd have to figure out what to say about where they are, then be ready if and when he makes a play for them."

I thought about everything that could go wrong with Wally's plan—and there was plenty—but nailing Mullins was tempting.

"Interesting; let me run this thing by Davis and get his take on it. He'd have to be in the loop anyway."

We put the stones back in their little bag and placed them in the evidence safe in my office. They'd be okay until we could get them to Coupeville, where they'd be someone else's responsibility.

Seventeen

It had been two days since he'd heard from Mullins, and the lack of progress was worrying. Here he was, the leader and Prophet of the FLDS, and now he was holed up in a Best Western hotel a stone's throw from the Las Vegas airport.

His aversion to the other travelers passing through this fleabag lodging had more to do with their aura of sinfulness than any fear of being noticed. Leaving his room only for food, he was content to while away the time watching reruns of *Leave It To Beaver*, *Happy Days*, and the constant stream of ghastly romance movies on the Hallmark Channel. With no televisions allowed at his compound in Colorado City, he was stunned to see how many movies existed around the Christmas fairy tale.

Joseph Driggs was raised in a strict Mormon household. His father was the bishop of his ward and spent more time on the business of the Church than he did with his five children.

As the oldest child of his family, he shouldered the burden of stricter rules than those following him. When he turned eighteen, and it was time to begin his mission, he was thrilled to leave home. He had been paired with Spencer Pratt, a member of his ward but a person he only knew casually.

Assigned to the poorer sections of El Paso for their proselytizing, the two young men quickly learned they had led sheltered lives. Subject to frequent harassment and physical threats by those they wished to convert, it wasn't long before Spencer gave up and returned to his home in Provo. Although missionaries were mandated to travel in pairs by scripture and secondarily for safety, Driggs ignored his father's pleas to return home and chose to stay in a far different city than the others in Texas.

Left to his own methods, he found communicating with those whose doors he knocked on easier without Spencer. He felt strangely at ease when speaking before a group of under-educated families and was surprised at how they absorbed his words and looked to hear more of them. As he became comfortable speaking before larger groups of people, he noticed his delivery became more polished and developed an almost poetic speaking style. He began to trust that he must have been divinely chosen because others believed in him.

He studied Joseph Smith's life and the origins of the Church of Jesus Christ of Latter-day Saints. While the Church officially discontinued the practice of polygamy, Driggs was convinced it was a mistake and vowed to return to the ritual that Smith introduced. He felt it *had* to be so if it was a directive from the Prophet.

After a year in the field, Driggs developed a substantial following, mainly from disaffected members of the LDS Church and a smattering of males who thought having more than one wife might be a fun way to live. Other organized religious groups began taking notice of this upstart., the so-called Prophet. They encouraged those in law enforcement to do something about the increasing number of men with multiple wives.

As pressure mounted on the group, Driggs looked at other areas to relocate to with his followers. He read about the FLDS settlement in Short Creek and announced to his flock that he would be moving there, and anyone who wished to follow would be welcome.

Over thirty-five members of his El Paso congregation followed him to Colorado City, four of whom were his wives. At first, the existing FLDS settlements in Short Creek resented the newcomers, but when they realized that twenty-five of the group were women, they welcomed them. When the dominant males in the group were looking for additional females to wed…well, it was always better to have more choices.

When he arrived, the FLDS Church in Short Creek was led by ninety-year-old Rulon Jeffs, who, probably because of his advanced age, paid little attention to Driggs and his flock. When Warren Jeffs assumed leadership less than two years after his father's death, the real animosity between the two factions began.

It started with a few of the men on Jeffs's side having wandering eyes at the recent arrivals. Although the Driggs settlement was several miles from the central FLDS Church, it was close enough for certain members to visit other certain members. Both Driggs and Jeffs tried to stop the cross-breeding, but alas, the heart wants what the body craves.

The funding for the FLDS Church came from the businesses and retail stores owned by the Church, mandatory tithing from its members, and, when the stars aligned, occasional funding from the SNAP program courtesy of Uncle Sam.

Because Driggs's group was late to the party, no such income streams were available save for mandatory tithing. This led to a more impoverished population of believers and eventually led to Joseph allowing folks with unpleasant histories to stay at their compound. This largesse was conditional on generous contributions from the visitors he considered objectionable, but because it was necessary, he was convinced it was due to divine intervention.

As the years passed, Driggs's group became the dominant faction of the FLDS Church. Because of the frequent boarders hiding from the law, their prosperity outpaced the Jeffs camp. In time, most of the original settlers abandoned him and started following the teachings of Joseph Driggs. He was officially *The Prophet.*

With an adoring congregation, a generous selection of wives, and an income stream more than he could spend, Driggs was convinced of his omnipotence. He became lazy and complacent and took for granted the complete obedience of his flock. When the first of his wives left the community, he was shocked. It was inconceivable that someone he'd taken care of, serviced regularly, and kept clothed and fed would leave him.

He chalked it up to an underdeveloped mind and a young woman who didn't know a good thing when she had one. When a second left, he became concerned and sent one of his assistants to track her down. The acolyte was successful and returned with the fearful woman. Driggs punished her by withholding favors, food, and clothing, and the balance of the wives club shunned her.

The number of followers and the occasional wife deciding to go out on her own slowly increased, and the need for an enforcer presented itself. Many of the drug kingpins who visited used the services of a man named Shane Mullins to keep their dealers in line. Driggs figured if ruthless, unprincipled men used him, he would develop a relationship with the man.

Over time, Mullins became his dedicated enforcer, one whose serious flaws and deviant behavior Driggs overlooked because of necessity. If members of his congregation were allowed to leave, how could they be saved? It was his duty to bring them back.

As he and Mullins became closer, they developed a symbiotic relationship in which each tolerated the other's worst attributes. Oddly enough, the tolerance eventually turned to acceptance and understanding, resulting in two horribly flawed individuals.

When Driggs received word of the FBI's impending raid, he and Mullins decided to make off with their ill-gotten gains. They converted most of the cash and drugs into diamonds for easy transport and planned to leave Colorado City for Tucson the day before the scheduled raid. That's when Hannah Stucki and her buddy managed to fuck things up beyond repair.

The last report from Mullins was both worrying and promising. It seemed the local cops on Whidbey Island found the diamonds Stucki hid on some ferry boat, but now they were in their possession. He pictured the police force on a little island in Puget Sound to be much the same as the inept deputies from the Mayberry cops. Surely, they'd be no match for Shane Mullins.

Eighteen

The story of the diamonds appeared in the Whidbey News-Times three days ago. Tom Davis had okayed the plan with the caveat that if the shit hit the fan, I would have to own it.

We decided it was best to keep the diamonds in our safe at the Freeland station for two reasons. First, it was far enough away from Coupeville to remove any association with the Sheriff should things go astray, and second, if Mullins were inclined to pull anything, Freeland would be perceived as an easier target.

I never thought anyone would break *into* a police station, but that whole business with the little guy on Lone Lake Road proved me wrong. I was glad it was in the past.

We ensured our CCTV cameras were working and stationed an extra deputy across the street at night, but otherwise, it was business as usual. Mullins going after the diamonds while in our custody was a long shot at best, but it was all we had.

We hadn't heard anything from Francis, which could have been either good news or bad; about that, all we could do was wait.

Wally and I busied ourselves with the day-to-day issues of our small station on the south end of Whidbey Island, all the while the specter of a looming Shane Mullins not far from my consciousness. After a few days passed, we assumed the hitman was not stupid enough to attempt to steal something from the cops. We needed to try something else.

"Maybe he's given up on getting the diamonds back and left the area," Wally suggested.

"Possible," I answered. "But he seems the type to keep at it until he gets what he wants, or he'll die trying. How about trying to reach Francis and see what he's been up to? Maybe he's got a line on Driggs."

"Yeah...sure, maybe."

Nineteen

Now that Mullins knew where the diamonds were, he felt better. It was simply a question of how to get them. He hadn't come this far in life by taking undue risks, yet disappointing Joseph Driggs was out of the question. The challenge was to find leverage over someone who could get the stones *for* him, thus keeping him out of harm's way.

Since the population of the small towns on South Whidbey was tiny, it was a challenge to remain unseen, especially if he wanted to observe those who had access to the diamonds. He couldn't do much about his height or mushed-up nose, but he could do a few things that might help disguise his distinctive features.

He noticed many islanders were retired and in their seventies or even older. It seemed most male citizens decided shaving was optional and facial hair, even though gray and uneven, was more prevalent than not.

While his beard grew longer, he spent a week in a dumpy motel on Aurora Avenue, a few miles north of Seattle. He picked up an oversized pair of glasses at a local drugstore and parted with his favorite Irish headgear, instead choosing a Seahawks ballcap to cover his wispy hair.

With the weather still in the fifties and overcast most days, he chose an oversized thirty-year-old London Fog raincoat from a local thrift store. By stuffing hotel towels around his midsection and hunching over his shoulders, walking with a shuffling gait, he was confident he'd fit in with the other old-timers on the island. The following morning, now driving a rented Prius, he boarded the 9:30 ferry for Whidbey Island.

The Island County Sheriff's Office in Freeland was a small, one-story building converted from a single-family home. Since Coupeville, the county seat, was less than twenty miles away, there was no need for anything more significant on the sparsely populated south end of the island. Upon his arrival in town, Mullins passed by the building and found little concealment to observe those coming from or going to the office.

He parked at a coffee shop around the corner and shuffled past several tables occupied by older folks discussing local gossip and the weather. He thought how different their lives were from his, sure that he'd go batshit crazy living such an uneventful existence.

Taking his coffee to the only vacant table, he pretended to read the local paper someone had left behind. His next decision was made for him when a short, stocky deputy arrived accompanied by a taller older gentleman wearing half-glasses on the end of his nose.

They greeted the barista like old friends, and they must have been because he proceeded to make their drinks without being told what they wanted. In constant conversation and stopping at two tables to chat, the two left the shop carrying four cups and a bag full of something. He watched as they, on foot, headed toward the station.

He waited several minutes before nodding at the closest table and asked, "That the Sheriff?"

"Nah, just Wally Turpin. He's second in command down here on the South End. You new on the island or just visiting?"

As he feared, the bottom half of the island was a small community where everyone knew everyone. It wasn't six degrees of separation here, more like one or two.

"Just up for a visit. Even though the weather's crappy, I thought I'd get away from the missus for a bit, you know, take some alone time." He did his best to hide his Irish accent.

The response had the intended effect; the two men, sensing a kinship, smiled and returned to their ramblings about the Mariners and their likelihood of ever getting to the playoffs. So far, he'd seen nothing that presented a problem.

***

Maggie stopped by the station to discuss her findings from the autopsies on the Gleasons. I filled her in on finding the diamonds, and we made small talk while we waited for Wally and Bruce to arrive with our lattes and scones.

Our dispatcher returned to his tiny alcove while the three of us sipped and chewed. I wondered why Maggie showed up in person rather than calling or emailing her findings.

We settled in, and she got right to the point: "I found several tiny pieces of metal mixed in with the tissue and bone from Marianne Gleason's face. A few were lead, and one was brass. As I said before, the damage was extensive, destroying her face and crushing her skull. The trace metal we found was buried inside the skull cavity."

"What do you think they're from?"

"My best guess is some kind of hammer. Years ago, some were made with metals other than steel. The lead heads were wrapped in brass and were used when sparking was a concern. Some shops still make bespoke hand sledges to order—any type and weight of head and a handle of any wood species."

"Any way to tell how old this one was?"

"Probably decades old, but that's a guess based on the mix of metals. Even the custom ones now are either all lead or steel."

My mind flashed back to the picture of Mullins we'd received from Sparks—the one showing a heavy sledgehammer in his right hand. I cringed at thinking about what it would do to a human being, what it *had* done to Marianne Gleason.

"What is it, Rog?" Maggie picked up on my cogitating.

"The guy we're looking for is known to carry a hammer like this. Hold on a sec while I grab the photo."

I retrieved it from the file and placed it on the table before Maggie. "This is Shane Mullins. Check out his right hand."

She stared at it for a minute, then shook her head from side to side, "If this is the son of a bitch who did this, I hope you get him before he can do any more harm. That hammer could be the one that did the damage."

"Thanks, Mags. We were pretty sure this is our guy, but this makes it definite."

"I'll do a little more digging on old custom hammers; maybe we'll find the source, but don't hold your breath. In the meantime, I hope you catch this asshole and soon."

We said our goodbyes to the ME, now more determined than ever to put an end to the brutal actions of one Shane Mullins.

***

He waited fifteen or twenty minutes, left his table and returned to his rental. Because his line of sight to the Sheriff's Office was obscured, Mullins was forced to drive by the one-story building in an attempt to gather information. He needed some leverage to recover his boss's diamonds.

His first pass was futile, with no activity visible at the station. Across the street was a back loading dock to the largest grocery store on the island, and he managed to park slightly behind one of the large tractor-trailers delivering produce.

It wasn't long before the door to the little building opened, and a short, thin woman wearing jeans, sneakers, and a ballcap departed. She got behind the wheel of an older, red Chevy pickup and backed up to exit the parking area. Unsure of her role or position within the department, Mullins assumed she must have some knowledge of where the jewels were. He followed.

Maggie Ryan was considering what kind of human would do that to another. She knew most of the details about the case and thought she had seen every manner of murder possible, but something about this guy was troubling. It was as if he enjoyed his work. As she pondered her next moves in the search for clues, she failed to see the dark blue Prius a few car lengths behind her.

It was less than a thirty-minute drive from Freeland to Coupeville, and traffic was usually nonexistent as it was today. With under two thousand inhabitants in the quaint historic town, Maggie knew most of them by their first name.

Completing her medical degree from Tufts University, with the help of an ROTC scholarship, she spent the next five years on active duty with the U.S. Navy, stationed in Oak Harbor. It was there she learned the skills needed to be a medical examiner. How her curiosity led her to examine dead bodies over live ones, she couldn't say. It might have been a keen desire to see bad guys put away, but the tiny clues and the excitement of discovering the one key fact that would provide closure to a loved one or family was more her raison d'etre.

When she heard Island County was looking for a full-time ME, she resigned her commission in the Navy and looked forward to living permanently on the island she'd come to love. Her home in Oak Harbor was only ten miles from the county seat, yet she continually searched for a place in Coupeville or nearby.

After a dozen years, she finally found what she was looking for. Just off Parker Road, about a mile east of town, she found a small cottage on two acres perched on a bluff overlooking Penn Cove.

The house was in dismal condition, and she'd dedicated herself to completely remodeling it for the past three years. Her social life was as bleak as her new home, giving her more time to spruce the place up. There had been a few dalliances while with Uncle Sam and one or two since, but nothing she cared about continuing. She had her work, her running, and her home, and at this stage in life, that was enough.

As she took the turn from SR 20 onto Main Street, she thought about the poor woman who Mullins had murdered and the barbaric nature of the crime. She was glad Roger and Wally were on the case.

It was late afternoon, and she planned to stop by Toby's Tavern to pick up some takeout for dinner. A few trim pieces at home still needed painting, and she couldn't be bothered cooking while that chore remained. Parking on Front Street, she noticed a dark blue Prius that passed behind her as she exited her truck. She could always tell the visitors in town because they never took the first parking space they found. Front Street was one-way, and on-street parking was always at a premium. Once a vehicle got to Alexander Street, there was no choice but to loop back around and try again. By then, the passed-up slot had already been taken. She chuckled to herself as she entered the tavern.

As she made her way down Ninth to Parker, her mouth began watering in response to the aroma of the crispy halibut burger sitting in the bag on the passenger side. In less than five minutes, she pulled into the carport, reached over to grab her dinner, and opened her door. That was when a large, calloused hand grabbed her around the mouth from behind, muffling her scream. She felt a sharp poke in her neck, struggled flutily, then tingling in her body, then nothing. The droperidol Mullins had used for years while recovering runaways still worked its magic.

Twenty

The cabin was rustic and smelled of old wood. A queen bed was shoved against a pine-clad wall, and a small writing desk with a lamp and a chair sat opposite. He presumed a stained, knotty pine door on the far side of the room led to the bathroom. One other item was shoved in the corner on the far side of the bed—a puffy, plaid dog bed.

Francis seemed unsure of his next move, but Henry...not so much. The three-year-old eighty-pound GSD vaulted into the center of the bed, turned three circles, then plopped down and stared expectantly at his human.

Jesus, he thought, *what have I gotten myself into*? He rested his muscular body on the small chair and looked at his new friend. "What do you think, Henry? What's going through that brain of yours?"

The shepherd perked his ears even higher and twisted his head, seemingly trying to understand. He held that pose for a few seconds, then lowered his head on his two front paws, his eyes never leaving Francis.

He had heard dogs could be smart, but this one almost scared him with its intelligence. He was out of his league, so he did what he always did when unsure—he took action.

He stood up, and as he did, so did Henry. "Come on, buddy, let's take a walk."

The large rust and black mass of fur jumped from the bed, stopped at his feet, and sat, still looking up.

"What? What is it?" Francis sensed the dog wanted something...*but what?*

After a few seconds of staring at each other, he got it. "The leash, right? The leash?"

Two sharp barks answered his question. Francis shook his head in wonderment at this marvelous animal as he snapped on the leash and headed out the door. "Let's go, boy, c'mon."

At dusk in Kanab, the surrounding rocks and mountains gave off an unearthly, deep red glow. Francis and Henry took one of the many trails through the boulders and small crevasses surrounding Dogtown. The temperature was a comfortable seventy degrees, and the wind was nonexistent. The quiet was broken only by the swish of Francis's boots through the sand and the rapid huffing of Henry.

He found himself talking to his companion, asking him about the case, where Driggs was, and what made Mullins such an evil man. Every time he paused, so did Henry. He was astonished at the animal's awareness and constant search for threats. He started to understand why GSDs were the workhorses for police, search and rescue, and the military. Still, though, as much as he liked him, he wasn't inclined to take care of a pet.

They circled back to the cabin just before dark. Opening the door, he saw a brown paper bag on the desk, several grease stains providing clues to its contents. On the floor next to the dog bed was a large bowl of water and another with kibble piled high. Francis had never heard of this place, but it was clear they had their shit together.

He scarfed down the still-warm hamburger and fries while Henry did the same with his dinner. Francis knew enough to take his pal for a short walk after eating to do his business.

They returned to the small TV-less cabin, with only each other for company. Francis thought it was silly for people to talk to their pets like humans, but now he found himself doing precisely that. He was tired from the day's events and the exhilarating walk and was looking forward to crashing early.

Making sure Henry was in his bed, he showered, brushed his teeth, shaved his head, and returned to the bedroom. Henry's bed was empty, and he was once again perched in the middle of the bed designated for humans.

"Henry...down, boy." Francis snapped his fingers as he said this.

The large shepherd dutifully stepped from the bed and went to his designated sleeping place. Francis climbed under the covers, switched off the bedside lamp, and immediately fell asleep in the room's pitch darkness.

At some point in the middle of the night, he turned over to get up to relieve himself but found Henry nestled next to him. The dog seemed determined to sleep in the same bed, so Francis turned the opposite way to get to the bathroom rather than protest. He wondered what thoughts were going through the dog's mind and why he seemed to latch on to someone like him.

He stumbled back to bed in the darkness, climbed back in, even pushing the animal over a few feet so he could fit, and soon fell back asleep. He didn't stir until daylight crept through the curtains the next morning.

Reaching over, he found Henry was no longer lying next to him. He sat up to see his new best friend sitting alertly in his dog bed, apparently awaiting instruction. "Ya know, Henry, you sure are an interesting fellow. How about I get you a little food? Then we can get to finding these Barlow people."

After Henry finished the last of his kibble, they headed for his truck. Francis opened the rear door of the crew cab and urged his companion to jump up into it, but the dog just sat there staring at him.

"What? You can't jump?"

When Francis attempted to help the animal up, he pulled away.

"C'mon, Henry, what's the problem? We gotta get going."

Frustrated, Francis opened the front passenger side to put his duffle in. Looking like an Olympian, Henry launched himself inside the truck and onto the passenger seat. He sat there alertly, looked down at his partner, and barked sharply as if to say, *close the damn door, buddy.*

Shaking his head, Francis threw his duffle into the back, closed both doors, and headed for the Best Friends Welcome Center. They arrived to find Terri standing by the entrance.

"Well, Francis, how was your night with Henry?"

They were standing on the step, Francis holding the leash and Henry practically glued to his leg.

"I'll admit, he's an amazing animal. He sure has a mind of his own, but we got along well."

"Would you like to adopt him?"

"I think he's wonderful, Terri, but I don't see me having a dog."

She looked disappointed but accepted his decision. "I understand. If you still want to talk to the Barlows, you can find them in the cafeteria, across the street."

He thanked her, handed her the leash, and turned to leave. As he did, Henry began a high-pitched keening that nearly buckled his knees. He stopped momentarily but then continued walking to find the two men who might be able to help him find Driggs.

Abe and John Barlow were not brothers, but if looks meant anything, they could have been. They were both slightly built and somewhere in their mid-twenties. They seemed to be gentle souls and appeared to love their jobs working with the animals at Best Friends. Unfortunately, they were of little help in supplying any information that might help locate Joseph Driggs.

The two men had discovered that caring for animals and spending time with others of like minds was far more rewarding than living with the FLDS's strict and sometimes bizarre rules and practices. According to the Barlows, Driggs may have had altruistic intentions at one time, but their impressions were that he grew increasingly greedy and self-absorbed as the years passed. They felt he would never be far from Shane Mullins, especially if money were involved.

Disappointed but determined, Francis returned to his rented truck across the street. As he opened the door to get in, he heard Terri yell, "Henry...HENRY, come...get back here."

He turned just in time to witness what a full-grown German Shepherd traveling at thirty miles per hour looks like. In a blur, Henry vaulted into the pickup, hopped over the console, and sat in the passenger seat.

Terri rushed over and said, "I'm sorry, Francis. He pulled the leash from me as soon as he saw you. Let me get him out of there."

Francis looked up at the dog, sitting silently and alert, his intelligent eyes begging to stay. He melted. He'd never had a dog or even a goldfish, but there was a connection with Henry he'd never felt with anyone before, human or animal. "Never mind, Terri."

"Huh? What do you mean?"

"It seems I don't have much choice here. I think he's adopted me, not the other way around. What do I need to do to take him with me?"

The paperwork was taken care of on the hood of his truck while Henry supervised and never moved from his shotgun position. Francis had planned to return his ride to the Las Vegas Harry Reid International Airport, but now, with his additional passenger, he opted to make the seventeen-hour drive back to Whidbey Island. He figured they'd make Twin Falls by nightfall, then do the ten-hour stretch the following day.

A little over an hour after leaving Kanab, they merged onto I-15 and settled in for the next four hundred miles. Henry had finally curled up on the passenger seat and was snoring quietly. Every time he glanced at his new pal, he felt a little twinge in his gut. He knew his buddy, O'Malley, owned a German Shepherd and was rarely seen without her. He began understanding how attached this breed could become to a single individual or family. He recalled what Terri had told him: "Remember, these dogs are pack animals, and if you and your family are their pack, they will defend and protect you until they die. It's their sole purpose in life."

She also told him how important it was to socialize Henry with others, including other canines. As the miles passed, the more he thought about it, the more he realized he was now responsible *to* and *for* another creature. It was the same way he felt about his brother...sort of. This was a little different. He wondered what Jake would have to say about his new roomie.

Twenty-One

It was the smell she noticed first. A mixture of coffee and stale body odor invaded her nostrils. Her arms ached, but when she attempted to move them, she found she couldn't. She was lying on her sofa, her hands fastened together behind her, her feet immobile as well. She instantly recalled the hand over her mouth and the sharp stick in her neck. She'd been out the entire night, and now, opening her eyes, she faced the guy in the picture she'd seen. Shane Mullins.

"Morning, sleepy head. I was starting to worry about the dose I'd given you, but you look just fine." He no longer attempted to hide his accent, and she thought she might have missed a word or two, so heavy was his Irish brogue, but his air of hostility was unmistakable. She was pissed, too, at her captor's drinking *her* coffee out of *her* favorite mug.

"What do you want, Shane Mullins?"

"Well, aren't you the smarty pants. And just how would ya be knowin' me name, lass?" Mullins seemed to enjoy his powers of intimidation and laid it on thickly.

"What do you want?"

"Not keen on making conversation, eh? Well then, let's get down to business. I want the diamonds your friends at the police have stored somewhere." He slurped his coffee—*her* coffee—as he delivered his demands.

"And how do you think I can help you get them?"

"You're resourceful...come up with something."

"Even if I knew where they were, I couldn't get them. I'm just the ME; they're the cops."

Mullins was quiet momentarily, then said, "Would you think they'd have a change of heart if I sent them one of your fingers?"

It was said with such calm and precision that she shuddered at his suggestion.

"Of course, if I did that, we'd need to leave your lovely little place here, and I'm not quite ready for that."

She held her tongue, mostly because she was scared shitless. She also had no idea how to get this man what he wanted. Her situation was dire, but she trusted Wilkie and his team. If only they knew of her situation.

It was eerily quiet in her house; the only sound was the ticking of her coffee maker.

"When I drove in here, I noticed how quiet the neighborhood was. Why do you suppose that is?"

"I have a few acres here, and most neighbors are still in Arizona or Palm Springs."

Mullins was quiet again while he processed this new information. After several minutes, he stood and walked over to the sofa, towering above her.

"Sit up."

After two attempts, she finally succeeded in getting her bound legs off the seat and managed a listing sit, her hands still taped together behind her.

He grabbed one of the wooden kitchen chairs and placed it in the middle of the sitting room, then walked over and lifted her as if she weighed nothing. She winced as he put her on the chair and wondered what he was doing.

"I need to check some things out, and I can't have you going anywhere." As he spoke, he grabbed the roll of duct tape he had used to bind her earlier and began wrapping it around her, fastening her to the chair. In a few minutes, she looked like a mummy, the chair all but swallowed up by the sticky gray tape.

"Tell me again which neighbors are gone."

Struggling to breathe because of the cocoon-like confinement, and she felt guilty about giving up her neighbors. "The three homes to the west are vacant, and so is the one just east of me. Why?"

He said nothing as he turned and left her alone.

Maggie considered herself an independent soul capable of competing, even excelling, in a male-dominated profession. But now, she felt helpless…and frightened more than she'd ever been.

***

Mullins backed down the long gravel drive onto Parker. Much like his birthplace, the weather here was drizzling again, but the towering firs and cedars lent an ethereal feeling to this island. He passed the first driveway to the west and turned on the next one. This gravel drive was poorly maintained and rutted with puddles. It was longer than his captive's and ended at a small log cabin that reeked of disrepair.

As he pulled up to the dilapidated porch, only the hybrid's mechanical whine disturbed the silence. He wondered how someone who could afford to winter in another state could allow their home to deteriorate to this degree.

Faint vapors were coming from a stack on the roof, indicating some heat source was keeping the home habitable. Smashing one of the sidelites to the right of the front door, he reached in and unlocked the deadbolt. He marveled at the trusting nature of the Whidbey Islanders.

Once inside, he flipped on a light switch and was surprised at what he saw. Unlike the exterior, the inside of the house appeared stylishly decorated and well-kept. The central room seating group faced a river rock fireplace that appeared well-used. A plaid sofa and two upholstered lounge chairs were clustered around a live-edge coffee table of sumptuous proportions. Several side tables held iron-forged lamps that appeared to have been handmade. *Yes*, he thought, *this will do nicely.*

He found the thermostat and raised the temperature ten degrees. Since he would be here for a while, there would be no sense in being uncomfortable. The adjacent kitchen on the far side of the room appeared tidy but well-used. A tiny magnet shaped like a clamshell held a calendar to the refrigerator door. Looking closely at it, he saw the first week of May circled and *return home* written in red.

Perfect, he said to himself; it gave him over a week to complete his business. By the time the owners returned, he'd be long gone. They'd probably be upset by the mess he would leave, but that was their problem.

***

"Oof." The air rushed from Maggie Ryan's lungs as Mullins tossed her over his shoulder like a sack of dog food. He'd cut the tape holding her to the chair.

"What are you doing? Where are you taking me?"

"Not for you to be concerned with, my dear. I'm still thinking about how to use you to get the diamonds, but whatever I come up with, we can't do it from your place. We need an alternate base of operations."

"What? Where?"

"Shut the fuck up, dearie, or I'll stick a rag in your mouth."

He carried her to his car and tossed her into the back seat. They arrived at the vacant neighbor's house in less than three minutes.

"This is the Gorman's place."

"I don't care whose it is. Let's go." He carried her into the house and tossed her onto the sofa.

"Are you going to keep me tied up?"

"Until I figure out what I'm gonna do, yes."

"How about if I have to go to the bathroom?"

"Your problem. Hold it."

Maggie stopped talking and took in her surroundings. At another time, it would have been a cozy, relaxing room, but her captor and her knowledge of his back story had brought her to a near panic state. While she tried to calm herself and think logically, something she saw reminded her of the danger she was in. Resting on the side table next to one of the chairs was a well-used and tarnished ancient hand sledgehammer.

Twenty-Two

"I'd like to speak to the senior deputy, please."

"And who should I say is calling?" Bruce rarely received calls like this and was wary from the start.

"Tell him it's Joseph Driggs."

"BOSS...Rog...it's that Driggs guy, the one Francis went looking for."

I was stunned for a few seconds. We'd had no luck with the diamond lure for a couple of days, and now we'd received a call directly from Driggs.

"Deputy Wilkie here..."

"Yes, Deputy, it seems you have something of mine, and I'd like them returned."

"And why should we do that, Driggs?"

"Several reasons, actually. First, the stones are my property; Ms. Stucki stole them. I'm told you recovered them from one of the ferry boats where she had hidden them."

The details were in the article we posted, so he could easily have gotten his information there. Still, I had to ask, "Ms. Stucki was murdered, Mr. Driggs, and we have reason to believe you ordered it to be done. That makes the diamonds evidence in our investigation of the crime."

"Yes, I heard about the unfortunate death, but I had nothing to do with it."

"Do you know Shane Mullins?"

"Yes. He was one of the visitors who came to our community occasionally."

"Our findings are that he and you are much closer than you let on. Several sources, including the FBI, have told us he does the dirty work for you. It's why you've been on the run and also why we're looking for him for several murders, including that of Hannah Stucki."

Driggs was quiet for a few seconds, then seemed to have reconsidered his approach. "Why don't we do away with this nonsense. I want the diamonds back by tomorrow night."

"Why should we do that, Driggs?"

"Because we have an acquaintance of yours...Margaret Ryan, I think her name is. As of now, she's unharmed under the care of Mr. Mullins. Unless you get my property to him by day's end tomorrow, I can't promise she will remain that way."

I was stunned, and so were Wally and Bruce, who had been listening to the call. "Maggie... why Maggie? She's just the ME; she's got nothing to do with this."

"Be that as it may, Deputy, she was a convenient target. I will call you back with instructions on where and when to deliver my property." The call was disconnected.

We stood there looking at each other, then, from Wally, "Jesus, Boss, he's got Mags. We gotta do something."

"I know, Wally, I know. Get Tom Davis on the phone, Bruce."

I told the sheriff what happened on the call and that Maggie was supposedly missing. He promised to send a team to her house immediately and let me know their report as soon as he got it.

Bruce returned to his duties while Wally and I puttered around, waiting to hear back from Coupeville. A half-hour later, he called, "Her house is empty, Rog, and there were indications of her being restrained. They found duct tape and a syringe. We're checking its contents now. Her truck is still there, so they must have gone in his. I've got a BOLO out for Mullins now. The problem is we don't know the timing of this. They could easily be off the island by now."

***

Francis arrived at the Early home, tired from the two-day marathon drive from southern Utah. He still had the rental truck but was too exhausted to return it until the next day. The last forty-eight hours had been exhausting, but his fondness for his new pal had increased tenfold.

His four-legged companion was great company and more intelligent than most people Francis knew. That morning, Francis called his brother to tell him when to expect him and that he was bringing a friend. Jake was curious, but he trusted his brother implicitly even though he couldn't fathom who Francis was bringing.

Jake heard Francis coming before he reached the front door. He was talking to someone named Henry. He heard his brother come in and then something scraping the walnut plank flooring. His mouth dropped as he turned the corner in his wheelchair. Three sharp barks signaled that the friend was now aware of the stranger in the chair.

Looking first at his brother, then at Henry, Jake was at a loss for words. Then Francis dropped the leash and said, "It's okay, Buddy, go meet my brother."

Henry cautiously approached Jake, sat at his feet, and lifted a paw to his knee. Still looking at the dog in wonderment, Jake gently took the paw and gave it a timid shake.

"I take it this is your new friend."

"Um...yup. This is Henry. He kind of adopted me. Really...he did."

Henry still hadn't moved. Jake released his paw, and the three-year-old dog and the seventy-year-old county commissioner stared at each other.

"He's magnificent, Francis. It feels like he knows what I'm thinking."

"Yeah, he sorta has that effect."

"Come on in and sit; you must be exhausted. I'll grab a couple of beers, and you can tell me about your trip."

So, the two brothers and their new roommate sat by a crackling fire while Francis related the events of the last four days. Their disappointment at not finding Driggs's whereabouts was more than offset by their joy at Henry's arrival.

"Any developments here while I was gone?"

"Just before you arrived, I received an update from Wally Turpin. It's not good."

"What...tell me what's happened?"

"Mullins kidnapped Maggie Ryan, the ME. He's holding her somewhere until we return the diamonds to him or Driggs. Davis and the deputies from the north end are working on it, but they think he's off-island."

"That sonofabitch. I leave for a few days, looking for the guy calling the shots, and they pull this. I'm going up there."

"Francis...no. Wait a minute. You're wasted, and you'll probably be in the way. Please do me a favor and spend the night here. If you feel the same way in the morning, then do whatever you like."

Torn between his sense of responsibility and awareness of his current state of depleted energy, he nodded to his brother. "Okay...you're right. I'll get some rest, then figure out what to do in the morning. Who's Ryan anyway? And why her?"

"She's the medical examiner. They think Mullins saw her when she met with Wilkie, and she must have been an easy target. They found evidence of her abduction at her house in Coupeville."

Francis shook his head as he stood and muttered something that sounded like "assholes." Henry bolted upright and followed Francis down the hallway to his quarters.

"Night, Bro. Thanks for looking after me." His shout echoed down the hallway as he turned the corner into his room.

***

The brothers sat together having coffee at seven the following morning. "How was Henry last night?" Jake asked.

"He didn't move, which was great because he leaned against me the whole time. He seems to like the connection. I let him out at six, and he inspected the property for you."

"Ah...good to know. What are your plans today?"

"I'm going to Coupeville. I know, I know, the cops are on it, and they know their business. But, you know me, Jake, I can't just sit by and wait for something else to happen. Maybe I can see something they missed because I see things differently. Whoever this Ryan woman is has got to be scared to death of Mullins, and I'm pretty sure he's not gonna simply let her go even if they turn over the diamonds."

"If you're sure about this, Francis, please keep Roger in the loop. He'll want to know what you're up to."

"Oh...yeah, I will."

In his F-150, he hopped on to SR-525 and began the twenty-minute drive to the county seat. It felt good to be in his own truck, and judging from Henry curled up on the passenger seat, his companion felt likewise.

As promised, he called Roger while on the road.

"Francis, glad you called. Any luck in Short Creek?"

He gave Roger the bad news and finally explained his reason for calling: "I'm going to Coupeville, Rog. I want to see what happened for myself."

Wilkie was quiet for a few seconds, then eventually responded. "You *do* know that the Island County cops are all over this, don't you?"

"Uh...yes, yes I do."

"And Maggie Ryan is someone everyone in the county adores. Right? And you *do* know they'll stop at nothing to get her back. Right?"

"I didn't know about her history, Rog, but I've still got skin in the game. It's because the woman had my name she ended up dead. I'm gonna get this creep."

Wilkie seemed to realize that his friend wouldn't take no for an answer, so he did what he could. "Do me a favor, Francis, and don't ruffle any feathers. I trust you'll keep a low profile. I'll have to pull you off if Davis calls about you. Got it?"

"Don't worry, Rog, they won't even know I'm around."

"Yeah...I'm sure."

He lost the connection shortly before the turnoff to North Main Street. With the elevation changes and the giant trees on Whidbey, cell service was notoriously spotty. He turned right, followed Main past the county buildings and Sheriff's Office, then took a right on 9th and drove the short mile to Ryan's address. At some point, 9th turned into Parker, but he never noticed.

He expected a crowd of sheriff's vehicles would be on site, but it wasn't so. With the entire property surrounded by yellow police tape, the little cabin was impossible to miss. It looked somehow lonely.

After parking at the driveway's entrance, Francis and his trusty sidekick ducked under the yellow tape and walked up to Maggie Ryan's house. The morning sky was shrouded in a marine layer offering intermittent sprinkles of moisture that neither man nor dog noticed.

The site was eerily quiet, and Francis poked around judiciously, making sure to keep it that way.

"Not sure what I'm doing here, Henry, but I'll bet the cops must have missed *something*."

Here I am talking to a damn dog, he thought. But then he looked down into Henry's face, saw the hanging tongue, the soulful, searching eyes, and the giant ears, and, once again, he felt that tug in his gut. He'd never understood how people could get so attached to their pets. *Now*, he did.

He walked to the bluff side of the house, where a side door had been left ajar. Henry trotted in ahead of him, immediately went nose to the ground, and began sniffing everything in sight. When he got to the sofa and chair, he barked once and looked up.

"What is it, Henry? You got something?"

Another bark, then a walk in a circle, then he sat and stared at Francis.

"You're done? That's it?"

Francis shook his head at the dog's inability to answer his questions, then, "C'mon Boy, let's vacate the premises."

They left the same way they had come, Francis leading the way. He turned as they reached the front of the house and noticed Henry was standing frozen, his nose high in the air...sniffing.

"What is it, Henry? What's up?"

Rather than answer, he bolted through the fir and cedar forest. Francis did his best to keep up. The young GSD was almost out of sight when he stopped and looked back to make sure his master was close behind. Immediately, when Francis caught up to him, Henry sat and looked up at him.

"What?"

Henry looked away for several seconds, then back to Francis.

"What are you doing, Henry? What the hell do you want?" Francis was irritated he had to spend precious moments chasing his dog through the woods.

With a high-pitched whine and a nudge to Francis's leg, Henry took several steps forward.

"Jesus, Henry...come on."

As he bent to grab the collar, he looked in the direction Henry was focused and saw a blue Prius parked next to a rustic-looking cabin. He'd already crossed one driveway, but this one seemed barely passable.

He and his companion edged to the side of the rutted two-track using the huge fir trees for cover. He turned to Henry and said, "You're kidding, right? Tell me you smelled something in Ryan's house and tracked it to here."

Henry stared at him, probably wondering if he'd made a mistake attaching himself to this slow-witted human. Clearly, this man wasn't aware that GSDs possessed 200 million more olfactory receptors than people. He strained to show patience with his partner, but it was becoming a challenge.

They continued closer to the cabin when Francis saw that a small window in the sidelite next to the front door had been broken. Henry had only been his companion for a few days, but he sensed the dog knew when to be quiet, so together, they crept toward the side of the house. The off-and-on drizzle soaking the needles and twigs underfoot made a stealthy approach less problematic, but still, they were cautious.

Finally, having arrived at the cabin's corner, he took a deep breath. A double-hung mullioned window to the left of the river rock chimney was just above his head. He could tell by looking at Henry that his canine friend was listening to something. His ears stood at attention, and his head turned upward. Edging closer to the window, he heard enough of the deep bass Irish brogue to be convinced that Mullins and his captive had traveled only a few thousand feet from Ryan's place. The problem now was what to do next.

The decision was made for him when he heard a door slam from the house's interior. Cautiously, he peered through the window and saw a woman trussed up and lying on a sofa. She struggled against the duct tape binding her but had little success so far. The door to the room began to open, so he ducked quickly.

This time, he heard Mullins clearly: "Good news. I got a text from Driggs, and he said the deputies would be leaving the diamonds at the drop-off tonight."

"Does that mean you'll be letting me go?"

"Well, darlin', that's what they *think* it means. The problem is I can't leave any witnesses now, can I?"

Her eyes followed his as he glanced in the direction of his hammer. She began shivering as he continued, "Of course, we'll need to keep you around for a little longer, you know…just in case something untoward happens. I've always enjoyed that word—untoward…how about you?"

Maggie knew this man was dangerous and had murdered more than a few people, but she wasn't sure he was psychotic...until now. She resolved to try to find a way out of this in whatever time she had left. The duct tape securing her wrists behind her back had started to stretch and loosen; maybe if she managed to free herself, she could escape. She kept quiet and continued her work.

Francis, huddled with Henry by the window, had heard everything and knew Ryan's time alive was growing short. He knew about the hammer, and he also knew there was a good chance Mullins was armed with the gun that killed Stucki and the Gleasons. Charging into the cabin wasn't in the cards, nor was calling the cops; there wasn't time to fetch them, and he doubted his phone would work.

As he contemplated his next move, he heard Mullins speak: "You'll have to wait here for me—hah—I need to try to reach the boss about the timing on this. The upper deck is the only place I can get service. Don't go anywhere."

As he clomped up the stairs, Francis stole another look through the window. This time, Maggie Ryan saw him, and her expression became one of surprise mixed with a dose of fear and then curiosity.

Being used to such reactions, he put his finger to his lips, telling her to be quiet. He wasn't sure how long Mullins would be gone, but he had to try to get this woman out.

"C'mon, Henry, stay with me." The dog and his human moved quickly to the front door and eased it open. The tiny squeak made him cringe, and he froze. Straining to listen, he heard faint grunts and dampened tones from above, mixed with Henry's rapid breathing.

Maggie's mouth hung open when she saw the size and full presentation of her possible rescuer and his dog. "Help me," she whispered.

Once again, Francis put his finger to his lips as he hurried over to her. For his part, Henry sat but remained on full alert. He'd been trained by the best and knew only one commandment: *Protect his human and his friends.*

As Francis began to work on the tape wrapped around her ankles, he became aware of the stillness in the room. No longer were their muffled sounds from above. A creak from an upper stair tread made them freeze. Henry stood and walked soundlessly over to the sofa.

First, his legs appeared coming down the stairs, and then his chest. Finally, Mullins's entire torso was visible. He looked in their direction. This man who had killed many and seen almost everything seemed not to understand what was before him. A large bald man with a tattooed face leaned over the sofa while a fearsome German Shepherd glared at him.

Without a word, he reached behind to grab the Walther P22Q stuffed in his belt. Whether it was his eyes or the twitch of his shoulder as he reached behind, Francis was never sure. What *was* certain was that, whatever the trigger, Henry sensed a situation brewing.

From his position by the sofa, Henry crossed the distance to the stairs in a blur. Standing on the second step, Mullins realized that the threat from the tattooed bald man was less problematic than the GSD missile speeding toward him. Just as he pulled his weapon, the animal launched himself the last few feet, and with 240 pounds of pressure exerted by one-inch canine teeth, Henry tore into the killer's upper thigh.

Mullins dropped the gun in between screams. He tumbled the last two steps with Henry still clamped on his leg. Blood was pouring from the wound, soaking both man and dog.

Momentarily frozen by the suddenness of the events, Francis went back into action. He tossed the still trussed-up ME over his shoulder and ran for the door. He wasn't sure how injured Mullins was, but he didn't care.

"Henry...Henry, leave it. Let's go, Buddy. Come-on."

Obediently, Henry let go of the leg but couldn't resist another lunge at this despicable human. As he snapped at Mullins's face, the man cringed in the corner of the stairway, still screaming and desperately trying to stem the flow of blood. Henry bared his teeth, uttered a frightening growl, then turned and trotted off.

Twenty-Three

"I don't know who you are, but thanks for getting me away from that guy." Her hands and legs still bound with tape, Maggie Ryan spoke from the back seat of Francis's crew cab. Henry sat in the front.

"It wasn't anything."

"I was talking to the dog, stupid. And if you don't mind, could you undo me?"

They had jogged through the woods back to Ryan's house. After placing Maggie on the back seat, they sped back to Coupeville and the Sheriff's Station. Now, in the county building parking lot, they both caught their breath.

Francis knew nothing about this woman but appreciated her sharp wit despite the circumstances.

"Come on...really? We *are* a team, you know."

He chuckled as he exited the truck and opened the rear door to free Maggie.

"Thanks...I mean it," she said again. This time, her gratitude was genuine. "Who are you, by the way?"

"I'm Francis Early, and this is Henry."

As he mentioned his companion's name, Henry turned and offered a soft little bark in greeting.

"Henry's a fucking hero."

"Hey, nice language there, Maggie."

"Listen, Buster, you go through what I've been through the last twenty-four hours, and you can say whatever the fuck you want."

Francis conceded the woman had a point, so he nodded in agreement, then said, "Yes...he *is* a fucking hero. I've only been with him for a few days, but I'm discovering he's a remarkable animal. Let's get you into the Sheriff's and tell them where they can find Mullins."

"If he's still alive, that is. With all that blood, Henry may have punctured the guy's femoral artery."

Maggie would know about these things, Francis thought.

***

It had been a few hours since I'd heard from Francis, so I assumed he was staying out of trouble. Then my phone buzzed.

"Rog, it's Tom Davis."

I was afraid I might get this call. "Tom, I tried to get Francis not to come up there, but you know how he can be. What has he done?"

"Well, for starters, he and his dog rescued Maggie Ryan. They're both here with me now, and so's the pooch. I've sent two squads over to the scene to round up Mullins. I'm waiting to hear from them."

"The pooch? What pooch?" I wasn't shocked that Francis was smack in the middle of a shitstorm again, but this was the first I'd heard of a dog.

"*Henry*...you know, Early's dog."

"I didn't know he had one."

"Well, he does, and according to their story, the dog did some serious damage to Mullins. Maggie thinks he might have bled out after they left."

"Jesus...they're both okay?"

"Maggie's still a little shaken up, but Henry and Francis seem fine. Everybody in the office loves the dog."

I felt slightly left out, but I was glad Maggie was safe. "What can I do?"

"For now, hang on to those diamonds. I'll ring you back as soon as I hear from the teams."

After we signed off, I filled Wally in on the developments.

"When did Francis get a dog?"

I laughed when the first question was about the dog. "Don't know. Guess we'll have to wait until we talk to him for that story. I want to get to Coupeville to interview Mullins if he's still alive."

The office phone rang before Wally had a chance to comment.

"Hey Tom...*what*? You're sure? Okay...talk to you then."

I turned to Wally, who had a troubled look on his face. "Mullins was missing. They said there was blood all over the place, and his car was still there, but he was gone."

"What? How?"

"There was a blood trail out the front door and across the porch. Also, some traces on the gravel in the driveway. The best they can come up with is someone came and got him out of there. No one saw anything, of course.

"They've alerted the ferries and the cops at Deception Pass. Davis put a team at the bridge entrance to check every vehicle that leaves the island."

"Whoa, man, that's gonna piss some folks off,"

"I agree, but we're talking about a guy responsible for multiple murders. "

"What can we do?"

I was thinking the same thing. "Let's get to Coupeville. I want to talk to Maggie and Francis. We're closer to this than the deputies up there, and maybe we'll learn something."

The historic town of Coupeville is a frequent landing spot for visitors to Whidbey Island. It became the county seat in 1881 due to its central location and ease of access by those trafficking on Puget Sound. Front Street is still occupied by several buildings of that era, lending an old-world charm.

We arrived in less than twenty minutes and went straight to the Sheriff's Office. We found Francis and Maggie sipping coffee in the seating area outside the inner sanctum reserved for those in uniform. As we entered, an intensely alert German Shepherd jumped to attention.

When a low growl emerged from the animal, Francis put a hand on his head and said, "It's okay, Henry...okay. He's one of the good guys."

Something about the shepherd stopped me from rushing over to Maggie and Francis, but I was sure the relief I felt upon finding them appeared on my face.

"Just stand there and let him sniff you for a few seconds. Henry...go."

The dog trotted over, gave Wally and me the once over, then returned to Francis's side and laid down.

"We good, Francis?" Wally asked.

"Yup," he said as he stood with Maggie, and the four of us hugged.

"You okay, Maggie? How are you doing?" I asked.

She sighed deeply and said, "I'm much better now. That guy was one scary dude. If it hadn't been for Henry...and well, I guess Francis, too, I hate to think what would have happened." As she said this, Francis and she exchanged glances that were difficult to decipher.

"I don't know how he did it, but Mullins got away. There was so much blood, Rog...we thought for sure he was a goner."

"Yeah, we heard from Davis; that's why we're here. Are the deputies still at the scene?"

"I think so. Let me go back there with you."

"You're staying here, Francis. I'm thankful—and so's Maggie, I'm sure—for what you've done, but let us take it from here."

Again, with the glances, then, "Okay, but you'll let me know what you find?"

"Yup, we will. And the next time I see you, I want the low down on Henry here."

When we arrived at the scene, it was crawling with deputies and one of Maggie's crime techs. The deputy in charge was a friend from another investigation who hurried up to us when we exited the cruiser.

"Roger, Wally, glad you're here; I know you guys have been carrying the load on this one."

Don Ericson was a top-notch investigator with the department for years. I was glad he was on site. "Anything worth mentioning yet, Don?"

"Judging from the tire tracks, another vehicle—looks like an SUV or something—was here. The Prius tracks are the only other fresh ones. We think Mullins was still alive—at least his heart was pumping blood—when someone helped him get away. There are drag marks and scuff marks over here where it looks like the other vehicle was parked. We think whoever it was helped get Mullins loaded up and then took off."

"Maggie thought the guy's femoral was damaged."

"Coulda been, there was a lot of blood. Cora, who's Maggie's assistant over there, agrees. She also said if whoever the rescuer was got a tourniquet on the leg right away and got help somewhere, he might have survived."

"Son of a bitch," Wally cursed, "I can't believe he got away."

"Yeah, well...for now, maybe. We *will* get him, Wally."

Twenty-Four

T he Ford Explorer was tan, and the windows were tinted just enough to make it difficult to see inside.

Driggs had driven to Seattle the previous day, spent the night in Mukilteo, and took an early ferry to Whidbey Island. He'd found the least attractive vehicle on the rental lot just in case, and now he was grateful for it.

After he'd spoken with Mullins, they agreed to meet up to finalize the plans for the drop. The woman who had been kidnapped wouldn't be a problem, he thought, if Mullins had anything to do with it. Right now, though, his associate was moaning and tightening the belt, stemming the pulsing blood from his leg.

He passed the pickup on his way to the property to meet Mullins. The strange-looking man behind the wheel looked like a tradesperson and his dog or a yard worker for one of the larger homes on the bluff. Only when he entered the house and saw the carnage did he make the connection. The semi-conscious Mullins was muttering and holding on to his belt, which was fastened around his thigh.

His connection to Mullins was complicated. On one level, the man was a valuable tool to be used when necessary. On another, though, Driggs respected the man's excellence in his profession. They had been associates for years, each understanding the other's needs and neither passing judgment on the other's shortcomings. Mullins was the closest thing to a friend he'd ever had. Now, if they didn't get help very soon, it was likely he would die. He helped him up and started for the door.

"The hammer," Mullins said through clenched teeth. "Get my hammer."

Driggs propped him against the wall, picked up the Walther, and retrieved the hammer. Then, they made their way to the car.

The nearby hospital was out of the question. Coupeville had the only one on the island's south end, and their presence would surely be reported if they sought help. A glance at the injured leg showed the bleeding had slowed to a trickle, which was encouraging.

"Shane...how are you doing?"

"What do you think? That fucking dog tried to kill me. Jaysus, this hurts."

"Looks like the bleeding's slowed a little." Driggs headed east on SR 20 because of a lack of any other options. He knew the ferry was out of the question, and north was the two-lane Deception Pass Bridge. He figured the cops would have that covered.

"I need somebody to fix this."

"Yes, I know. Any ideas? We can't go to the hospital for sure. This place is so goddamn small, everyone knows everyone else."

The two-lane arterial was the only means of getting from one end of the island to the other, and combined with SR 525, it covered almost fifty miles from the Clinton Ferry Terminal to the Pass Bridge. With dusk approaching and a fine mist falling, visibility was limited, and they nearly missed the sign.

"What's a WAIF, Driggs?"

"I don't know. Why?"

"We just passed a sign that said, WAIF. I know I've heard some islanders talk about it. Pull over when you can; I'll look it up."

They pulled into a church parking lot while Mullins fumbled one-handed with his phone.

"Give me that, Driggs," said, taking the phone.

With a few swipes, he pulled up the website for the Whidbey Animals' Improvement Foundation. "It's a shelter for animals, so what?"

"Turn around; maybe they have a vet there to fix this."

"You're crazy, Mullins; they'll turn us in for sure."

"Yeah...maybe, but first, let's get this fixed, and we'll worry about that later. At least there will be fewer people there than at the hospital."

After retracing their last two miles, they turned into a gravel parking lot surrounded by tall firs and cedars. As they did so, two pickups and a sedan were leaving for the weekend. They pulled up to a large structure and turned off the ignition. Several more vehicles departed while they waited, leaving only a late-model pickup and a very old Ford Bronco.

"Looks like everyone's going home for the evening."

"For your sake, I hope there's still a vet here. Let's go."

They made it to the entrance with a hobbled Mullins leaning on Driggs, but it was locked, and a "Closed" sign was posted in the window.

"Shit," Mullins mumbled as he pounded on the glass with his open hand.

In seconds, a young woman wearing scrubs and a surgical mask walked up to the door, first pointing at her watch and then at the closed sign. Then she saw Mullins's condition and immediately opened the door.

"What happened? Why are you here? You should be at the hospital."

"We need help," Driggs said.

"We take care of animals here. Right now, the vet and I are in the middle of surgery. Take your friend into Coupeville; it's not far."

Driggs sighed and pulled the gun from behind him. "I'm sorry, Miss, but we need to see the vet...now."

Her eyes widened in fear as she stared at the weapon.

"Turn around and take us back where you came from." As he said this, he turned and locked the entrance door.

The young assistant obeyed the order and headed for the surgery. As she walked, Driggs spoke again: "Easy there, young lady. As you can see, we can't move very fast, and I wouldn't want to trip and have this gun go off."

The threat had its intended effect, and she slowed enough for them to follow her down a wide corridor, allowing access to several exam rooms. After a left turn, they reached a set of double doors, bright lights spilling from their large windows.

"What was it, Annie?" The woman hunched over a large golden retriever asked while still attending to her work.

"Um...Doc...these people forced their way in."

Turning from her work and immediately noticing the gun, the veterinarian's surprise caused her to gasp through her mask. "What are you doing here? This is a sterile area."

"Sorry, Doc, but my friend here has had an accident, a dog bite, and he needs attention," he nodded toward the blood still oozing from Mullins's wound.

"I am an animal doctor. I don't work on humans, and I'm in the middle of something right now."

"Yes, I can see that, but I need you to stop what you're doing and attend to my friend...now." He raised the Walther for emphasis.

"I told you; I don't work on humans."

"Yes, well, you're going to make an exception in this case."

With gray wisps of hair escaping from her cap and tiny wrinkles around her eyes, it was evident that the vet had more than a few years under her belt. She sighed and turned to her assistant: "Close him up, Annie. He should be fine now. Make sure to swab the suture with antibacterial ointment when you've finished."

Then she turned to Driggs and Mullins, "You two follow me. I'll do my best, but I'm no people doctor."

She led them to one of the exam rooms they had passed on their way in and had Mullins lie down on the exam table. Leaving the belt where it was, she cut away the pant leg until the entire wound was exposed.

"I'm guessing you pissed off a big dog, Right?"

"Just keep working," Mullins gasped through gritted teeth.

She grunted and continued to pour sterile water over the entire area, washing the blood away.

"Yup...looks like whoever did this--probably a shepherd—had a hell of a bite. You're damn lucky he only nicked your femoral artery. Otherwise, you'd be dead."

"I'll use a local on the bite; that should take care of the pain for a while, and then I'll do my best to patch up the artery. You're gonna have to take it easy for a few days, though, because if you mess up the repair, you could start losing blood again. Also, you've gotta keep the area clean when you leave. If you get it infected, it'll be a real mess."

She injected the local anesthetic into the area and tightened the tourniquet. Then, she poured betadine over the entire wound, including the adjacent tooth punctures, and began sewing the puncture wound. It was tedious work, and Driggs eventually took a seat.

"It's the best I can do. This man needs a hospital."

"Yes, well, that's not going to happen."

"Would you please leave now?"

"Well...here's the problem. We can't have you telling anyone we were here, so we have to make sure you can't do that."

"What do you mean?" Real fear showed in the veterinarian's eyes.

"Sorry, Doc. We appreciate your help, but we can't have you talking to anyone. Let's get your assistant over here now."

"Please...I promise we won't tell anyone."

"Sorry, we need to be sure, and there's only one way."

"They'll find out eventually."

"Yes, but we'll be gone by then."

Mullins eased out the pistol and pointed it at the women.

"Shane, wait." Driggs held his hand in front of the weapon.

"What? Growing a conscience?"

"Look, they saved your life. Let's lock them up in one of the dog pens. They'll be stuck there until Monday, and if we haven't worked things out by then, it won't matter."

Mullins reluctantly agreed. He waited, still hobbled, while Driggs marched them into the rear warehouse area where a dozen large kennels were located. A few dogs in various stages of recovery began barking at the new arrivals. He put them into the last one in the row, shut the gate, and threw the deadbolt. It offered a slot for a padlock, but none were available since the occupants were usually four-legged animals without thumbs.

Driggs thought for a moment, then said to the two captives: "If you move, I'll have Mullins come back here and shoot you. I'll be right back."

He jogged back to the front and out to the car and grabbed what he needed.

"Be right back," he said as he passed Mullins on his way to the kennels.

When he reached the cage holding the veterinarian and her assistant, he raised the sledgehammer and bashed the mechanism latching the gate. After two additional whacks, it was fused shut. The only way out for them would be when someone cut the chain links with bolt cutters.

The captives were terrified but alive. "Thank you, ladies," Driggs called out as he returned to Mullins. "You are two very lucky women."

Twenty-Five

We could do little at the crime scene, so we headed back to the Freeland station. With a roadblock at the pass and the ferry docks at Clinton and Keystone on full alert, I was confident Mullins would be found if he attempted to leave the island. The wild card here was whoever helped Mullins escape. My first guess would have been Driggs. I couldn't imagine him coming to Whidbey Island to meet with his henchman, yet there weren't many other possibilities.

We arrived in Freeland shortly after dark and went inside the station to close the week. I was surprised to see Bruce still on duty.

"How come you're still here, Bruce?" Wally asked before I had a chance.

"Tom Davis thought it would be a good idea to handle the radio for a few hours in case Mullins was sighted. He told me he'd make it worth my while."

Since Bruce was a volunteer, I wasn't sure what Davis had promised, but I let it go. The Sheriff was probably right to cover all the bases. We briefed Bruce on everything we knew, filled out our daily activity worksheets, and began to leave.

Bruce stopped me before I got to the door. "Who's on this weekend?"

Wally and I took turns sharing weekend duty for our jurisdiction, and this one was mine. "Yours truly, Buddy."

"Nice to know we're in good hands, Rog. I'm gonna hang out for a couple of hours, then call it a day. Good luck with Mullins; I'll see you Monday."

I chuckled at Bruce's sarcasm, saluted him, and left for home. It had been an eventful day.

***

Mullins dozed fitfully while Driggs drove south for no particular reason. They failed to ransom the woman for the diamonds, and in the process, Mullins almost was killed. They abducted a veterinarian and her assistant and locked them inside a dog kennel for the weekend. They were stuck on this stupid island with no way to escape without getting caught.

Driggs had seen how violent a man Mullins was. He knew what he'd done for his past clients and was aware that while he was exclusively his enforcer, he'd also done some terrible things. While his motivation had morphed from a man of God to a mercenary, tempted by the things money could provide, he still fancied himself a good person. He was relieved when Mullins had allowed him to spare the lives of the two women.

While most of the world thought the lifestyle of the FLDS members strange and downright aberrant, his strict adherence and dedication to Smith's teachings had always blinded him. Now that money had taken an exalted position in his psyche, he fleetingly wondered if, with all that had passed, he may have been misinformed or, rather, uninformed about the true meaning of life.

Whatever the case, he was determined to find a way to get the diamonds...*his* diamonds. As he passed Greenbank and one of the few phone booths left in America, a simple plan began to take shape in his mind. *Why complicate things*, he thought, *just walk into the podunk Sheriff's Office with the gun and get the damn things.* Most people didn't know what he looked like anyway.

He nudged the dozing Mullins and told him to direct them to the Freeland station. They approached it just as a Sheriff's cruiser pulled away.

***

Bruce Strickland was sixty-three years old. He'd retired from Microsoft seven years before and moved to Whidbey Island with his wife and golden retriever to escape the increasing congestion of the burgeoning Seattle metropolitan area.

Initially, he enjoyed the peace and quiet of island life. But then his wife joined a book club and took up golf, and he found himself puttering around the house to pass the time.

"Find something to do," she told him as she left for the golf course one day. "Maybe you should volunteer for something."

He spent a few days looking at options when he overheard a couple of deputies at Crabby Coffee lamenting that they'd lost their dispatcher. Apparently, because the district was so small, the position was volunteer. Bruce felt his position as head of corporate communications for the giant software company would make him a perfect fit.

Police activity on South Whidbey is relatively tame. After a few weeks on the job, Bruce wasn't sure he'd made the right decision. Then, the episode with the warlock who lives on Lone Lake Road happened. Suffice it to say, the whole affair was paradigm-shifting. He learned much about himself under pressure and became a close friend to Roger Wilkie and Wally. He couldn't imagine life without his job—even if he never got paid.

He was hopeful that this Mullins character was hurt enough not to be a threat to anyone else. He knew he was on the island somewhere and understood Roger was unsure about how he'd escaped. He felt things would quiet down, but he stayed over to be sure. If something came up, his boss would need to know.

Hearing a knock at the door, he stood and went to the side window. He knew Roger had locked it on his way out, and he couldn't imagine who'd be calling at this hour. On the step stood a short, slightly chubby fellow with thick glasses. A ballcap was pulled down, probably to keep the drizzle from misting his glasses. The man looked vaguely familiar, but Bruce couldn't place him. *It was likely just some local complaining about something,* he thought.

A small caliber gun was thrust in his face the moment he opened the door. Stumbling backward, he tripped and fell on his ass.

"Is there anyone else here?" Driggs asked.

Bruce remembered where he'd seen the guy as he slowly pulled himself up using a nearby desk. It was in one of those pictures that Roger had received from Francis's buddies.

"N-N-No."

"Good. I'm guessing you know who I am and why I'm here."

"I do."

"Excellent. Now, how about you go and get my diamonds."

"I can't. The chief deputy is the only one who knows the combination to the safe."

"What's your name?"

"B-Bruce...Bruce Strickland."

"Okay, Bruce Strickland. I'm not a violent man, but my friend is. Last chance to do this quietly: OPEN the safe."

"I told you...I can't."

As the words left his mouth, the door opened, and the imposing figure of Shane Mullins hobbled in. In his hand was his favorite weapon.

"Problems, Joseph?"

"Bruce, this here is Shane Mullins. I'm sure you've heard of him. Shane, Bruce here is somewhat reluctant to assist us in getting my diamonds back."

Bruce backed farther into the room, his eyes never leaving the sledgehammer he'd heard so much about.

Without another word, Mullins limped over to the volunteer dispatcher and smashed three pounds of lead and brass into his right shoulder, tearing through flesh and demolishing the entire upper arm and collar bone and destroying the socket. Bruce collapsed from the pain.

"Damn it, Shane, we need him conscious."

"Hold your horses, Driggs. He'll be fine. Mullins hopped over to a water cooler and filled a paper cup. He returned and threw the contents into the fallen man's face. Bruce's eyes fluttered, but he collapsed again when he tried to move. Mullins repeated the process until his victim was aware enough to speak.

"Sorry about that, Sir, but my associate has little patience. Now, unless you'd like further encouragement, the combination please."

Bruce recited the safe's combination numbers through drool, moans, and spittle. When he was finished, he passed out once more.

"Jaysus, Joseph, the man's a lightweight."

Driggs ignored the comment, strode to the safe, and turned the dial. "I hope this works because it appears our friend here is no longer useful."

Starting over twice because of shaking fingers, Driggs managed to open the safe's heavy door. The lower shelf contained reams of documents, but a cream-colored cardboard box sat alone on the top shelf.

"Got it!" The former Prophet of the FLDS grabbed the box and ripped off the top. Inside was the purple bag taken from his compound in Short Creek.

"There seem to be some missing, Shane."

"How can you tell?"

"The entire stash was taken, and I know it was more than this."

"A lot more?" Shane was getting impatient.

"No, but more than what's here."

"I can't imagine the cops taking any. Maybe the woman who stole them did something with them, so let's take what we've got and get going." As he spoke, he headed for the unconscious man and raised his hammer.

"Leave him, Shane. We've got what we came for." He said, heading for the door.

"What about him? He can ID us," he nodded at the passed-out man

"Shane...if they don't know who did this, then they're even dumber than I thought. Leave him; he's not going anywhere soon."

They hurried to their SUV and took off for the highway.

***

The day's events had left me exhausted and more than a little concerned about the two violent men still somewhere on the island. The Deception Pass Bridge was a likely escape route, but the on-site inspection teams practically eliminated that option. The Clinton and Keystone ferry terminals were also on alert, leaving no real option for Driggs and his accomplice.

Andie did her best to cheer me up, but my focus was elsewhere. We had a light dinner, and as I prepared for an early bedtime, I thought about Mullins's need for medical treatment. He *had* to find it somewhere and soon.

I called Bruce to tell him to start looking for anywhere that could provide the medical assistance he needed. When no one answered at the office, I tried his cell, but there was still no answer.

"Maybe he's hitting the sack early...like you." Andie offered an explanation.

"Yeah...maybe, but he's always answered, regardless of the time."

"Try Carol. Here, use my phone; the number's in there."

Carol was Bruce's wife and *always* knew where he was.

"Hey, Carol. It's Roger. Is Bruce there?"

"No. He said he would stay at the office for a few hours, just in case. Did you try there?"

"Um...yeah, but I couldn't reach him."

"His cell?"

"Not there either."

"That's not like him."

I didn't want her to worry, so I said, "Maybe he stepped out for something to eat."

"Nope...he wouldn't."

I suddenly had a bad feeling. "I'll run by the station and check, Carol. I'm sure it's something simple."

"Call me right away."

I said I would. I got dressed again and hurried out the door. Andie overheard it all, and she, too, was looking concerned.

"Keep me in the loop, Rog," she yelled after me.

I gave her a thumbs up and spewed gravel, swerving down the drive.

***

Still shaken from her ordeal, Maggie thanked Francis for taking her home from the Sherrif's Office.

"Could you come in, Francis? Just to be sure?" She asked.

Along with Henry, he followed her in; she shuddered slightly at the sight of the duct tape still wrapped around the chair to which she was tied.

He moved ahead of her, cleaning up any other reminders of the traumatic event, while she fidgeted in the small kitchen, then said, "Coffee, Francis?"

"Sure, sounds good." He was glad for the distraction it offered.

They sat on the sofa, Henry at his feet, and quietly sipped their coffee until Maggie said, "Francis...I was scared to death. I've never been that afraid before. I thought I was better than that."

He looked at her with understanding, and she leaned into him. Putting his muscular arm around her shoulders, comforting her, he said, "None of us know how we'll react to an event until it happens. You were stronger than most people would have ever been."

She nodded her thanks and quietly wept for a minute. Then she pulled away and faced him." So, Francis, tell me about yourself."

Slowly, at first, he told her of his childhood with his much older brother, Jake. He spoke of his troubles with drugs, his skirmishes with the law, and his eventual imprisonment at McNeil Island. He related the saga of the drug kingpin and his assassin who assaulted them at their home a few years ago and how he got involved with a serial killer who tried to poison the entire island, which was the beginning of his relationship with Roger Wilkie.

When he was finished, she saw this man in a different light. He'd been through much, yet still had one of the kindest dispositions she'd ever encountered.

She told him of her career with the Navy and her subsequent employment by the county.

They talked about their lives on Whidbey and their love of nature. Soon, they began finishing each other's sentences and laughing frequently. When the subject of her kidnapping came up once more, he remembered his commitment to apprehending Mullins. It was getting late, and he wanted to reach Roger to catch up on the search.

"Excuse me, Maggie, I need to make a call." Henry stirred as he stood to use his phone.

***

I pulled into the small parking lot next to the station. Bruce's car was still there, the door slightly ajar. Something uncomfortable swirled in my gut.

"Bruce," I shouted as I hurried inside. The first thing I noticed was the open safe. Then I saw a small puddle of blood, and beside it, my good friend and volunteer dispatcher crumpled against the side of a desk.

He moved his legs slightly and moaned. He appeared semi-conscious, and I could see why. His right upper arm and shoulder had been dismantled. Then he opened his eyes and recognized me.

"Rog," he said in a voice I could barely hear, "It was Mullins, and Driggs was with him. I'm sorry, but I gave them the combination."

"Don't worry about that, Buddy; let's get you some help."

I called the EMTs first, then Carol. I told her Bruce was hurt but not in mortal danger and asked her to contact Andie. She said she'd meet us at the hospital in Coupeville.

The emergency techs on Whidbey Island were second to none—they had to be. With only the small regional hospital in Coupeville, they were experts on all kinds of trauma, heart attacks, and strokes. They were the primary line of care and often the difference between living and dying for those who chose to live on this beautiful slice of planet Earth.

They administered to my friend in less than ten minutes, and in another ten, they were on their way to the hospital. My phone buzzed when I got in the cruiser to follow them. It was Francis.

I told him what had happened. He cursed when I told him about Bruce, once again taking undeserved responsibility simply because a dead woman was told to contact him. He told me he'd see me at the hospital and disconnected.

Twenty-Six

With the diamonds back in their hands, Mullins and Driggs considered their journey to this strangely shaped land in Puget Sound a success. Now, they had to find a way off this stupid island.

"We can't go north because the bridge is covered, and we're pretty sure the ferries are a no-go, right?"

Mullins nodded his agreement, then offered, "Maybe we could steal a boat."

"Not likely. It's dark; we don't know where to find one, and there will be cops everywhere."

"So, what?"

"Check your phone again; see if there's any other way off. Maybe a water taxi or something."

They continued driving north until Mullins gave up his search. "There's nothing. Two ferries and the bridge; that's it."

"Two Ferries?"

"There's the Clinton one we got here on and another one from a place called Keystone."

"Where does it go?"

"It says Port Townsend. Looks like from there, we can drive wherever we want."

Driggs pondered this momentarily, then asked, "You think anyone knows what we're driving?"

Mullins shrugged, "I dunno…maybe, maybe not."

"How big a place is this Keystone?"

"From what I can see, it looks pretty tiny. They use a smaller boat, and it doesn't make that many trips."

"What about cameras?"

"The site shows a couple. Right now, only a few cars are in the lot, and they sail in twenty minutes. It's the last trip tonight. There's only one booth, too."

A few minutes passed, then Driggs seemed to reach a conclusion: "We're screwed if we stay on the island, and we might get noticed if we leave. But, maybe our chances are better on this little boat."

"Okay, and if the shit hits the fan, we can handle whoever's tending the booth."

Driggs always marveled at his associate's ability to cut through the distractions, even if he was a bit crude. "Yes, Shane, that too."

They followed SR 525 until the turnoff west to the Keystone ferry. It was pitch black, and they had ten minutes to catch the last run for the night.

They drove right up to the ticket booth without even a one-car wait. The attendant, who appeared to be in her late thirties, seemed distracted by something on her phone. She looked up and said, "Roundtrip for two?" as she peered over Driggs to make sure there was an additional passenger.

Driggs said, "Yes," hoping to discourage any other questions.

"Any seniors?" she asked.

Not realizing there was a senior discount for ferry passengers, he was momentarily confused.

"Seniors?" she asked a bit louder.

"Uh...no...none...no seniors."

She made change from his fifty and handed it back. "Lane one, on the right," she said, looking more closely at the passenger this time.

Because the 9:30 sailing was within minutes, their vehicle was waved directly onto the *Kennewick* without stopping in the holding lot.

Nora Browne had been texting her fifteen-year-old son when the tan Explorer pulled up. The damn kid was supposed to be at home in Oak Harbor, but her Life 360 App showed his location to be at his buddy's house. His gaming skills were impressive, and any chance to annihilate his peers in person was hard to pass up. A single mom, she did her best but frequently questioned her mothering skills when her teenage son was involved. She'd ordered him home and wondered if she'd been too strict. Thankfully, she would be leaving shortly.

The Explorer driver seemed a little nervous; he wasn't a frequent ferry rider. From what she could see of the passenger, she noticed several brown stains on his jeans, which appeared torn in places.

She'd seen all kinds leaving the island and would have thought nothing of it except for the bulletin she received. All points of departure from Whidbey Island were to be on the lookout for two suspected murderers who were armed and dangerous. *Could it be them?*

Hoping she wasn't raising a false alarm, she phoned her supervisor, who immediately passed the alert on to the Sheriff's Office.

They were directed to the center car deck by one of the deckhands. Since it was the last sailing on a Friday night, only a half-dozen vehicles were on board, and they pulled up behind them. Driggs turned off the ignition and glanced at his watch.

"We should be leaving soon; it's nine-thirty."

Mullins grunted in agreement and reclined his seat back.

Another ten minutes passed with no other vehicles loading and the ferry tied to the dock. Driggs started to get nervous.

"Shane?"

"Yes...what?" he said drowsily.

"I'm getting a bad feeling; we haven't moved. What if she called the cops?"

Mullins sat back up and was now on alert. "She might have, huh?"

"Ideas?"

"Let's get this boat underway, I say."

"How?"

Mullins began opening his door. Just before exiting, he turned to Driggs and said, "We pay the captain a visit...that's how."

They took the stairs to the passenger deck and located the "No Entry" flight to the bridge. Because the crossing was only thirty-five minutes, most drivers stayed in their vehicles, but a handful of walk-ons wandered about, looking for a comfortable place to sit during the trip.

When no one was watching, they slipped over the small chain stretched across the steps and climbed to the bridge level of the two-hundred-seventy-foot vessel. They arrived at the top deck, where they were alone. There were bridges at both ends of the ferry.

"Where is he? Which end?" Mullins asked.

After thinking it through, Driggs said, "Gotta be the end nearest the dock. I think he'd want to be able to see the dock as he's leaving."

"Let's go."

With Mullins still limping, they moved along the darkest side of the deck, arriving at the bridge without detection. Driggs had the Walther while Mullins carried his trusty sledgehammer. Standing on each side of the door leading to the bridge, Driggs gave the go-ahead to his partner, who slammed the heavy hammer into the locking mechanism that secured the door.

As it swung wide, he hurried inside to find a seated first mate and a shocked Captain Danny Collins holding a cell phone to his ear.

Twenty-Seven

Bruce was treated in the ER while Wally, Francis, and I stood in the waiting area. At Francis's insistence, Henry was allowed in as a service dog. The EMTs told us that as bad as it looked, he would be okay. They acknowledged there would be surgeries and months of physical therapy, but in the end, our buddy would be fine.

Ten minutes after we arrived, my phone buzzed. It was Tom Davis, and he was excited.

I listened to the report he'd received from the Keystone Terminal and told him we were on our way and to make damn sure the *Kennewick* didn't sail until we arrived. There was no way to dissuade Francis and Henry from coming.

Wally drove while I spoke with the toll booth operator who had sounded the alert. Her description of those in the Explorer convinced me we had the fugitives trapped.

I called Davis back to let him know, and he gave me some disturbing news: "I was on the phone with the captain when something happened. I heard shouts, then nothing. When I tried to call back, it wouldn't go through."

"Shit," I said. "Who's on duty on that run tonight?"

"Captain Collins, I think it was."

"Danny Collins? What's he doing on that route? He's usually on the bigger boats."

"Don't know, Rog. I told him he had to stay put until you arrived when something interrupted him."

None of this sounded good, and we had just blown through the toll booth gate that Nora Browne had left open for us. Wally sped through the vacant holding lot, took a screeching right turn at the ramp to the *Kennewick*, and vaulted aboard just as it began to rise.

Crossing the churning waters below, we landed with a hard thud on the steel deck, scattering the two shocked deckhands in the process of securing the giant mooring lines. Wally slammed on the brakes, and the four of us jumped out.

I informed the deckhands what was happening and told them to head to the crew's quarters until I came to get them. Seeing Wally and me in uniform, Francis's imposing look and alert police dog seemed more than enough to get them to comply. Before they left, they gave me an idea of how many walk-ons and drivers were on board.

We hurried up to the passenger deck, where the passengers were as shocked as the deckhands. As we headed for the stairs to the bridge, my phone buzzed. The ID said it was Danny, so I held up my hand to stop the others.

"Danny?"

"Yes, I figured you might be in the loop. I'm telling you to stay away from the boat. Your friends here have forced me to get underway. They..."

I heard rustling as the phone was taken away.

"This Deputy Wilkie?"

"It is," I could tell the speaker was Driggs.

"We've had to commandeer the ferry. If you and the rest of law enforcement stay away from the boat, we'll be out of your hair. If you interfere, things could get messy."

It was clear Driggs and Mullins didn't know we were already onboard, so I tried to keep him talking. "You injured my friend. He's in the hospital."

"Yes...well, it couldn't be helped; we needed information. At least he's still alive."

"How do you expect to get away? When you land in Port Townsend, cops will be waiting for you."

"I don't think so. If that happens, there will be an unfortunate loss of life on this boat. If I were you, I'd let us go and let these poor folks live." The phone disconnected.

I filled my associates in on my conversation with Driggs and told them he didn't know we were on the ferry. At least we had that going for us. We turned from the stairs to the bridge to find a place to talk. As we did, we found ourselves facing a small group of passengers who appeared worried.

"What's going on, Officer?"

"It's deputy, ma'am. We had a report of an altercation onboard, but it seems we were misinformed." Wally took the liberty of answering for us.

It seemed to mollify their concerns, so we retreated to a table away from the rest of the passengers to devise a plan. Since we were now crossing the Strait of Juan de Fuca and knew our two adversaries were busy with Danny, little would happen over the next twenty minutes.

First, I called Tom Davis and told him the situation. He was relieved we were able to make the ferry and told me not to take any chances and to please not let anybody else get killed. He said he'd take care of alerting the Port Townsend police, and now that the killers were on the high seas, the Coast Guard would also be involved.

The wild card in this scenario was what Driggs and Mullins had planned for their escape when we docked at Port Townsend. It seemed they'd be trapped, but Driggs had proven himself adept at getting out of tight situations, and I was determined not to underestimate him.

***

The wheelhouse was cramped. Usually, only the captain and chief mate were stationed there, and adding the two criminals made it claustrophobic. Jeff Galbreath, the diminutive chief mate, was now curled up in a corner.

When they barged into the operations center, their first action was eliminating any threats. Galbreath, a hundred thirty pounds soaking wet, was an unlikely one, but just in case, they'd tied his hands tightly behind him using electrical cords torn from several radios. Now that he was out of the picture, it was up to Danny Collins to steer and navigate the *Kennewick*.

"How are we gonna get out of this, Driggs?" Mullins looked concerned now that he'd had a moment to think about their predicament.

Captain Collins also looked to Driggs to see what he had to say.

"Keep your eyes ahead, Captain; worry about your duties, not us," Driggs said, then added, "Give me a few minutes, Shane. I'm trying to work something out."

What seemed like an eternity, but in reality, only less than five minutes, he spoke again: "We can't land there, Shane. It'll be impossible for us to get away. If we had been able to make it on board quietly, then maybe...but now that the word is out, they'll be waiting for us."

***

Chief Warrant Officer Ron Wheeler had been on active duty with the U.S. Coast Guard for ten years. Originally a Southern California native, he had been stationed in the Northwest after his basic training and never left the area. He loved it, even the fickle winter weather.

He had only been captain of the Coast Guard Cutter *Osprey* for less than a year, but in that time, he and his crew had been called upon for numerous hazardous rescues. Docked at the Union Wharf Pier in Port Townsend, he and his crew looked forward to a restful weekend after a challenging recovery in Neah Bay, just inside the entrance to the Strait of Juan de Fuca.

A fishing boat from the Makah Reservation lost power and was in danger of being tossed on the rocks. The fierce currents and gale winds hampered their efforts, but Wheeler and his crew successfully saved both the boat and its crew. They were exhausted as they pulled into their slip. Then, CWO Wheeler got the call from Lieutenant Commander John Oden.

"Ron, we have a situation." It was never a good sign when there was a "situation."

"Yessir, what have we got?"

"You heard about the murder on the Clinton ferry, right?"

"Yessir."

"And the other one in Freeland, yes?"

"I do, Sir."

"Well, it seems the two guys responsible have hijacked the *Kennewick,* and it's mid-channel now."

There was silence as Wheeler tried to picture what was happening.

"Ron?"

"Yessir?"

"I need you and your crew to get out there and monitor the situation. Escort that ferry into Port Townsend and report to me what's happening. We'll decide what to do when we know their demands."

It had been his first mission remotely like this, and Wheeler was on untilled soil. He was a disciplined and intelligent officer, though, and he was confident his training would allow him to make the correct decisions.

"We got this, Sir. We're leaving now."

The *Osprey* left the dock and headed to greet the *Kennewick*.

***

The remaining radio in the wheelhouse squawked, and news of the *Osprey* heading to intercept the *Kennewick* filled the room. Captain Collins looked at Driggs with a slight grin and said, "What now, Driggs?"

The former cult leader back-handed Collins with the Walther, smashing his lips and knocking a tooth onto the instrument display. Not only did it stun Mullins, but it also seemed to be a shock to Driggs. The smart-ass grin by the captain had been enough to stir a primal need for retaliation that he hadn't before experienced, let alone acted upon.

Collins stumbled, grabbing his shattered mouth, but regained his balance and stood by the steering console. He was understandably silent.

"How long before they get here?" He asked Collins.

"Maybe ten, fifteen minutes," Collins mumbled through torn, bleeding lips.

"Is there any way to get off this thing?"

"You could jump," It seemed Collins hadn't lost his sense of humor.

Driggs lifted the Walther once more, enough for the captain to concede. "No, wait. You could use a lifeboat; we could full stop and launch it. They have enough power to get you wherever you want."

Mullins pointed at the chief mate, "Does he know how to do this?"

Collins was slow to answer, not wanting to get Galbreath any more involved, but the mate spoke first.

"I do; I can take you there and get it in the water. We drill for this once a month." His dedication was one of the reasons Collins always had him on his crew.

"How do we get there without dealing with the passengers?" Mullins asked.

"Easy," Collins answered. "We tell them it's a drill and to assemble on the auto deck. It happens occasionally, so it shouldn't be a problem. Then you can take the stairs down to the main deck where the boats are."

"Do it. NOW." Driggs made up his mind. " Then both of you are coming with us. Shane, please take care of this equipment when he's finished."

Mullins grinned as he took his hammer, waited for Collins's announcement, and in less than a half-dozen strokes, demolished the radio, radar displays, and GPS location equipment.

***

Folks, this is the captain. We're having a required rescue drill. We'll need all those on board and those in their vehicles to assemble at the aft end of the auto deck. It will only be for a few minutes, and then we'll be back on our way to Port Townsend. Thanks for your cooperation.

I was shocked to hear Danny's voice, but I knew something was happening when the two-thousand-ton ferry slowed its progress. So did Wally, and Henry looked more alert than before as if that were even possible. Francis asked, "What does this mean, Rog?"

"I'm not certain, but let's pretend we're part of this and make sure all the passengers are accounted for. If these guys want hostages, we're not going to let them take any. Let's get down there fast."

The folks exited their cars and pickups and shuffled to the aft end of the deck, a few looking perplexed and several appearing to have just woken up. The three of us and Henry took positions that afforded us good visibility but also made the thirty or so individuals nervous. We did our best to give the impression it was nothing unusual, but too many of them could see this was anything but.

***

The *Osprey* got underway immediately and reached its top speed of twenty-five knots in less than three minutes. Wheeler calculated he'd be alongside the *Kennewick* less than eight minutes after their departure.

He was still uncertain what would be required of him and his crew, but he was ready.

Twenty-Eight

Sitting idle a third of the way across Admiralty Inlet, the *Kennewick's* bridge was untended. Driggs had forced both Collins and Galbreath to accompany them. They reached the deserted main deck without incident, and the first mate led them to the lifeboat station.

"You...get in the boat," Driggs said to Galbreath.

"Why? You two will be better off without me."

"GET in the boat," Driggs emphasized his demand with the pistol.

Danny Collins wasn't sure where this was headed, but at least it seemed the passengers would be spared. He asked, "Why am I here, and why are you taking Jeff?"

"You are here to ensure we get into the water in one piece, and your mate is with us to ensure this boat is operating properly. If there are no issues, you'll both be unharmed."

Mullins seemed to prefer to do some harming, but he deferred to Driggs.

Once the first mate lowered the lever securing the lifeboat to the davits, it dropped smoothly and gently into the water sixteen feet below. Collins could do nothing but watch.

"Start the engine, please," Driggs directed Galbreath.

Seconds after the ignition button was pressed, the throaty rumble of the D-4 Volvo Penta inboard engine roared to life. Driggs positioned himself behind the wheel while Galbreath looked on from the stern and Collins from above.

"There is a radar reflector on board?" Driggs asked.

Galbreath looked disappointed but answered, "Yes."

"Please throw it over."

The first mate complied with the order as they drifted away from the Kennewick.

"Now...over you go."

"What? It's freezing in there."

"Shane, please encourage the young man to get off this boat."

As the brutal accomplice approached Galbreath, hammer in hand, he decided hypothermia was a better way to go than a bludgeoned head. He jumped off the orange lifeboat that, within seconds, powered off into the night.

***

I didn't like what was going on. We were on the cavernous auto deck while the ferry was motionless in the water. At first, there was mild excitement among the passengers, but that quickly dissolved into gripes about why they weren't moving.

Several were interested in Henry, and being a good sport, he allowed them to pet him. While this was happening, Francis sidled up to me and quietly said, "You do realize the passenger deck is empty. There's gotta be something going on up there."

Of course, he was right, but the safety of the passengers was still a concern. I walked to Wally's position and said, "We'll check on the main deck. Can you handle these folks?"

"No problem, Boss. Stay safe."

We took the stairs to the deserted main deck. I wondered if we were wrong when I saw movement on the port side of the deck. It was Danny...alone.

We rushed out the side door, and I yelled, "DANNY!"

As he turned, I saw his bloodied mouth. "Danny...what happened? You okay?"

Rather than answer, he pointed into the water where a writhing, half-swimming Jeff Galbreath tried futilely to make it to the boat.

"Rog, throw him that lifesaver on the bulkhead; if we can get him out fast, he should be okay."

Francis sprung into action and launched the bright orange donut toward the first mate.

"Pull him toward the aft end of the boat. There's an access break in the rail where we can pull him up."

While Francis managed to comply, I asked, "What about Driggs and Mullins?"

"They took the lifeboat. Headed off back the way we came. The Coast Guard should be here any second. Hopefully, they can track them down."

"Are you okay?"

"Probably need some dental work, but yeah…okay. Let's get down below and get Jeff aboard."

When we returned to the auto deck, Wally was pulling Jeff out of the water. Several passengers assisted while the rest looked on, likely wondering how a person could still be alive in the frigid waters of the sound. That he'd been in the water for a few minutes was the only reason for his survival.

We told the passengers there was no need to worry and to return to their vehicles while Wally and I went to the bridge with Danny. Francis and Henry took it upon themselves to warm up Jeff and make sure he was okay.

As we entered the wheelhouse, the brilliant spotlights of the Osprey illuminated the entire ferry. If the passengers thought the whole event was simply a man overboard, they now knew it was something much more.

We needed to reach the Coast Guard cutter's commander, but when I saw the destruction of the comms gear in the wheelhouse, I knew we had to find a workaround. I called Davis on my cell and told him to contact the *Osprey* and have them call me.

In less than a minute, CWO Wheeler was on the phone. He called me Deputy Wilkie, so I figured Davis had given the introduction. "Here's what's happening, Chief: I guess you know Driggs and Mullins hijacked the *Kennewick*, or you wouldn't be here. They took off a few minutes ago in a lifeboat and headed east. Can you catch them?"

Rather than answering my question, he focused on the passengers and crew. "Is everyone onboard okay and unharmed? Is any medical assistance needed?"

"Everyone's good, Chief. Please tell me you can get these guys."

"We're going to do our best, Deputy; we'll get this thing moving as fast as she'll go. Thing is, those lifeboats can haul ass, and they're ten times as maneuverable as we are. If you folks are good, we're peeling off to go after the bad guys. Chief Wheeler, out."

Danny got underway again and was focused on getting to Port Townsend. Jeff Galbreath, an olive wool blanket over his shoulders, came through the smashed door just as I signed off with the *Osprey*.

"I hope they get those two, but it's gonna be difficult. They had me toss the reflector over before I went in the water."

I turned to Danny and asked, "They'll still give off a radar signature, right?"

"They will, but it will be faint, and if they stay close to the shore, there will be a lot of clutter. It might not be easy."

"Shit," I muttered under my breath, "Any idea where they might go?"

"None. They'll probably stay inside Admiralty Inlet because the seas are calmer, but that still leaves a million possibilities. Those fuel tanks are full, so that doesn't help either."

Twenty-Nine

They were in the shadow of the *Kennewick* as the enormous spotlights of the *Osprey* illuminated the water. Their direction wasn't as important as staying out of sight of the cutter.

Driggs wasn't much of a boater, but he'd driven small runabouts before, and this thing was easy. He guessed it would need to be if passengers ended up driving it in case of an emergency. It was fast, too.

The closer the *Osprey* got to the ferry, the wider its shadow was and the more time it bought them. Driggs wasn't sure the cutter could still see them on their radar, so he held the throttle down, putting even more space between them. Mullins held on to two of the many handholds while Driggs pressed the craft to its limits. The sound's calm waters allowed the craft to plane in seconds, accelerating even faster. Once they were beyond the ferry's shadow, they headed around the Fort Flagler peninsula, where the land mass effectively blocked any chance for radar to acquire them.

***

Chief Wheeler was pissed. He didn't know what to expect when he reached the *Kennewick*, but he was glad the passengers and crew were safe. That he allowed the two killers to escape, though, angered him mightily.

The smaller lifeboats were fast and could turn on a dime. These characteristics contributed to their reputation for lifesaving but also made them difficult to chase down. Once they headed into the south sound, he knew their chances of corralling them had disappeared.

He reported his situation to his CO and told him there was little chance they would capture the hijackers. It was assumed the killers would be once again on land, and it would be up to the local jurisdictions to find them. There were too many opportunities for them to vanish.

***

Driggs quickly learned the nuances of the lifeboat. Because of the overcast sky, there was little ambient light at ten p.m., so they stayed as close as he dared to the shore. Enough cabins and cottages had lights on for him to navigate, although he still had no idea of his direction or the identity of the surrounding land masses.

Those new to the waters of the Pacific Northwest are seldom aware of the remarkable range of tides and currents. When the moon aligns just right, this difference can exceed fifteen feet. Often, minus tides expose large outcroppings of rocks seldom identified by buoys or markers, while higher ones allow them to lurk just beneath the surface. The locals know this, of course, but visitors from other parts of the country are unaware, especially those from the Southwest, and even more, especially those non-boaters who happen to be killers.

While Driggs was trying to keep close to the east side of Marrowstone Island to escape radar detection, he heard and felt a loud scraping noise, as if a giant claw had grabbed the aft end of the lifeboat. He immediately turned toward the open water, guessing they had managed to drive over one of those submerged but shallow unseen rocks.

The boat shuddered, and the steering became balky, but they slowly headed away from land. He managed to get up to fifteen knots before the wheel, instead of being stiff and difficult to turn, suddenly spun freely in his hands. Worse yet, turning it did not affect the boat's direction. When he increased the throttle, nothing happened. The engine was running, but they'd lost the prop.

The irregular shapes of the islands, inlets, and peninsulas that populate the Puget Sound region make it difficult to determine which land masses are islands and which are connected to the mainland. Driggs and Mullins were oblivious that they were now rudderless somewhere between Marrowstone and Whidbey Islands, entirely at the mercy of the notoriously fickle currents.

Mullins, content to let his boss handle the navigational duties, realized something was wrong shortly after encountering the rock. Still holding his injured leg with both hands—during the activities of the past few hours, it had started seeping blood again—he asked the obvious: "We're fucked?"

"Things could be better, but at least we're off that damn island. If we're lucky, we'll drift someplace where we can find a car and get away from this god-forsaken place."

Mullins had even less experience with boating than Driggs and knew nothing about tides or currents. "How long before we get to land?"

"I don't know, Shane. It's up to a higher power."

It had been some time since Driggs had referred to anything remotely religious, and since he had no desire to go there, Mullins let it pass. He'd rather sit down and wait it out than engage with Driggs. On some infinitesimal level, he figured there was something wacko about his partner.

They coasted mid-channel for the better part of an hour, then slowly began drifting toward another land mass. This one had a smattering of lights from homes on the shore, but because they were approaching eleven p.m., there were only a few.

As they edged closer to shore, Driggs finally realized that the boat had oars lashed to its sides. *It's a lifeboat; of course there are*, he mentally scolded himself.

He ripped the Velcro straps away, lifted two heavy wooden paddles, and passed one to Mullins. It took several tries, but after much swearing and grunting, each managed to fit the pin into the oarlock. Mullins seemed exhausted from the ordeal, but it was more likely due to his loss of blood over the past twelve hours. They wrapped their hands around a grip and began edging their way to land. First on their agenda was finding a place to crash.

The closer they got to the shore to their east, the denser the houses looked. While the beach looked easy to navigate, there was too much risk of being seen. Even though the heavy oars made steering the craft difficult, they continued south. They passed a gigantic sandy bluff so white it was visible even in the dark, overcast night.

The bluff gradually sloped downward, and if houses were on the shore, they were either vacant or the lights were off for the night.

"I'm done, Joseph. We gotta beach this thing. I can't keep rowing." Mullins was used up.

Driggs agreed; he, too, was wasted: "Okay, Shane, let's head in here."

They nosed the lifeboat into the soft sandy beach and grounded it with barely a whisper. It was after midnight. While they were struggling with the unwieldy boat, the constant drizzle was unnoticeable, but now, with the temperature hovering around fifty degrees, the chill penetrated their soaked clothing.

As they headed away from the shore, Driggs suddenly thought, "Shane, let me have your hammer for a minute."

Mullins, never without his weapon, handed it over reluctantly. "What for?"

"I'll be right back." Driggs turned back toward the lifeboat, climbed aboard, and smashed several holes in its fiberglass bottom. After stepping back onto the whisper-quiet beach, he shoved the orange craft back into the sound. With the tide ebbing, it was sucked into a swiftly moving current immediately, even as water rushed in through its damaged hull. By the time it sank, it would be in much deeper water.

The bluffs here were noticeably lower than the enormous one they passed, yet they were still steep, and, in the dark, the climb was treacherous. Mullins had a tough time saddled with his injured and now bleeding leg.

They eventually reached the top and found themselves on a large expanse of manicured lawn. Over a hundred feet away sat a whitish farmhouse-looking building large enough to house several families. The only illumination was from an outdoor spotlight affixed to a utility pole to the side of the house.

"Looks empty," Mullins's exhaustion was complete.

"I'll find out, Shane; stay here." Driggs wasn't in the best shape, but his ordeal over the past few days had shown him a reserve of energy that surprised him.

He moved to the back porch, where the screen door was unlocked. The door to the house was another matter, but after all he'd been through, he no longer cared. He used the butt end of the pistol to shatter a small bottom windowpane, waited a full minute to see if alarms or people would react, then reached inside and retracted the deadbolt. He took a chance and switched on a small lamp.

From what he could see, the kitchen looked like something from a magazine. A twelve-burner range sat against the back wall while a rectangular island of Carera marble took center stage. A side wall held a masonry fireplace flanked by two leather side chairs. After living for years in shabby housing in Colorado City, Driggs wondered if he'd made a mistake. Maybe those who forsook the literal teachings of Joseph Smith for the pleasures and riches of this world knew something. He immediately shoved his thoughts back into the deep recesses of his mind and went back outside to fetch his partner. Along the way, he discarded his vulgar musings, attributing them to lack of sleep and exhaustion. *Then again, maybe the diamonds would be the vehicle for his conversion.*

Thirty

scorted by the *Osprey*, the *Kennewick* docked in Port Townsend only half an hour after its scheduled arrival. Since its communication equipment was in shambles, contact between those on land and the bridge was made by cell phone. Repairing and replacing the equipment in the wheelhouse would take all night.

Danny Collins was taken to Jefferson Healthcare Medical Center, where an on-call dental surgeon was provided to repair the damage Driggs had done. Because our passage was the final one for the evening, we could either spend the night in town or drive the five hours it would take to get home without a ferry crossing. The choice was a simple one.

We located a small hotel in town that was available due to the off-season. When they heard of our ordeal, they provided our stay gratis—Henry included. The first ferry to Whidbey Island was at 6:30 in the morning, and we'd be on it.

We'd been so close to apprehending Driggs and Mullins, and now no one knew where they were. We sat in the lobby bar, nursing beers and discussing the situation. I had spoken to Tom Davis, and he assured me every law enforcement agency in the Puget Sound region would be looking for them, but unless somebody found the lifeboat, it would be a massive search area.

Francis and Henry left for their room while Wally and I sat quietly. Eventually, he broke the silence, "Hey, Rog...some fun this job, eh?"

I shook my head and grinned. My second in command was always able to knock the sharp edges off any situation. It was only one of the reasons I loved having him by my side.

"You've got that right, Pal. How about we call the women in our lives and tell them we won't be home tonight." I was certain Andie was worried that I hadn't yet called, and I wanted to put her mind at ease. The changing look on Wally's face told me he was thinking likewise about Kate. We finished our beers, said our good nights, and headed for a short night's rest. What tomorrow would bring, I had no idea.

***

When I finally made it home the following morning, Andie was at the door to greet me. Since he lived in Greenbank, Wally agreed to drop Francis and Henry off in Coupeville to pick up his truck. I only had time for a shower and a change of clothes before heading back to the station for weekend duty, but hugs from my favorite person in the world boosted my morale.

Before I left, I told Andie about all we'd been through. The previous night's call had been brief, and she listened intently while I filled in the blanks. She was especially shocked at what happened to Danny Collins and Bruce and was beginning to develop an intense dislike for the two criminals who were consuming the resources of the Island County Sheriff's Department.

It was quiet in my office, the coffee tasted great, and I looked forward to a day of routine reports and ordinary island crime. I was still angry that we couldn't corral Driggs and Mullins, but based on the direction they were headed, they'd be someone else's problem soon.

Then my cell phone buzzed. It was Tom Davis: "You working?"

"It's my turn, Tom; what's up?"

"First, good work last night. You didn't get the fuckers, but none of the passengers were hurt, and Danny's gonna be okay."

"Uh...you called to tell me *this*?"

"Nope, I called to tell you we just sent a team to WAIF. One of the volunteers phoned to tell us they thought they recognized Mullins from his picture on the TV. When she was leaving yesterday, she saw a car pull into the lot and thought the passenger was Mullins, but she didn't realize it until this morning when she saw the news."

"And…"

"And guess what they found…"

"Tom…I'm tired; just tell me."

"Okay, okay…yeah, sorry, of course. Anyway, the vet and her helper were locked in one of the kennels. Seems like they forced her to work on Mullins's dog bite. She said it was pretty bad, and she did her best to patch him up, but she also said unless he took it easy and kept the thing elevated, it could start bleeding again."

"They both okay?"

"Yes…tired and thirsty, but okay."

"So, you're telling me that with all their running around, we might have a seriously injured Mullins on our hands?"

"Yup…that's what I'm saying. What do you think it means?"

I thought about it briefly before answering, but Davis was antsy."

"You there?"

"I am… If I were in their shoes, I'd look for a place to hunker down. And sooner rather than later."

"Kinda what I was thinking, too. We've got the entire region looking for that lifeboat, but no luck so far. The thing is, there are lots of part-time places around the sound. Folks go away when the weather's bad and don't return until May or June."

"So maybe they'll hide out somewhere. Unless, of course, the neighbors notice something, but there are plenty of large parcels without neighbors."

"I agree. Since there's still a chance they're on Whidbey, we should start looking at accessible places along the beaches. I'm thinking it would have to be on the south end, so that's yours."

"Got it, Tom. It's a long shot, but we'll tell the troops to check on vacant places with beach access."

"Sounds good. Get some rest."

He disconnected, and I began preparing a bulletin for the on-duty deputies to follow up and check any vacant properties.

***

Francis and Henry settled in the pickup after Wally deposited them in the county complex parking lot. He, too, was wasted from the previous evening's activities. It dawned on him that over the past several days, he'd begun to think of his approach to life as *we* instead of *I.*

When his companion looked up at him, he felt a twinge in his gut. Henry's love was unconditional, and Francis had often provided his fierce, protective instincts for others but never had anyone done so for him. He'd begun to trust the shepherd implicitly.

As he headed south, he had a sudden thought. The excitement of the last twenty-four hours had left little time for reflection, but now, with time slowing down, he thought about his encounter with Maggie Ryan. She was different than any woman he'd ever met. Independent yet intensely committed to her work, his brief visit with her after her encounter with Mullins left him wanting to see her again.

The thought of seeing her erased his weariness, yet he still felt like a teenager calling her.

"Maggie? It's Francis."

"Francis who?"

He wasn't sure he'd heard her correctly. *How could she not know*, he thought.

"Um...you know...from yesterday."

"Oh...*that* Francis. Yes, yes, I seem to remember now. You're the guy with the dog, the one who saved my ass. Is *that* who this is?"

It finally dawned on him that she was jerking him around. He'd heard some folks from the East Coast could be sarcastic; he guessed it was an acquired trait that, with any luck, he'd learn to appreciate.

"Sorry, Miss...I guess I've got the wrong number," he thought he'd try it.

"Don't you dare hang up, Francis."

"Hah...gotcha!"

When he heard her throaty laugh on the other end, he remembered why he liked her.

"Where are you?"

He told her about the previous night's exploits and how he was now in Coupeville.

"Come on over; I'll make you breakfast," she said, disconnecting the call without giving him a chance to reply.

"Well, Henry, looks like she likes us," he said to his attentive companion as he tuned his truck around and headed toward her little cabin on the bluff.

He stepped up to the front porch with Henry at his side. Before he could knock, the door opened, and Maggie greeted them. Dressed in faded jeans and wearing a blue Tufts University sweatshirt with the sleeves pushed up, her head barely reached his chin. Her almost white hair was gathered in a tight ponytail, giving her a professorial look. It was the first time he'd seen her without her glasses and ball cap.

Unsure of how to physically greet her, his discomfort was relieved when she bent down to hug Henry. After several seconds, she stood, put her arms around Francis's muscular neck, and hugged him tightly. "I'm glad you called, Francis, and thanks again for saving me. I was scared to death."

Surprised and reassured that she thought of him as something more than a friend, he gently squeezed her back, or so he thought.

"Hey, Big Guy, easy there," she squeaked out.

"Oh...geez, sorry," he said as he released her.

She laughed easily as if she were sharing a joke with an old friend. "Don't be sorry, just a little lighter on the hugging," she said, pulling his head down and kissing him on the mouth.

"There...that better?" She said, pulling away with an ear-to-ear grin.

"Um...yeah...lots." It was a different path than he had walked before, but somehow, this woman left him at ease taking it.

They both stood at the threshold, quietly looking at each other. Eventually, Henry tired of the human nonsense and barked loudly. *There had to be food in this house somewhere.*

They both laughed nervously at first and, on some level, thankful that time was no longer standing still. Maggie ushered them in ahead of her and quietly closed and locked the door.

Thirty-One

Mullins had collapsed on the sofa in the family room. He managed to slow the bleeding by keeping his leg propped up on several of the loose pillows used to decorate the place and had fallen into an exhausted sleep.

After turning on another lamp, Driggs found a flashlight in one of the kitchen drawers. He inspected enough of the house's interior to get them through the night without turning on any more lights. He located a bathroom and the seating groups in the family room, and that was all they needed. He helped Mullins elevate his leg and then crashed on one of the other sofas in the room.

The following day, he awoke to sunshine streaming through the windows while Mullins was still snoring twenty feet away. The room they were in was huge. Its ceilings had to be fifteen feet high; it was at least twenty-five feet across and fifty feet long. A ledge stone fireplace was centered on the far wall, surrounded by white bookshelves.

Driggs mused that whoever owned this house had some serious money. The fact that it was only a part-time home was a further testament to the owner's wealth. He went to the kitchen and found a cache of K-cups with *Starbucks French Roast* printed across the top. *How convenient,* he thought, as he located the brewing machine on the far counter.

While the coffee was brewing, he rummaged through a stack of mail and newspapers piled on a portion of the counter that appeared to serve as a desk. It seemed that someone was picking up the occupants' mail and bringing it in for them.

The owner's name was Peter Tomlinson, but that wasn't what caused him to freeze. It was the address. They were back on goddamn Whidbey fucking Island. All they had been through to escape this birdshit-shaped strip of land had been in vain. They had the diamonds, sure, but they might as well have been in prison. He could only imagine what Mullins would say when he found out.

He spent the next hour investigating the rest of the house and property. It was extensive. There was an attached garage with what looked like guest quarters above, a garden shed, and a fenced chicken coop, and the closest neighbor could only be seen from behind the garage. The drive to the main road was a winding thing composed of crushed rock and featured a wrought iron gate now closed. They couldn't have chosen a better place to hide out,

Someone looked after the property during the owner's absence, but it *was* the weekend. It was possible they'd have a couple of days without being interrupted, although they would need to be vigilant.

Driggs returned to the main house to find Mullins sitting on the sofa, his leg still elevated, and drinking coffee. "Nice place you've got here," he said from his perch.

When Driggs didn't answer immediately, Mullins sensed a problem.

"What is it?"

"We're still on Whidbey Island."

"WHAT? How do you know that?"

"Look at the mail on the counter in the kitchen. This is a Whidbey Island address.

"Shit!"

"Yes...shit is correct. We still need to get off this rock...how's the leg, by the way?"

"The bleeding's stopped, so I think keeping it elevated is working."

"Another problem is someone is picking up the mail and bringing it in. It's the weekend, so we may be okay, but we should be careful."

"Perfect."

Driggs had been thinking about the situation on his tour around the property and had come up with a plan: "Let's stay here until Monday morning. There's food, plenty to drink, and it's warm. You can rest that leg."

"Yeah...but where do we go on Monday?"

"They have no idea where we are. I sunk the lifeboat so they wouldn't find it, and by Monday, things should have calmed down a bit. They'll have to quit soon if they're still blocking the bridge. The locals won't put up with it. Besides, for all they know, we've drowned or landed somewhere else."

"How do we get there?"

"I haven't looked, but there has to be a car or two in the garage. I'll check later and look for keys."

With a plan in place, the two criminals began to relax. The stress of being on the run had started to leak away, and the unpredictability of their immediate future was quietly pushed to the back burner.

***

I was surprised when Wally strode into the station shortly before noon; it was his weekend off.

"Hey, Buddy, to what do I owe the pleasure?"

"Kate had to do some things in Langley, so I thought I'd drop by to see how things are going."

I told him about my conversation with Tom Davis and the possibility that Driggs and Mullins might still be around. While thinking it unlikely, Wally agreed that if they were, they'd be laying low.

"I'm guessing no sign of the boat?" he asked.

"None yet. Davis said the Coast Guard and State Cops are looking, but no luck so far."

"I suppose it's possible they drowned. That water is awfully cold."

"I agree, but then the boat would show up."

"So...what? They sunk it on purpose after they came ashore somewhere?"

"More likely, I'd say."

"So where could they be?"

I reached behind me and grabbed a map of the entire Puget Sound. We spread it on my desk and tried to figure out the possibilities.

"We know they were last seen heading south in Admiralty Inlet," I stated. "And their boat had plenty of fuel."

"That means they could be as far south as Seattle?" Wally asked, now realizing the many possible landing areas for the lifeboat.

"It's possible, but I agree with Tom that they'd try to get back on land as soon as possible.."

"Okay...let's say they were on the water for an hour or less. Where could that put them?"

"That still leaves endless choices. From Marrowstone Island to Whidbey to as far south as Hansville or even Edmonds. They might have even gone down Hood Canal. It's a huge search area."

Wally was quiet for a few minutes. He seemed to be trying to think like the bad guys. He finally said, "If I were those guys—remember they're Southwest folks—I think I would be uncomfortable on the water, especially at night. I'd try to get to land as soon as possible."

It made sense to me, and I said so.

"He continued, "If we're guessing correctly, it'd be more likely they're on Marrowstone or Whidbey, maybe even Hansville or Port Ludlow."

"And the boat?"

"Like you said, they sunk it."

We thought about the scenario we came up with for a few minutes, and then I stated our only option: "We could be right, Wally. I think it's likely, but all we can do is check out the possibilities here on our patch. I'll get this out to the troops and tell them there's a good chance they're still on Whidbey. Maybe we'll get lucky."

Thirty-Two

Billy Barnett had lived on Whidbey Island for over thirty years. He took early retirement from Boeing fifteen years ago to help his wife, Barbara, during her battle with Alzheimer's. After six months of doctor's visits, both on the mainland and the island, he had to admit defeat.

Her condition had deteriorated rapidly, and the prognosis was dismal. Finally, admitting he could no longer care for her, he admitted her to a memory care facility in Freeland. After less than three months, she mercifully died.

Over the intervening years, he had learned to deal with the grief, but it never disappeared. His comfort these days came from his daily walks with his eight-year-old golden retriever—a gift from his daughter--and his visits with his neighbors, the Tomlinsons. They were a dozen years younger and traveled extensively.

He thought them a bit stuffy when they moved next door six years ago and knew they had to be wealthy because the property had been on the market for over three million. A rumor had it that they paid cash for the place. A month after their arrival, Lucy—his golden—signaled someone was at his front door.

"Excuse me; I'm Peter Tomlinson. We've recently moved next door, and we're having some of the neighbors over this Saturday to introduce ourselves. We would be happy if you could join us."

He was surprised by the invitation, but there was little joy in his life, and he couldn't imagine mingling with happy people now...maybe never. With Lucy by his side, he thanked George for the invitation but declined, explaining he had things to do around his house.

"I understand, but come by around six if you change your mind. It's very informal, just a meet and greet." Barnett watched after him as his new neighbor walked back down the driveway. He closed the door and leaned against it, taking a deep breath. "What do you think, Lucy? How about these folks? They're the newbies, and they're inviting *us* over."

Two days passed, and it was Saturday morning. Billy and Lucy walked along the beach at the bottom of the bluff. It was overcast, of course, but the quiet lapping of the sound on the driftwood-piled beach gave him a sense of peace. Then he heard another dog barking ferociously.

When he reached the point where the beach turned into a small cove, he saw his new neighbor throwing a ball to a young German Shepherd. The dog froze when he saw them, then turned and charged after them.

"Bruno...BRUNO, get back here," yelled Tomlinson. Bruno paid no attention. When he was five feet from a shaken Billy Barnett, Bruno stopped on a dime and sat. He kept barking.

Tomlinson finally caught up to them and apologized profusely. "I'm sorry, Billy. We've just had him for a few months, and he's still getting used to the island. He's friendly but has a big bark, and we've yet to figure out how to control it."

During this explanation, Bruno began sniffing Lucy and Barnett, and within seconds, the two dogs ran off into the freezing waters of Puget Sound.

Barnett relaxed when he saw they were having fun, then turned to his neighbor and said, "Looks like they'll be pals, George. I gotta say, though, that guy would scare the crap out of me if I didn't know he was friendly."

"I know, I know...I'm sorry...again. Hey, Billy, the offer is still open if you want to come by tonight. Bring Lucy with you. They'll keep each other company.

Lucy and Billy made it to the Tomlinsons. He met several neighbors he never knew he had and discovered that he and Ronnie, George's wife, graduated from the same high school, albeit twelve years apart. It was the first time since his wife died that he had enjoyed an evening.

Since then, they had become close friends. When Lucy passed away, the Tomlinsons were the first to offer condolences, and George invited Billy to accompany him and Bruno on their beach walks. When they traveled, Billy took care of Bruno and collected their mail. It was the least he could do for his best friends.

Billy's home was a small, ranch-style affair, and his half-acre property ran in a pie-shape from Whal Road to the beach. On his east side, Tomlinson's encompassed over five acres, and the five thousand square foot home was one of the more impressive structures on the island's south end. The properties were bordered by thick stands of fir and cedars, with an impassable undergrowth of blackberries and dense clumps of salal.

Peter Tomlinson and his wife traveled frequently as investment bankers for a large New York firm. With additional homes in Portugal and Hawaii, it wasn't uncommon for them to be gone for months. Billy dog-sat for Bruno so frequently that he developed a bond with the animal nearly as strong as he shared with Lucy.

The rare spring sunshine wasn't lost on Bruno. He picked his leash from the basket by the door and brought it to Billy while still in bed. At seventy years old, his joints weren't as flexible as they used to be, and it took him twenty minutes and two cups of coffee to loosen up. All the while, Bruno sat by the door, leash in his mouth.

The beach was deserted, as usual. The soft southerly breeze brought scents of saltwater mingled with pollen from thousands of spring blooms scattered throughout the islands and the mainland. Bruno ran and jumped playfully the moment he was released from his leash. He found a piece of driftwood to his liking and tossed it high before darting and diving into the frigid water.

As they walked past the Tomlinson residence, he noticed something seemed off. When he dropped their mail off yesterday, he was sure he had checked the thermostat to ensure it was set at sixty. There was no sense in heating the place while they were out of town, yet clouds of water vapor poured from the furnace vent on the roof. He supposed the temperature had dropped below the setting, triggering the system, but it seemed unlikely.

The access to his neighbor's property from the beach was a rugged climb up the bluff, and he knew better than to attempt it. Instead, he retreated the way they'd come, taking the rickety stairs to his property and then taking Wahl Road to the gated entrance for the Tomlinson's.

Walking around the gate, they approached the house cautiously. Bruno seemed to sense Billy's angst and mimicked his wariness. They continued to the water side of the house and stepped through the screen door onto the porch. Seeing the shattered windowpane, Billy had little doubt that someone had broken into the home. Bruno must have sensed it as well because, just then, he began barking uncontrollably.

***

Startled by the sudden ear-splitting barking, Mullins sat up so quickly he almost started his leg bleeding again. "Driggs...what the fuck?"

Driggs bolted from his chair and ran to the window. "Shit...there's an old timer out there with a dog. He's checking out the door we broke in."

Mullins stood but stayed by the sofa. "Maybe he'll leave."

"Not once he's seen that broken window. He'll either come in or call the cops."

"You need to take care of him, Joseph. I'm not moving so well."

For all his transgressions with the law, Driggs had never killed anyone. Sure, he knew Mullins had done so for him, but he rationalized that his soul was spotless since he never pulled the trigger. But now, faced with the prospect of being caught, he became slightly less concerned about his place in the hierarchy of eternal souls.

The old guy was peering through the door while the damn dog kept barking. He pulled out a set of keys and seemed to be searching for the right one.

"Shit...he's got a key, and he's coming inside," Driggs said.

Still standing by the sofa, Mullins became insistent: "Joseph...you've got the gun. Do something." The barking dog seemed to be affecting him.

Reluctantly, Driggs took the gun from the side table and waited behind the pantry wall. He hoped the guy would decide to leave, but it wasn't to be."

The door opened quietly, but Bruno blasted inside, oblivious to Billy's calls. He headed straight for the tall man standing near the sofa in the spacious great room. The man, recalling his last altercation with another German Shepherd, let out a shout worthy of an Olympic shot-putter after a gold medal throw.

"Driggs...DRIGGS, get the goddamn dog...shoot him!" Mullins screamed.

Ignoring the old timer, Driggs rushed into the great room and began shooting at Bruno. A seasoned gun handler would have had difficulty shooting a bobbing and weaving GSD intent on doing damage to its prey, so it was no surprise that Driggs's bullets hit much of the furniture and chipped a few stones in the fireplace but only succeeded in frightening the animal, who wisely ran out the same door he'd come in.

The shock of seeing the two outlaws, one shooting wildly at Bruno, froze Barnett where he stood. While he watched the dog escape the mayhem, Mullins grabbed his hammer and limped over to him. As Billy turned from seeing Bruno's tail disappear--thankful his sidekick managed to get away--the three-pound vintage sledge shattered his skull.

Thirty-Three

There was only silence as the gun smoke settled and the two criminals surveyed the aftermath. Stuffing from one of the pillows, hit by a stray bullet, floated in the air. Mullins, his bloody hammer by his side, looked down at Barnett's lifeless body while Driggs looked on in shock, the now empty Walther dangling from his right hand.

Shane...Jesus...why did you do that?"

Mullins looked up, shook his head, and limped over to the bullet-ridden sofa before he answered. "Would you rather have had him call the cops?"

"Of course not, but..."

"Then he had to go. You sure as shit weren't gonna hit him."

Driggs, still wide-eyed at the display of violence, couldn't tear his eyes from the corpse's mashed head, now leaking blood and brain matter, forming a small puddle on the kitchen floor. "What now?"

"Now we're safe, at least for a few days."

"What if the guy has a wife or lives with someone? They'll miss him."

"Look him up on your phone. This is a small community; he'll probably be somewhere on that thing. Check his pockets for his license. C'mon, Joseph...you can do this."

Gingerly rifling Barnett's pockets, Driggs located his wallet containing his driver's license. After only a few Google searches, he found an obituary for the wife. He saw, too, that the address was the next-door property. There was mention of a daughter living in Michigan in the obit, but that did not seem to be much of a problem.

"I think we got lucky, Shane. It seems he lived alone, and he's picking up the mail and looking out for things here. He had the key, after all. The only loose end is the dog who ran off."

"Fuck 'em. Maybe he'll get hit by a car. I think those shepherds have it in for me."

Rather than talk about which dogs had it in for his partner, Driggs changed the subject: "What about him? We can't just leave him here."

"Drag him into the garage; we'll only be here two more nights."

Driggs, wanting to stay as far away from the demolished mess of Barnett's head, grabbed the body by the legs and attempted to pull him back toward the door. He failed.

"Help me, Shane. I can't do it alone."

"You're gonna have to, Joseph. I can't do much with this leg, or it'll start bleeding again," he yelled from the sofa.

Try as he might, Driggs could only move the body a few feet. The old timer was slightly built, but moving a hundred and fifty pounds was still an uphill battle for someone with The Prophet's physique.

He *had* to figure something out. There was no way they could stay in the house with a putrefying body lying on the kitchen floor. He left the dead man and walked through the great room to the adjacent hallway. Mullins yelled after him, "Hey, where are you headed?"

"If I'm going to move that thing, I'll need something to help. I'm taking a look in the garage."

Flipping on the lights as he opened the door, he wasn't surprised to see two expensive examples of German engineering. He wasn't sure of the vehicles' years, but it was clear that the BWM sedan and the Porsche Cayenne were recent editions.

Other than the two cars, though, there was little he could see that would help him move the body. He exited the garage through a side door and walked toward the fenced garden area containing the shed. Upon entering the small barn-like structure, he saw a collection of gardening tools that would embarrass Home

Depot. Smack in the middle of the room was a shiny John Deere X500 lawn tractor. *This could work*, he thought.

He collected several coils of rope from hooks on the wall and tossed them in the basket on the back of the small tractor. Turning the key to start caused the machine to lurch forward and stall. After several tries, he realized the brake pedal needed to be engaged to get the thing running. He slid the small barn door aside and drove to the porch on the bluff side of the house.

The little tractor wasn't the quietest thing in the world, but the only neighbor was on the kitchen floor. Driggs wasn't concerned. He backed the green and yellow machine up to the porch, got off, and took the rope inside. After wrapping several turns around the corpse's legs, he tied the other end to the hitch at the tractor's rear.

Slowly, he began to pull the body toward the door. Things were progressing nicely until one of Barnett's legs became stuck against the door jamb and couldn't make the turn. Driggs swore under his breath, dismounted, and stepped onto the porch. He'd become used to the dead body, thinking of it only as an inanimate object now, no longer a human being.

Stepping over the dead man into the kitchen, he kicked the leg solidly, unsticking it from the jamb. The body lurched forward a few inches the moment the leg was released. Back on the tractor, Driggs pulled the cadaver out of the kitchen, across the porch, and down the single step. He was elated at his progress but realized he was only halfway home. He needed to put the damn thing somewhere.

Inspiration struck. With Billy Barnett now tied to the John Deere, Driggs drove across the yard, the dead man's head bouncing along the uneven ground. He continued through the garden and straight into the shed. By pulling forward to the opposite wall, Barnett's corpse barely cleared the threshold of the sliding door, but that was enough. He turned off the key, climbed down, stepped over the old timer, and reached for the door. As he did, he tripped over the mower deck and sliced his hand on a nearby pruning shear, putting a damper on his successful accomplishment.

Nonetheless, proud of his triumph, he walked back to the porch and into the kitchen, where all that remained was a drying trail of blood and tiny gray specs of something. Wrapping a handful of paper towels around his already coagulating injury, he awaited Mullins's approval of his efforts.

***

Bruno was as scared as he'd ever been in his life. When he and Billy approached the door, he sensed danger. Thousands of years of breeding and instinct-honing had given him the skill to process disassociated smells and sights to determine how and when to go into protection mode.

He'd charged into the house to protect Billy, his pack leader. Then came the yelling by the tall man who smelled very dangerous, and all those booms came from the smaller, chubby guy with his own smell. That's when he turned and ran. He felt awful. His only job was to protect. And he failed.

He'd run as fast as he could, and now he was back on the beach...somewhere. He stood still for a moment and sniffed the air. There were so many smells...most were familiar, but there were sooo many. It was sensory overload.

He took his time and began to separate them. Finally, he isolated one. It was faint, but he was sure it was a quince tree. Billy's yard had a quince tree mixed with apple and pear trees. He'd bitten into one once but spit it out. It wasn't very pleasant. But he knew the smell; once he knew it, he could never forget it.

He trotted down the beach in the direction the smell became stronger. It was a long walk, but he soon began to notice familiar driftwood and things he smelled every day. He was home. He ran up the steps to Billy's house and waited by the door. He knew his buddy would return.

Thirty-Four

We heard nothing on Saturday. The Washington State Patrol and the Sheriff's Departments in the counties adjacent to the sound were now involved. At the request of the State Patrol, the FBI also lent its expertise, deploying USERT, its Underwater Search and Evidence Response Team, but still no sign of the lifeboat.

I called in two teams of deputies from their weekend off to canvass those homes and communities with beach access along the suspected route. Even Wally, still tired from Friday night's adventures, stuck around. With so many inlets and coves around the sound and with the lifeboat's range, the possibilities for ditching it were endless. I still thought it was more likely Driggs and Mullins would have attempted to get off the water as soon as possible,

Reports from the field were negative. The part-time homes were vacant, as they should have been, and those occupied were by the legitimate owners. There was nothing more we could do.

I took some time to visit Bruce in the hospital. He'd spent the morning in surgery, having his shoulder reconstructed, and was still deliriously happy from the meds flowing into his veins. He slobbered and told me how much he loved me and his job, and for a minute, I was tempted to record the session to hold over his head at a later date. I patted him on his good shoulder and told him to get some rest.

Without much else to do but monitor reports, I let Wally handle the second shift. I looked forward to a home-cooked meal and a relaxing evening with Andie.

Sunday was a duplicate of Saturday. Cloudy skies, with a zero percent chance of news of the fugitives' whereabouts. I was chatting with my second-in-command over coffee when I suddenly thought: "Hey, Wally, where is Francis? How come we haven't heard from him?"

"Ruh-rho...this can't be good. Have you talked to Jake?"

"I'll call him now; there's not much else happening."

Wally sat by while I spoke with Jake Early. He only heard my side of the conversation, but that was enough for him to attack me with questions after we were done.

"Where is he? Did Jake know? He did, didn't he, and he's gone and stepped in shit again, right?"

"Easy...easy there, Big Guy. It seems our good buddy, Francis, spent the night in Coupeville."

"Huh, Coupeville? How come?"

"Brace yourself, Wally. It appears Francis...yes, that Francis...spent last night with a woman who lives there."

"What? How would he know anyone there? *I* hardly know anyone there. I mean...geez... I think the only people I know there work for the Sheriff's Department. I mean, Maggie lives there, but she's too...she wouldn't, uh...it's Maggie? *Maggie Ryan?*"

"Yup...Maggie Ryan."

"Well, holy shit...who woulda thunk it."

"Jake spoke with him this morning. Called him because he didn't come home last night, and that's unusual; he was worried. Francis spilled the beans...said she was incredible, and he'd never known anyone like her. Even said she loves Henry and the feeling is mutual."

"Huh...Francis and Maggie. Well, I guess there *is* someone for everyone. I mean, she's sharp as they come, and well...Francis is too. I just wouldn't have pictured them together...but now that I think about it...yeah. You know, they're both smartasses, so there's that."

"Wally?"

"Yeah?"

"Don't try to figure it out. You found Kate, didn't you?"

"Uh...yeah."

"And how many folks think she's nuts for being with you?"

"Um...lots. Okay, different subject...how about those M's?"

We both laughed loudly at the go-to question in the PNW, then turned our attention to the lack of progress we were experiencing.

***

With no news by Monday morning, I called for a meeting. South Whidbey Island is approximately fifty-nine square miles, and the number of officers patrolling it varies, depending on staffing and need. Besides Wally and me, four additional two-person teams were present.

I updated everyone, which only took about twenty seconds. I told the teams what Wally and I had discussed and how we thought chances were good that our targets might still be in the area. "I realize you've been thorough in your canvassing, but let's do it again. Start with the most accessible areas first and knock on every door. If nobody answers, look around and look in the windows. If someone's been there, it should be obvious. We've been given a blanket warrant because of the violent nature of the crimes and the danger posed to those living here. Use it, but don't abuse it."

I'd worked with everyone present and was comfortable giving them this authority. It was a small community, and since the officers lived among those they served, there was greater trust in them than in many large urban areas. It was a more genteel approach to law enforcement, and it worked.

Thirty-Five

"I think it's time we got out of here, Shane. I checked the garage yesterday, and the owners were kind enough to leave the key fobs in the vehicles. Which would you prefer, the BMW or the Cayenne?"

By Monday morning, Driggs and Mullins had had enough of hanging around. The freezer had supplied them with more than enough to eat, and lounging on the sofas and watching mindless TV seemed to recharge their batteries. The leg had finally stopped seeping as well.

Hygiene wasn't near the top of their list of concerns, but even *they* had become aware of their rank state. Peter Tomlinson was six feet tall and of average build and weight; after showering, they visited his enormous walk-in closet. While underwear was no problem, his other clothing fit neither man. His jeans were five inches too short for Mullins, but they were transformed into acceptable below-the-knee shorts with a few cuts. Driggs wasn't as fortunate. Because none of Tomlinson's casual wear could contain his forty-inch waist, he was forced to settle for a pair of sweats that fit snugly. Now, at least, they could sit in the same vehicle without being overcome by bodily off-gassing.

"You pick; you're doing the driving. I'm better off taking it easy with this leg."

They stood beside each other inside the garage, deciding which hundred-thousand-dollar vehicle to select. Besides pickups and rental cars, Driggs had little experience with those driven by the rich and famous.

"I've always wondered what driving a Porsche was like. Let's take the Cayenne."

After opening the garage door, they climbed into the caramel leather interior and closed the doors. The SUV *smelled* expensive. Its instrument panel rivaled that of the lunar lander as far as Driggs was concerned. After ten minutes of pushing buttons, pedals, and levers, he felt confident enough to get underway.

"You know where we're going?" Mullins asked.

"Yes. No more ferries, so the only other option is that bridge up north. If we're lucky, they won't still have the checkpoint."

"If not?"

"I don't know; let's talk about that if and when it happens."

The route was simple: get on the main road and stay on it until they arrived at Deception Pass. Even if there were a little traffic, they'd be there by one.

***

It had been the best weekend of Francis Early's life. He had no idea what stars aligned to allow him to fall into Maggie Ryan's life, but he was thankful for it. Maybe all that went before—the schoolyard fights, the drugs, McNeil Island, his brother's kindness, all his friends on Whidbey—maybe it all happened so he'd be ready for her when they met. However it came about, he'd make damn sure he didn't screw it up.

They had spent the last two nights together, and unless he was misreading her terribly, she was as reluctant to part as he was. He was sure of it when she came up behind him and wrapped her arms around him.

"Francis, I have an idea."

"You do? And what would it be?"

"Do you have to get back today?"

"Uh...no, not really. I think Jake has things under control. I was going to stop and see Roger, you know, see what's happening with the search for your buddy, Mullins."

"Hey...knock it off, pal," She punched him in the arm as she said this. "He's a creep, and I hope they put him away."

He turned around and gave her a gentle hug. "I know, Mags, I do. It's why I want the fucker found. It's why I won't give up until he is."

She put her head on his ample chest and sighed. "Can it wait one more day?"

"Sure, what did you have in mind?"

"Let's go somewhere. It's a beautiful day, and I'd love to go hiking and forget about all the nastiness."

"On the island?"

"Of course, there are plenty of places to hike. We can do Ebey's or Dugalla or Goose Rock or a bunch of other places."

"How about Henry here? Do they all allow dogs?"

"Most do, especially if they're on leash."

"Do you have a favorite?"

"Well…it's a beautiful day, and I haven't been to Goose Rock in years. The last time was when I first came to Whidbey Island after living in Boston. I remember thinking what a special place to come with someone you care about. I was by myself then, but I still remember the view and wishing I had someone to share it with. I do now, and I'd like to take you there."

Francis made a valiant effort to stop himself from tearing up—real ones, not tattoos--but was unsuccessful. Several splashed on top of Maggie's head. She looked up at him, her eyes glistening too. She grabbed him around the neck and squeezed him fiercely before pulling back and looking at him. "Come on, Francis, enough with this sappy stuff; plenty of time for that later. C'mon Henry, you too."

Traffic was light, and they reached the Deception Pass Scenic View parking lot in less than half an hour. This early in the day, they easily found a spot. Maggie's backpack was roomy enough for their water and protein bars, treats, and a collapsable water bowl for Henry. Francis took the pack while Maggie held Henry's leash as they crossed the road to the Goose Rock Perimeter Trail, which began the two-and-a-half-mile round trip. The highlight would be the summit of Goose Rock, the highest point on Whidbey Island.

***

"Let's get out of here, Wally. If nothing else, we can give the troops a hand."

We took off in my cruiser and headed for Double Bluff. The name comes from the enormous bluffs—up to three hundred feet high—formed by thousands of years of the erosive process by the area's winds, rains, and tides. With Mutiny Bay to the north and Useless Bay to the east, the beach at Double Bluff is popular with tourists and locals.

Most beachgoers aren't aware that the smaller bluffs to the west are home to several of the pricier properties on the island. With the patrol teams headed to other places, excluding these homes from our list of possibilities fell to us.

We proceeded to Wahl Road by taking Fish Road off the highway to Mutiny Bay Road. The properties on Mutiny Bay, often called Whidbey's "Gold Coast," run into the millions and belong to the families of many of the principals of the economic engine that made the Pacific Northwest famous. Since most had their own security and were not so isolated, I was less concerned about them.

We passed Dirt Road and Deer Foot Lane as the road turned west. It occurred to me that whoever came up with the names for most of Whidbey's smaller roads must have been on a bender for a few days, realized he or she had to come up with a bunch of names in a hurry, and then used whatever popped into their head at the time.

On our left, a gated entry leading to a well-maintained driveway appeared, with the name Tomlinson on its mailbox. I turned to Wally and asked, "Do you know them?"

"Nope. Heard the name before, some banker thing, but never met them.."

"Should we check?"

"Let's stop by Billy Barnett's place next door. He's come out of his shell a bit since his wife passed and I think he looks after Tomlinson's place when they're gone. We might be able to kill two birds."

Turning into the Barnett driveway, we saw a young German Shepherd standing on the front step. Barking wildly.

One look at Wally told me he'd rather sit this one out. He said, "Maybe you should take this one."

"What...you scared of a little doggie?"

"Nope. Just thought you'd like to get some field experience."

"I thought you knew this guy."

"I do...it's just..."

"The dog."

"Yeah...maybe."

"Look...it's a shepherd, right?"

"Yes."

"You know about them...right?"

"What about them?"

"They're SHEPHERDS! They guard the flock. They're extremely loyal to their pack leader. That's what this one's doing. If we show we're not gonna threaten anyone or anything, he should lighten up a little."

"Okay...show me."

"Wait...you said you knew this guy?"

"A little, yeah."

"So that's his dog?"

"I don't know. I didn't think he had one anymore, but maybe he does."

"You're not being much help here, Wally."

"Maybe he's dog sitting...I don't know."

I shook my head and opened the door. The dog was going apeshit but looked more scared than anything. I moved to the front of the car and knelt. I began to speak in a soft, high-pitched voice. I'd read about these dogs and knew a little about them because O'Malley had one. Come to think of it, Francis did, too. It was like an epidemic.

The shepherd hesitated, and his barking slowed, but he was still anxious. I kept talking in a soothing voice, and little by little, he edged closer. Eventually, he came alongside and sniffed me all around. He let me scratch his ears and pet him. I motioned for Wally to get out, and he did so hesitantly.

The dog erupted again when the door opened, and Wally's face turned ashen.

"Just stand there," I said. "Let him sniff you."

Wally became a statue. The animal barked even louder than before and strode up to my partner, who was frozen. The noise suddenly stopped; the only sound was the dog sniffing around Wally. Then he stopped and walked back to me.

"All better now?" I asked.

"I guess...he's a scary dog."

"Nah, he's just doing his job. Let's look inside."

We looked through the windows and saw nothing unusual.

"Seems odd, this dog just sitting on the step with nobody around," Wally said.

"How well do you know Barnett?"

"I've met him a few times in town and at the Mutiny Bay Club. Everyone says he's a stand-up guy."

"Not like him to leave a dog outside then?"

"Probably not."

As we walked around the house, the dog ran to the side of the property and began barking again,

"What does he want now?" Wally mumbled.

"I don't know. It seems he wants us to go with him." As I walked in his direction, he moved farther away.

"Come on, Wally. Let's see where he goes."

We followed him down the driveway and to the gated drive next door. We walked around the side of the gate and followed the driveway to the Tomlinson home.

"Yikes, this place has gotta cost a bundle."

I nodded my agreement and tried to catch up to the dog, who had run to the back of the house. The barking was nonstop now. As soon as I saw the broken window in the door, I knew we were in the right place.

I drew my weapon, and Wally did the same. I was confident no one was home because the dog would have alerted them if they were, but no need to take any chances. We opened the door and saw a dried-up blood stain in the middle of the kitchen floor.

"Call it in, Wally. Let's get some people here: the techs and a couple of deputies to control the site. Find the remote and get that gate opened."

Thirty-Six

While we waited for backup, we cleared the rest of the house, careful not to touch anything. Nothing seemed to quiet the dog, however. He stood by the door and continued to bark.

The German Shepherd's bark is unmistakable. It is piercingly loud and difficult to ignore. I walked outside and tried to quiet him: "Hey there, boy, what's the matter? What's bugging you?"

As I spoke, he backed away much like he had done earlier. As I approached him, I noticed furrow-like drag marks in the gravel where it met the lawn leading to the fenced garden area. He turned, trotted forward a few steps, then turned back to make sure I was following. *This was not a stupid dog.*

As I approached the garden shed, I caught a whiff of something I'd smelled before. The dog was now whining at the sliding door. I knew what I would find, so I yelled for Wally to join me before I went any further.

When he caught up to me, he wrinkled his nose and said, "Shit...you think Barnett's in there?"

"I think the dog *knows* he is."

"Damn...I hate this. Let's get to it."

We reached the shed and slid the door aside, revealing Billy Barnett's body. The dog began licking what remained of his face and whining simultaneously. I gently pulled him aside and looked for something like a leash. As I did, I noticed several drops of blood on the concrete floor near a wall full of garden tools.

"Looks like he's been here a couple of days. Why would those fuckers kill a harmless old man?" Wally was getting worked up at the senselessness of it all.

I untied one of the ropes and threaded it through the dog's collar so we could control him. "He probably stumbled on them when he was checking the house or dropping mail off. The dog could be Barnett's or the owner's here, and he was caring for it."

We heard sirens approaching. There was a lot to process here, and I looked forward to having Maggie's take on how Barnett was killed. Although, judging by the state of his bashed-in head, I was sure I already knew.

The dog had finally stopped barking and was sitting, staring at the body. I took him to a nearby tree and temporarily fastened the rope to keep him away from the scene. Two Sheriff's vehicles pulled up, and Cora, Maggie's second-in-command, jumped out.

"What's up, Roger?"

"When we called, it was a break-in; now, it's a murder. Where's Maggie?"

"She took a day off."

Wally's look told me he was on the same page I was, and we both had a good idea of where she was.

Cora caught our non-verbal transmission and said, "What... I'm not good enough for you?"

Cora was an excellent crime scene tech in whom I had complete confidence. Maggie's history with Driggs and Mullins was the tipping point, though, and I told her so.

Somewhat mollified, she answered: "I'll see if I can reach her, but I don't have any idea where she's gone."

I could hear her leaving a message when Maggie's phone went to voicemail. She looked up, shrugged her shoulders, and smiled, "Looks like you're stuck with me. I understand your position, too, so I'll run everything by Maggie when we catch up. We should hear from her by the time we get the body back to the morgue so she'll have a first-hand look."

"Thanks for understanding, Cora. Let me know your first take as soon as you're ready. There's some blood on the floor in the shed, too."

"If that poor guy's head is bashed in like you said, I'd be surprised if there wasn't."

"No...it's on the other side of the mower...away from the body."

"Don't worry, Roger, I'm on it. We'll get everything bagged and checked in."

Wally and I continued to canvas the house and property while Cora did her thing. We reached the garage, where a new BMW was the only vehicle present. The place was plenty big enough for several others, so it made sense the killers took off in one of Tomlinson's cars. We needed to know the make and model, and fast.

Locating the property owners was paramount, but I didn't know where to begin. I charged one of the deputies with the search, but he seemed to be banging his head against a wall. They traveled a great deal and were wealthy. Several search engines identified George as a senior vice president with an offshore investment bank who preferred anonymity. According to the little biographical information available, the couple had no children. A Facebook page by Mrs. Tomlinson, Ronnie, showed a picture of the two of them and a young German Shepherd. The caption read: *Our new family member, Bruno!*

"At least we know his name now. Wally, find a way to contact Tomlinson's employer; if he's a big shot there, they'll know where he is. Tell them it's an emergency. Tell the deputy working on the locate to file a request with DMV to find out what the missing vehicle is."

I was worried if we didn't find out soon, the two killers would get off the island. I called Tom Davis and told him to reinstate the traffic stop at the Pass bridge as soon as possible. Maybe we wouldn't be too late, but I had a bad feeling.

While checking off all the boxes I needed to address, I looked at Bruno. Laying with his head tucked between his paws, he looked drained and sad. His pack leader, at least when his owners were gone, was dead, and he'd been outside for two days. The poor thing had to be hungry and thirsty and now had no place to live. I took him into the kitchen, filled a bowl with cold water, and put it in front of him. He drank greedily, so fast that I took it away lest he regurgitate everything. Then I called my wife.

I told her what we'd found at the Tomlinson's and that they were out of town. Then I asked, "Andie, would it be a terrible imposition if we took care of this guy, at least until his people are back?"

"Are you kidding? Of course not. I'm coming over right now to get him. You do the cop stuff, and I'll take Bruno off your hands. There's no way he's going to a shelter. I can't wait till he meets the goats."

With one less issue to worry about, I called Francis. I was certain he would know where our ME was.

***

They had taken the perimeter trail around the island's tip and worked their way up the east side of Goose Rock. At just under five hundred feet, the summit, the highest point on Whidbey Island, offered 360-degree panoramic views of the entire Puget Sound region. Even the star-crossed couple managed to take their eyes off each other to appreciate it.

"I can see why you thought this was a special place, Maggie; it's spectacular."

Her answer was a hug and a kiss, and Francis willingly accepted.

As they headed down the steep west side of the high point, their cell phones pinged, notifying them of incoming messages that had not been received earlier because of the lack of cell coverage.

They both felt a sense of urgency as they stopped to read the messages. Maggie spoke first: "They killed an old man, Francis. Just some guy watching his neighbor's house."

"I know. Roger says they took off in the owner's vehicle—they don't know what it is yet—and might be headed this way. The sheriff called the staties to set up a checkpoint this side of the bridge."

"If it's all the same, I'd rather not run into that guy again. Being tied up and threatened once was enough. Besides, they'll need me when they get the body to the lab."

As they reached the trailhead, they heard sirens and watched as two State Patrol cruisers whisked by.

"No worries, Mags, you're not getting out of my sight. Come on, let's get to the truck; we're heading back to Coupeville."

They crossed State Route 20 and reached the small parking area seconds after a dark blue Porsche Cayenne pulled into a space at the end of the lot. While Maggie climbed into the passenger side, Francis held the rear door open for Henry, who seemed preoccupied, sniffing the air maniacally.

Thirty-Seven

The Porsche was a dream to drive; Driggs could see why it cost so much. Mullins dozed as he drove, enjoying the quiet, peacefulness of the insulated passenger compartment. Shortly after they passed the Deception Pass State Park entrance, two State Patrol vehicles zipped past, lights flashing and sirens blazing.

Mullins stirred at the sound, instantly realizing their worst fears were now a reality. "They know we're on the run. They must have found the dead guy."

Driggs nodded in agreement and said, "You're right. But they don't know what we're driving, or they would have pulled us over."

"But what now? Once they start checking every car that's headed for the bridge, we're screwed."

Without answering, Driggs turned left into a small parking area less than two hundred feet from the bridge and the State Patrol officers.

"What are you doing?" Mullins asked.

"Look, Shane, there's no way we're driving across that bridge. They're stopping every vehicle."

"Yeah...I can see that."

"What else do you see?"

"Nothing...just some cops stopping every car."

"Look at the sides of the bridge."

"Yeah...so...people walking."

"And?"

"And what?"

□"The cops aren't even looking at them. It's like if they don't have a car, they don't care about them. We can walk across the damn bridge."

"What do we do when we get to the other side?"

"We can figure that out then. At least we'll be off this island."

Mullins looked unsure but finally relented. He asked, "We split up, right?"

"Yes, no need to attract attention. Take off your cap and hunch down like you're an old man. People will ignore you."

Mullins heard the excited sounds of other families and children when he opened the door. Because the Deception Pass Bridge and the adjacent park attract over three million visitors a year, not a day passes without a crowd. It was one of the reasons the roadblock was such an inconvenience and likely why little attention was paid to those brave souls traversing the 150-foot-high span on foot over the turbulent whitewater below. The narrow crossing is memorable, too, for the blustery winds ripping through the narrow channel.

Mullins stretched as he stood outside the Porsche. He pulled his collar up and removed his scally cap, tucking it in his pocket. Hunching over, per Driggs's suggestion, he made his way to the bridge, still limping slightly.

He heard someone shouting above the visitors' din as he approached the narrow sidewalk on the bridge's east side. Ignoring it, he walked on toward the other side and freedom. Then he heard it again. Someone was calling for *Henry*, whoever that was. It wasn't until he heard more shouts, then the screams of young children, that he turned to the disturbance.

It was the dog...the same goddamn dog who almost killed him. The charging German Shepherd was only a dozen feet from him, his teeth bared and spittle flying from his mouth. Mullins was petrified. He reached inside Tomlinson's coat pocket for his hammer, but the damn pocket was so small the handle of the sledge became twisted in the fabric.

Only a quarter of the way across the bridge, Mullins had nowhere to run, even if his leg was sound. Dozens of onlookers froze in their tracks while every vehicle on the bridge stopped as the muscular black and tan canine launched himself toward the man who had once before threatened his pack leader.

His sledgehammer now forgotten, Mullins did the only thing he could do. He raised his hands to protect his face and head. The move was logical but not in the dog's mind. What Henry remembered was the thick muscle at the top of the man's leg and how it felt when he sunk his teeth into it. He tried it again.

Mullins's shriek could be heard above the wind and the rushing waters below. He backed into the rail behind him and tried to shake the dog from his leg. Arching his back on the rail gave him slightly more leverage, but that was when Henry decided to let go. The ninety pounds of GSD on his leg was agony, but the dog's weight kept Mullins from tumbling over the rail. All those present that day would never forget the screams of the tall Northern Irishman who had ruined so many lives as he plunged into the freezing waters of Puget Sound.

***

The short, plump man in the Nike sweats and hoodie looked on in horror as his cohort disappeared from view. Rather than follow Mullins on the east sidewalk, he chose the west side, going against the traffic.

The patrol officers had abandoned their roadblock and were ushering onlookers off the bridge's east side while talking constantly on their radios. The dog that had attacked Mullins now trotted to a large, bald man face down on the ground with a petite, studious-looking woman standing by.

Driggs turned away from the mayhem and followed closely behind a group of visitors also trying to vacate the scene of the tragedy. Mullins had always been an unforgiving enforcer, but their relationship had become the one constant in his life, and he now felt unsure of his next steps.

He arrived at the small parking area just north of the bridge on Pass Island in less than fifteen minutes. He wasn't sure how long it would take for the authorities to determine the victim's identity, but he knew it would be soon, and when that happened, they'd be looking for him.

The three people ahead of him walked to a parked SUV with British Columbia license plates. When he looked at other cars in the lot, he noticed several were also from Canada.

Relying upon his ability to preach and persuade, he approached one of the Canadians and said, "Excuse me. The man attacked by the dog back there was a good friend. It was such a nice day, and we thought we'd come down and see the bridge. I need to get back to Bellingham to talk to his family. Are you heading that way?"

Rather than immediately buy into Driggs's bullshit, one of the men asked, "How did you get here...I mean, you know, if you need a ride now?"

Driggs was quick on his feet: "The fellow who went over the bridge had the keys with him. I called a locksmith, but they said it would take a few hours. I need to talk to them before they hear the news."

The doubt seemed to ease from the Canadian's face as he looked to his companions, who nodded their assent. "Okay," he said. "Hop in."

They dropped Driggs off at the airport at his request. It was on the way home for the Vancouver residents, who bought the explanation that he was visiting his friend and now needed a rental.

Mullins was always prepared with fake licenses and credit cards and now Driggs was thankful for them. He rented a Ford Explorer from Avis, telling the attendant he'd return the vehicle by the following weekend, and headed south on I-5.

***

Francis had seen Henry do that nose-in-the-air thing before and was instantly on alert. "What is it, Boy...what are you smelling?"

He barely got the words out when Henry bolted for the bridge. So many people were milling around that Francis became concerned his buddy would scare some innocent bystander. Yelling at the top of his lungs, he ran as fast as he could, catching sight of Henry as he approached the sidewalk on the side of the bridge. There, he saw the back of an older man walking without turning around. And he had a limp.

Francis couldn't identify the man until he turned to see what the commotion was. He knew Henry had done so seconds earlier and was determined to stop his escape. By the time he reached his dog, it was all over, and the State Patrol was ordering him to get on the ground.

Maggie pushed through the growing crowd and got her ID before the police. Even though she explained everything as quickly as possible, the troopers were reluctant to allow Francis up. Only when Maggie had Tom Davis call the State

Patrol did they believe he was one of the good guys. Sadly, Francis was used to it. He understood their concerns, but it still pissed him off.

Thirty-Eight

The coroner's vehicle had departed the scene, and Wally and I were about to leave the Tomlinson property when I got the call from Tom Davis.

I wasn't surprised the fugitives had chosen the bridge to leave the island, nor was I shocked that Francis had somehow managed to be in the middle of things again. What caught me off guard was that Mullins was there without Driggs. I found it difficult to believe, and Wally did too.

Davis wanted us to assist the State Patrol on-site because we were closer to the investigation. What bothered me mostly was that, according to Davis, Francis was the principal source for ID'ing Mullins. It wasn't that I doubted him, but I knew recovering a body from a fall off the Deception Pass Bridge was iffy at best.

Over the years I've lived on Whidbey Island, finding someone who had fallen in those swirling waters could take weeks, if at all. The enormous tidal swings and extreme currents could carry a body miles away; some were never found.

It was a forty-mile trip, but we got to the bridge in less than thirty minutes because of our lights and sirens. The bridge had been closed, and those looking to leave the island had to be turned away and directed to the ferry system. I could imagine how long the lines would be.

The troopers were happy to have us take over the interviews. They had plenty to do with the massive traffic pileup caused by the bridge closure. We shouldered our way through the onlookers and finally reached Francis and Maggie, still standing on the bridge with Henry sitting casually by their side. The patrol officers had already photographed everything, so we didn't have to deal with that distraction.

"Hey, Rog, Wally, fancy meeting you here."

I shook my head and purposely ignored him while turning to Maggie. "You okay, Mags?"

Despite the circumstances, I had to admit she looked a dozen years younger and had a glow about her. "I'm great, Roger, thanks to my two protectors here." She hugged Francis's arm as she spoke. Wally looked at me, unsure of how to react.

I turned to Francis, "Okay, tell me what happened and leave nothing out."

He told me the same thing he had to the state troopers and that he was sure it was Mullins when he turned around. He said Henry knew for sure.

"How about you, Maggie? Did you get a good look at him?"

"No. I only managed to get here after it was over. Everyone was running the other way."

"Did you see Driggs at all, Francis?"

"No. The only reason I even saw Mullins was because of Henry. After he got a whiff of him, he took off after him like a missile."

"And you're a hundred percent sure it was Mullins?"

He looked disappointed I was questioning him, but he answered in the affirmative and said, "Do you think I could have been mistaken?"

"*I* don't, Francis, but, oddly, Driggs wasn't around, and we may never find the body."

He nodded, understanding my position, but left little doubt in my mind: "It *was* him."

I clapped him on the back and said, "Nice work."

"It was Henry; all I did was witness the thing."

I was glad the murderous bastard was gone. Regardless of what anyone else thought, Francis was a hundred percent dependable.

As we headed to the parking area, a text came in from the DMV. I read it aloud to the four of us: "Says here the missing Tomlinson vehicle is a blue Porsche Cayenne."

"You mean like that one on the end?" Wally pointed.

We got within twenty yards of it when Henry started baking and charged toward the vehicle. A nearby family ushered their two youngsters inside their SUV quickly, fearful that the dog who had just facilitated a man being jettisoned from the bridge might have designs on their kids.

Francis grinned at me and said, "What do you think, Rog? Any doubt about who that was now?"

We taped around the vehicle and alerted the Sheriff's Department to have it towed to Coupeville so we could process it. If both Mullins and Driggs had driven it to where it now sat, then Driggs couldn't have been far away.

I alerted the State Patrol and the police in Anacortes to watch out for Driggs. Unfortunately, while Mullins's picture was plastered all over the networks, few images of Driggs were available for easy identification. We notified the Border Patrol, too, if he tried to escape to British Columbia. The Coast Guard was already on site in the waters below the bridge; I had doubts about them finding the remains of Shane Mullins.

***

An hour and a half after picking up his rental, Joseph Driggs turned east on I-90. While holed up at the Tomlinson's, Mullins had contacted a former associate who knew a guy, who knew a guy, who would turn the diamonds into real money. Mullins said the guy had connections with offshore banks that would allow deposits without any disclosures to regulators. That was why he was on his way to Spokane.

Thirty-Nine

It had been three weeks since Shane Mullins disappeared from the Deception Pass Bridge, and still, no trace of a body. The Tomlinsons were shocked when they heard what had happened at their home and returned from their travels as soon as they were able.

They were grateful when Andie returned Bruno but upset at the murder of their good friend and neighbor. Peter and Ronnie offered to be available and make their property accessible whenever we needed to see it. They took the responsibility of notifying Barnett's daughter and ensured she stayed in their guest suite when she arrived to handle the arrangements for her father.

Danny Collins had recovered entirely from his oral surgery, and Bruce's convalescence had accelerated to the point where he was once again a fixture at the office.

Since the prints taken from the Tomlinson home and the Cayenne were perfect matches for Driggs and Mullins, there was no question that Mullins had perished. The whereabouts of Driggs, however, was another story.

What few photos were available of him—and these were years old—were shown on the news stations locally and nationally without success, save for the occasional false lead.

A clerk from the Avis Rental location at the Bellingham airport thought Driggs might have rented a vehicle from them but wasn't sure. Her report became more credible when the rental turned up at the Spokane airport long-term parking after more than a week overdue. The local police took fingerprints and found that Driggs had driven the vehicle.

But that was where the trail ended. He could have taken a plane or driven anywhere; we had come up empty so far. The murders and assaults, save for Danny's busted mouth, were attributable to Mullins, so we all felt good about him being taken off the board.

But, for my money, Driggs was the wizard behind the curtain, the one pulling the strings. Stucki would not have been murdered, nor the Gleasons, without Driggs ordering it. Mullins was always a bad apple; as Driggs's hitman, though, he became more focused and more lethal. The former Prophet kept his hands clean, but he might as well have done the killings and assaults himself. I would turn over every stone to bring him to justice.

***

After caring for his financial needs and obtaining freshly forged identification documents, Driggs drove to Spokane International Airport and parked his rental car in the long-term lot.

He purchased a three-year-old Jeep Renegade from a used car dealer and had them deliver it to the airport. Telling them over the phone he was arriving after having been out of the country for a year, he made sure the transaction would be untraceable. The dealer could have cared less; he made enough on the deal to be unconcerned about the buyer.

Driggs could have taken a plane anywhere but chose not to. He needed to change a few things first. He negotiated a two-month stay at a VRBO in Missoula online, never having to see or meet the owner. For what he had planned, the five-acre property suited his needs perfectly.

With fake accounts at Amazon and Nutrisystem, he meticulously planned his monthly calorie intake. He'd also ensured the property had a small workout room with several pieces of cardio equipment and free weights. With hundreds of weight loss plans online, he chose one of the more ambitious diet and workout regimens.

At the end of six weeks, after adhering strictly to his diet and working out three times a day, he had dropped twenty pounds and developed muscles where there had been none. His face was thinner, and his waist had dropped to thirty-five inches from forty.

He ordered a complete overhaul of his wardrobe online, choosing a western theme. The boots gave him an extra lift of one inch, aiding his longer, leaner look, and even though he was pushing fifty-five, he appeared years younger.

It was time for his next appointment, and thankfully, it was in a location much more to his liking. After two days of mindless driving, he arrived at the Ritz-Carlton hotel in Rancho Mirage. This would be the perfect location for the next six weeks to relax and recover from his upcoming procedures. After living where he had during his previous life, he found the treatment by the hotel staff almost too much. If he asked for something, it was handled immediately. The food was impeccable, and every person on the staff had a smile glued to their face. The decadence went against his moral teachings, but it sure was enjoyable.

The clinic he had researched was located in a strip mall in the southeast part of town. The doctors were recommended by the same individual who fenced the diamonds.

The sign in the window said *Licensed Therapist by appointment only*. When he entered, the young woman behind the small reception counter looked up from whatever she was doing and asked, "Mr. Swanson?"

His research had shown these people were professional, and it appeared so.

"Yes...that's me."

"Excellent, Sir. Could you provide me the letter of introduction you received?"

"Of course." He was surprised when his Spokane contact gave him the letter and told him he would need it. He handed it to the receptionist, who took a few seconds to review it.

"Mr. Swanson, if you'll follow me, please." She locked the entrance before turning and walking through a passkey-secured door behind the counter.

As he followed, she asked, "Have you had anything to eat today?"

"No, I haven't."

How about anything to drink for the past two hours?"

"No."

They walked down a long, well-lit but eerily quiet corridor, stopping at another open door.

"Please take your clothes off and put on the gown. The split goes in the back. You can lock your things in the locker behind you. When you've finished, have a seat and leave the door open."

Ten minutes later, as he sat in the reclining chair, a young, handsome, Hispanic-looking gentleman dressed in scrubs entered.

"Mr. Swanson?"

"Yes."

"You understand completely the surgeries you have requested?"

"I do."

"And I see you've wired the requested funds to our financial institution?"

"Yes...you know I have, or I wouldn't be here."

"Certainly...well, let's get things going. The nurses will be in to get your IV started, and then you'll be wheeled into the OR."

After assisting him onto a gurney, the nurses started an IV. They told him to expect a tingling in his arm and tongue, and then he would feel nothing until he awoke in recovery. They were right.

When he regained consciousness, it took him several seconds to remember where he was. He recalled being told they would keep him overnight to ensure no complications. When he attempted to feel the bandages on his face, it was useless because of his bandaged fingers. They said once the anesthesia wore off, his face would ache, but the fingers would be more painful.

Everything he read regarding the procedures recommended against doing them all at once, but since it was necessary to do it covertly, he opted for the whole enchilada. What he hadn't counted on was the pain from his left ass cheek. The thing was on fire. Who would have thought that using the skin from that hidden body part to replace his fingerprints would be so debilitating?

He kept telling himself it would all be worth it eventually; unfortunately, eventually was far, far away. A few tears escaped his sutured eyes and soaked into the bandages covering his face.

The first week at the Ritz-Carleton was agony. He was thankful his dieting had shrunk his stomach because the thought of having to void his bowels in his condition without any assistance was too painful. Slowly, his face swelling began to subside, and the pain from the removed skin on his ass ebbed. His bandaged fingers caused some lingering difficulty, and the challenge of doing any simple chore was almost too much. The constant rebandaging resulted in several waste containers full of bloody bandages that he disposed of in an off-site container after dark.

By the third week, he felt almost normal. He was stunned at what he saw when removing his face bandages. Between the sutures and the swelling, his reflection looked like a cast member from *Night of the Living Dead*. At the end of the fourth week, though, much of the swelling had subsided, and he found himself looking at a new person. Gone were the bags under his eyes, and his pug nose now appeared more regal. His weak jawline was transformed into a Daniel Craigish mandible.

He knew few current photographs of him were in circulation, but now, even those would be useless. His lack of any identifying fingerprints rendered him invisible.

Forty

After three months, the Sheriff's Office in Freeland returned to pre-Driggs and Mullins normalcy. With no new leads to follow and no reports of any sightings, we were forced to admit Driggs had escaped. The net had been cast wide and far, with every law enforcement agency involved having zero results. The man had disappeared.

Instead of starting each day with a laundry list of places Driggs might be, I worried more about mid-summer ferry traffic issues. Typically, lines were longest leaving the island on Mondays when folks were returning to their homes on the mainland for the week. At times, the line could be a two—or three-hour wait, the latter often teasing folks into turning around and heading for the Deception Pass bridge to drive around Saratoga Passage.

With the gray, drizzly spring a distant memory, the island was coveted because of its almost always sunny weather and mid-seventies daytime temperatures. Fishing, crabbing, hiking, biking, and golf were the daily activities that kept the population occupied and mostly out of our hair. Of course, occasionally, one or two residents were overserved at a local watering hole, and it was our job to keep them off the roads and out of harm's way.

Now that the national exposure from the Mullins episode had abated, we were more occupied with traffic accidents, infrequent break-ins, robberies, lost dogs, and escaped farm animals. It was uniquely different from my LA detective days, and I loved it.

Bruce was fully recovered and back at work, and Danny hadn't missed a sailing. After Billy Barnett's daughter spent a few weeks at the Tomlinson place settling her father's estate, she, Peter, and Ronnie became good friends. She abandoned her Michigan life and moved into her dad's home. Her IT skills and ability to work remotely were always in demand, even more so in the tech-savvy Pacific Northwest.

Francis and Maggie were now inseparable. During most weeks, they stayed at her cabin in Coupeville and spent weekends at the Early estate near Goss Lake. Francis still fulfilled his duties as house manager for Jake, who welcomed Maggie with open arms. Having a woman's touch around the place brightened things considerably, and he was thrilled for his brother.

Although at peace with their new life together, the uncertainty of Driggs's whereabouts frequently surfaced in Francis's thoughts. It seemed he had vanished, but if past experiences were predictive, it was a safe bet the evil evangelist would turn up when it was least expected.

On a warm, clear morning in the latter half of July, Francis, Maggie, and Henry drove to the off-leash beach just east of Double Bluff. They had been here before, and Henry loved the smells, the soft sand, and running and splashing in the water. It was early in the day, and there were few other visitors. They held hands and sauntered along the beach, sharing the joy most dog owners experience watching their loved ones' expressions of sheer delight.

Henry emerged from the water, violently shook the salted drops away, and trotted to a driftwood log, likely possessing the nasty smells dogs enjoy. As Maggie and Francis caught up to him, they heard a distant bark piercing enough to penetrate the sounds of the birds and the lapping water. In the distance was another shepherd accompanied by a blonde-haired woman clad in jeans and a hoodie. As her unleashed dog bolted toward us, Henry took notice and went into protection mode, barking wildly and moving aggressively in the other animal's direction.

The woman began running after her dog, yelling at the top of her lungs, "BRUNO...BRUNO!" The dog, of course, paid no attention, not when there was an opportunity to play with one of his kind.

Henry was now face-to-face with the on-rushing shepherd almost fifty yards ahead of us. Both animals' barking had decreased in volume, and serious sniffing was now in order.

"Bruno...you naughty boy. I'm sorry, he's usually better behaved. I think it's because he senses he has something in common with your dog. I'm Nancy Barnett, and that guy is Bruno. I'm giving him some exercise while my neighbor is out of town."

The two dogs played a "chase me" game and ran in circles through the sand and water. Whatever earlier unease was replaced by the sheer joy of finding a new friend to play with.

As they introduced themselves, Francis recalled Wilkie's reports during the search for Driggs and Mullins, and the light bulb clicked on: "You're Billy Barnett's daughter."

Suddenly wary, perhaps at the imposing man before her, she replied, "Yes...and how do you know this?"

Maggie sensed the anxiety and took over: "We're sorry about your father, Nancy. I'm the county medical examiner, and Francis sometimes works with the Sheriff's Department. We were both involved when those two fugitives were at the Tomlinson's and killed your dad."

Looking down at her feet and then gazing at the dogs, she seemed more vulnerable now. "It's been rough. My father and I were never close, and when I heard he had been killed, I regretted not having tried harder. After I came here to settle his things, I began to see what he liked about living here, so I stayed.

"The Tomlinsons have been great and we've become good friends, but they're gone a lot. My *best* friend is Bruno...he's a wonderful pal...uh, geez...didn't mean to ramble on like that."

Maggie reached to put her arm around Nancy's shoulder and said, "No worries, kiddo...we're your new best friends. It seems I'm spending more time at Francis's place than mine these days, so let's get together whenever you can. The dogs--that's Henry, by the way—can play, and we'll get some needed exercise. Right, Francis?"

Displaying a less than sincere rendition of a wounded soul, he answered, "Why yes, Maggie, that's exactly what I was thinking, you know, that I needed exercise."

It was enough to break the ice and get the three laughing. They exchanged phone numbers and spent the next hour strolling the beach together.

Forty-One

After the euphoria of his new and improved looks began to subside, Joseph Driggs, aka Adam Swanson, felt alone in the world. His stay at the swanky hotel grew tiresome and monotonous, so after six weeks, he packed his belongings and left. Now that his sidekick was gone and he no longer had to worry about money, he was rudderless.

While on the run and during his convalescence, he read whatever he could find online about the FLDS. His outlaw reputation had decimated the ranks of his followers, most of whom reverted to the Warren Jeffs group. That was until Jeffs was convicted of sexual assault of a child and would spend his remaining days in a Texas prison.

With the headless FLDS in disarray, most believers were now scattered across the country. A few men, with their wives and their children, still lived in Short Creek, eking out whatever existence they could, and the more Driggs thought about it, the more it made sense. He hopped into a recently purchased silver Porsche Cayenne—he'd developed a fondness for the German car—and began the drive to Colorado City, Arizona. All his life, until recently, of course, he'd preached the gospel and the true ways of Joseph Smith. Now, a new prophet, Adam Swanson, would carry the torch.

Slowly, the remaining followers of Warren Jeffs and Driggs began paying attention to this new Prophet named Swanson. The former Driggs acolytes noticed a familiar timbre and cadence to his voice. Some said he sounded a little like the old leader, but others quickly pointed out how vastly different they looked. Besides, Driggs was hiding somewhere, ducking the law.

Little by little, his flock grew, and he began taking on additional wives. After two years, the FLDS in Colorado City was stronger than ever. The northern half of Short Creek, Hilldale, was no longer a party to the movement. Smaller splinter groups of believers across the country began to hear of the new Prophet through like-minded friends and acquaintances. Computer use among those in the fundamentalist sect was still discouraged for fear that outside influences might tempt those following the True Word.

Because the Prophet needed to be all-knowing, Driggs secretly spent hours online, ensuring the search for him was finally weakening and keeping up with the public's perception of the FLDS. A search for Driggs now brought only one or two sentences, and those were from his original escape from Whidbey Island.

He began to receive requests from groups in neighboring states to speak to their FLDS settlements. They had heard of this new Prophet and were anxious to listen to his divine take on the meaning of the gospel, according to Joseph Smith. Seeing an opportunity to consolidate and solidify his movement, Driggs began to travel to these groups and preach his beliefs.

The rapt attention and adoration of those he visited were intoxicating and addicting. Since most of his followers were poor and uneducated, they seemed to think a man living in luxury and driving a vehicle worth well over a hundred thousand dollars was not contradictory.

It had taken Driggs/Swanson a long time to reach this plateau in life, and he was enjoying the hell out of it. He now had eighteen wives, many of whom were in their late teens and twenties, and while keeping them pregnant and serviced properly could be a chore, he didn't complain. There were the occasional disagreements between a few of them, but a stern glance in their direction was all it took to end the dispute.

The FLDS settlement in Colorado City was isolated from mainstream America because not only the LDS Church but society, in general, frowned upon the practice of polygamy. This isolation posed considerable difficulty when state and federal agencies attempted to prosecute those involved. Taking cues from the original FLDS colony, the splinter groups also selected remote areas to settle.

When any attempt to halt the custom of multiple wives arose, First Amendment rights and religious freedom were the first line of defense.

One of the largest settlements was the YFZ Ranch in Schleicher County, Texas. When government pressure on the breakaway religion increased in the early 2000s, several members moved from Short Creek and established a foothold on 1,700 acres near Eldorado. In the spring of 2008, Texas authorities mounted a major raid on the property, removing over four hundred children from the ranch. The State Supreme Court ultimately returned the children, citing the state did not meet the burden of proof; eleven men were imprisoned for sexual assault and bigamy.

Warren Jeffs was still the Prophet of the FLDS at the time, and from his cell, he ordered the Texas settlement closed and the members to smaller scattered groups around the country. South Dakota, Colorado, Minnesota, Utah, and, strangely enough, Whidbey Island, near Coupeville, were some of the destinations.

Now that Driggs/Swanson had solidified his leadership of the breakaway cult, his presence was in great demand among these smaller congregations. He began visiting them with two of his trusted lieutenants. The intoxicating idolatry Driggs was experiencing became addictive. Many of those gullible enough to be swayed by the self-serving teachings of this new Prophet left their loved ones and fell under the spell of this charismatic preacher, much as Hannah Stucki did.

The men in these outposts, however, were from two different persuasions: There were a few true believers, but the majority were driven by the opportunity for sex with numerous women, many of whom were on the youngish side. It's possible that, in the early days of the FLDS, the founders genuinely attempted to spread the Good Word. Still, its custom of having multiple wives and living in remote areas was too tempting for many men with nefarious intentions.

Forty-Two

S ummer had come and gone, and we were in the tiny, sweet spot between fabulous and truly terrible weather. It was October on Whidbey Island. Most days were cool, crisp, and sunny, but the occasional rainy patch hinted at what would come in November and December.

Those were the months when south and southwest winds brought over a quarter of the year's rain and some of the fiercest gales in the Northwest. Thirty- to forty-mile-per-hour winds were common, and occasional gusts exceeded sixty to seventy miles per hour. This was one of the reasons the population dropped by as much as thirty percent during the winter, and it was also one of the reasons our crime rate diminished accordingly.

While there was still the infrequent drunk and disorderly individual and the rare burglary, it was mostly deer/auto accidents and vehicles slipping on ice patches. After two years, our thoughts of finding Driggs had faded, and only when we ran into Francis did the subject come up. He and Maggie were a couple now, and there were talks about tying the knot.

They still split their time between Coupeville and Jake's property, and the twenty-mile distance between them was not an insurmountable challenge. Today, Francis made an unannounced stop by the station, and he, Wally, and I were sitting in the conference room over coffee, munching on the donuts he'd provided.

"Any news on Driggs?" came the inevitable question.

"I think we'll never find out about him," I said. "At least we know for sure about Mullins." The killer's body—or what was left of it after the crabs, seals, and other marine life had a go at it—had washed ashore on Lopez Island a few months after he'd fallen from the Deception Pass Bridge. A few of his fingers were still attached, and his prints and his DNA confirmed it was Mullins beyond any doubt.

"Yeah, I'm glad they found him, but Driggs was the main dude."

"We agree, Francis, but it's been two years without a trace. Anything could have happened. He could be hiding in another country, or he could even be dead. The money he could get from the diamonds was substantial, so he could buy his way almost anywhere."

"I know...I do...I just hate it when someone gets away after causing so much grief. Would you mind if I did some snooping around?"

"Snooping? Like how?" Wally asked.

"Not sure. Maggie and I were heading for the sun as soon as the rains came. Maybe we'll visit Southern Utah and check out Short Creek. I want to take Henry to his buddies at Kanab for a visit, too. I want to show Maggie that place; she'll love it."

I figured Driggs was in the wind, and we'd never hear from him again, and I also figured there was little trouble Francis could get into. "Why Short Creek?" I asked.

"I don't know. Maybe because that's where all this started, and maybe someone there has heard from him. I don't expect to find anything, but we'll stop by as long as we're near there."

"How long will you be gone?"

"Everything's buttoned up at Jake's, hell he's pretty self-sufficient now anyway. We're planning on a few weeks, but I suppose it could stretch into a month. We'll see what happens."

"What about Maggie's job?"

"She's got gobs of PTO stored up, and if anything happens, Cora's got it covered."

Francis, Maggie, and Henry left the second week after our conversation. It was three days before the first atmospheric river of the season. It was going to be a long, wet winter.

***

Henry began barking furiously when the pickup pulled up to the Best Friends Welcome Center. Standing on the top step near the entrance, Terri assumed it was an animal the owner wanted nothing to do with and reluctantly approached the vehicle. When the door opened and the GSD bounded toward her, she exploded with glee.

"HENRY...Henry...good boy, how *are* you?" She knelt and furiously rubbed his ears, trailing her fingers through his thick fur. She hugged him tightly.

"Guess he still remembers you, eh?" Francis said as he climbed down from the truck.

"Francis...it's you. What are you doing here?"

"We wanted to get out of the rain, so we thought we'd take a road trip." As he spoke, Maggie came around from the front of the pickup.

"And uh...this is Maggie."

"Hi, Maggie. I'm Terri Millar. How long have the two of you been an item?"

A slight shade of pink found its way to Francis's face, and he said, "What makes you say that?"

"I may be a dog person, but I can sure as hell tell when two people are in love."

"But you've never met her or seen her."

"No...but I saw how you looked at her when she came around the truck. That's enough for me. Now tell me, Maggie, it had to be the dog. I mean, that's the only way you could have fallen for this guy, right?"

Sensing a kindred spirit, Maggie replied, "How did you know?"

The three laughed heartily, and she invited them for dinner that evening. Henry too.

Because it was mid-week, the cabins in Dogtown were only partially occupied. When Terri told them they could stay at one with an extra-special discount because they now owned a graduate, they jumped at the chance. It was the same cabin where Francis had stayed when he first met Henry, and as soon as they pulled up, the dog went ballistic. If there was ever any doubt about Henry's memory, it was emphatically put to rest.

Terri's place was a small ranch house just south of Hog Canyon Road. When they arrived, the sun was setting over the tall crimson cliffs, and the display of color was mesmerizing. Their hostess met them at the end of the driveway. "Pretty spectacular, huh?"

"It's incredible, Terri; I've never seen anything like it," Maggie gushed.

"It's one of the reasons I love it here. It can be lonely at times, but my work at Best Friends keeps me busy, and I bring some of the dogs home with me when they're still insecure. All in all, I wouldn't trade it for anything."

Francis briefly wondered how an intelligent, attractive woman could live alone in such a remote area but cast the thought aside quickly. It was her life to choose; if he'd learned anything, it was to help when he could and leave things that weren't his business alone.

They chatted about the foundation over dinner and made small talk. Francis asked about the Barlows, and Terri said they were still working at Best Friends, which led to the question Francis had hoped might come up.

"Is that FLDS group still in Short Creek?"

"They are. After Driggs disappeared and Jeffs went to prison, their numbers dwindled by half, but then some new preacher arrived and now their membership is bigger than ever."

"A *new* guy?" *It couldn't be Driggs*, Francis thought. Have you ever seen him?"

"Only once, at the grocery store. He had a few of his wives with him and a couple of guys who almost seemed like bodyguards. I'll never understand those folks believing what they do. It seems so manipulative."

"That's probably because it *is*," Maggie chimed in.

"What does this new guy look like?"

"Short, skinny, seems a lot younger than Driggs or Jeffs."

It sure didn't sound like Driggs. "Does anyone know anything about him? Where he came from?"

"Francis...remember me? I work at Best Friends...you're the detective. I've got all I can do to keep up with the animals. Maybe the Barlows know something; they'll be in tomorrow if you want to talk to them."

"Sorry, Terri. I'm still upset that Driggs managed to get away. If it's okay with you, I'll talk to them."

"Maggie, is he always like this?" she asked with a smile.

Maggie rubbed his massive shoulder and said, "Yup, he's a pretty focused fella...but he's my guy." As she finished, she punched him in the arm, put her fingers to her lips, and mimed zipping it.

The rest of the evening was spent with Terri, telling tales of the Foundation and the area's local color. They arranged to see the Barlows the following morning and called it a night.

Terri had contacted Abe and John ahead of time, and when Francis, Maggie, and Henry arrived, they were both in the cafeteria. After introducing Maggie, he told them everything that happened on Whidbey Island. They had seen a few things in the national headlines, but most of the details surprised them.

"We know Mullins is dead, but we can't find any clues about Driggs's disappearance. I wondered if you guys had heard anything from anyone you know in Short Creek."

They looked at each other briefly before Abe spoke: "We still have some friends there, but we don't see them often. The last we heard, there was a new Prophet by the name of Adam Swanson. The members seem to be very excited about him."

"Have you seen this Swanson?"

"No, of course not. We're outcasts, and they don't allow us on the property."

"Do you know how long this new guy has been there?"

"No, but I think at least a year or two. We don't hear much from our friends."

Francis felt he was wasting time, but he couldn't help himself. He thanked the two brothers, then said goodbye and thanks to Terri, who promised to visit if she ever got to Whidbey Island.

The trio loaded into Francis's pickup and headed south on Highway 89 toward the turnoff for Colorado City. During the hour-long drive, there was little conversation in the truck, each of the occupants lost in their thoughts about the futility of their inquiries. Henry's panting was the only sound save for the road noise.

Finally, Maggie asked, "Do you think we'll get anywhere, Francis?"

"Probably not, Mags. After we talk to the Hildale cops, we'll call it quits and head to St. George. Snow Canyon's a great hiking spot there; I'd like to show it to you and Henry. After this last attempt, I'll have to accept the bastard's disappeared."

Maggie brightened at this direction, reaching over and squeezing his arm. "That sounds great, Francis. Let's get this over with."

Maggie waited with Henry in the pickup while Francis walked into the same Hildale Police Department he'd visited two years before. The same desk sergeant reacted as he had when he first encountered the big man. Then he recognized him.

"It's you again."

Francis smiled, remembering their first encounter. "Yes, it is. How have you been, Sergeant?"

"Very good, Sir; what can I help you with?" The cop was all business, just like the last time.

"You recall last time I was here looking for Driggs, correct?"

"I do."

"Well, I'm here now doing the same thing. Have you heard anything about him? What's all this about some new leader at the FLDS?"

"About Driggs, Sir, we know as much as you do. He disappeared after all that stuff on Whidbey Island, and we've never heard from him again. That new guy over in Colorado City is a weird dude. He's got a big house and lots of money, but his followers have nothing. They don't seem to care much, though. They do whatever he tells them to."

The money thing got Francis's attention: "He's rich? Where'd he get it from? What does he look like?"

"Nobody knows," he answered. "The guy just shows up, and folks start listening to him. It's like he's some divine being or something. He's got this captivating voice."

"Sorta like Driggs?"

"Yeah...I guess. But he's nothing like Driggs. That guy was short and frumpy, looked like that Costanza guy on TV. This one's a skinny dude, good-looking, maybe a little taller than Driggs. We've checked him out but can't find anything on him. It doesn't bother us as long as he stays over there and doesn't break any laws. Gotta say, though, strange how those folks follow him blindly."

Part of Francis wanted to continue the search, but he felt he was at a dead end, and he knew Maggie had had enough. He thanked the policeman and headed back to his truck. He was with a woman he loved, and for whatever reason, she seemed to feel the same. He tucked the thoughts of Joseph Driggs back into a far corner of his mind, and the three of them headed to Snow Canyon. He'd seen it from a distance. And if the pictures he'd seen of it were anything close to reality, it would be a spectacular afternoon.

237

Forty-Three

I t was mid-November when Francis returned from his trip to southern Utah. We had received postcards from almost everywhere they'd visited. Snow Canyon, Zion, Bryce Canyon, Capitol Reef, and several other parks were now posted on our bulletin board. He was sun-tanned and smiling when he stopped in to report on his findings.

"Looks like you had quite the trip, Buddy." Wally got to him first.

"It was terrific. Those parks are unbelievable...makes you feel pretty insignificant."

I had only visited Zion, but if the others were anything close, I knew what he was talking about. We sat around the conference table and sipped coffee. "Anything on the FLDS or Driggs?" I thought it best to get the cop stuff out of the way before we got sidetracked.

"I hate to admit it, but it was a dead end. The FLDS is stronger than ever—some new guy running things now—but not a sniff about where Driggs is."

"I hear there's even a group near Coupeville," Wally said.

Francis shook his head slowly and said, "I heard that. I think it's only a few families now, mostly women and children, but I guess they're true believers; at least the women are."

The three of us were lost in our thoughts for a few seconds until Francis brightened up and said, "Oh, by the way, Maggie and I got married while we were away."

We both looked at him, stunned by the news, then stood, slapped him on the back, and congratulated him. "Why the secret?" I asked.

"Not a secret, just low profile. We spent a couple of nights in Vegas when we were close by. We saw an ad on TV about how easy it was to get married there, so we said, 'Hey...why not?' and we did it."

"Where are you two going to live?" Wally asked.

"For now, we'll do the same thing we've been doing. When spring comes around, we'll probably look for something near Greenbank. She'll still be close to work and it's only ten minutes from Jake's. Jake's throwing a big bash for us around Christmas; I'll let all of you know as soon as we've got a date."

"That's great news, Francis. We're all thrilled for you."

While Francis was at the Sheriff's Office, Maggie was at Double Bluff Beach. She still had a few days left before returning to work and wanted to see Nancy and Bruno. The cold drizzle ensured the two dogs and the two women had the beach to themselves as they strolled, bundled up, alongside the massive piles of driftwood cast upon the shore by recent storms.

Nancy was overjoyed at the marriage news and promised she'd be at the celebration regardless of the date. The two GSDs could have cared less and were up ahead inspecting an ancient Dungeness crab carcass.

***

The FLDS settlements throughout the country's western half had grown throughout Driggs's tenure. To say they prospered would have been inaccurate. The larger colonies grew most of their food, and many worked for church-owned businesses for little pay. Regardless of their income, they were required to tithe regularly.

Swanson (Driggs) and his trusted lieutenants monitored the church's finances closely, ensuring sufficient income for the hierarchy at the expense of the poorer members of the community. His regular visits to these satellite locales were designed to encourage maximum giving while promising his hapless followers eternal salvation.

With the funds from his diamonds safely deposited offshore, he had complete freedom to mold the church into a money-making enterprise that benefitted only himself and a few chosen ones. *If only Mullins were alive to see this*, he mused.

The only remote parish Driggs had yet to visit was near Coupeville on Whidbey Island. A few of his confidants wondered about this most impoverished outlier and why their leader ignored it.

The incidents on Whidbey Island had left him scarred, in spite of his surgeons' work and the dedication to diet and exercise that had transformed him into another person. The former parishioners he now saw regularly had no inkling of who he was, yet there was still a fear of returning to the island where he almost lost his life and where Mullins had died. He vowed to get past it.

He scheduled a visit shortly before Christmas. It would be the perfect time to remind his island flock of their duty to tithe and how it would cement their place in heaven after they left this earth.

Forty-Four

Three days before the celebration of Francis and Maggie's wedding, I received an email from Julie Houser of the Bellevue Police Department. It said, "Hello, how was I?" and told me to call the manager at the Bellevue Club Hotel. It had been a long time since our visit to the expensive boutique inn, and I couldn't imagine why I should call them. But I did.

The manager was Dan Spurgeon, who had been on the job for three weeks. He started with, "Officer, I'm sorry to have bothered you, but I think we have something that pertains to one of your cases."

I had no idea where this was going, so I said nothing.

"Well...when I took over this position, we did a house cleaning, and we came across something."

"Okay..."

"Our safe here is an old one with lots of small shelves, nooks, and crannies."

"Well...Mr. Spurgeon, that's nice to know."

"And we've found a small package wedged at the very back near the bottom."

"Also good to know."

"And one of our long-time employees says she remembered a couple of years ago talking to one of your deputies about another package addressed to one of our guests...a Hannah Stucki."

Suddenly, the alarm bells went off. "Yes...go ahead, please."

"Well, this one is addressed to her, too. I remember she was the poor woman who was killed on that ferry. I thought you should know about this."

"Thank you very much, Mr. Spurgeon. Could you put it somewhere safe? We'll be down to pick it up in the next couple of days."

"Of course, Sir. Call us when you're coming, and we'll have it ready."

I told Wally about the call and asked him what he thought.

"I don't know. I would have thought they'd have seen it when Kate and I were there. But...I guess if it were really small, it could have slipped behind some stuff. If she sent herself one package, I suppose she could have sent another."

"If it's more of the diamonds she took from Driggs, what's the difference? He's long gone; Mullins and Stucki and the Gleasons are dead. What the hell do we do with diamonds from dead people if that's what it is?"

"Party?"

"Good one, Wally. Whatever it is, I guess we need to pick it up."

"I'll go."

"Nah...you stick around. I'll go tomorrow and take Andie for a little Christmas shopping while we're there." Bellevue was the go-to place for fancy stores and destination shopping. The ferry travel discouraged off-island travel around the holidays but as long as the package needed fetching, I'd score points by offering to take my wife for some retail therapy.

***

Jake Early's massive log ranch was ablaze with Christmas lights. Francis had spent the better part of Thanksgiving week installing them and then reinstalling them after Maggie's input. It was the perfect setting for the holiday bash celebrating Francis and Maggie's marriage.

His wife had become close friends with Nancy Barnett, and the two GSDs were also best pals. That Henry sometimes preferred Maggie bothered Francis only a little, the trade-off being she would be safe anywhere with the shepherd at her side. The two women had taken it upon themselves to organize the preparations for the event.

The day before the party, a trip off-island to Costco and a nearby rental store was necessary to gather food, drink, and place settings for the forty or so people attending.

Francis's buddies from McNeil would all be there, as would most of the island's deputies who weren't on duty. When Terri Millar from Best Friends received an invite, she took a few days off and decided it was a perfect time to visit the funny-shaped island in the middle of Puget Sound. The O'Malleys would also be there, along with many of Jake's associates from the Island County government.

***

Joseph Driggs, aka Adam Swanson, preferred driving his Porsche Cayenne to visit the far-flung FLDS settlements on most of his journeys. It was more comfortable than flying, and those in his flock seemed more attentive when he showed up in the expensive automobile.

He couldn't understand how people with few worldly possessions would idolize a rich man who required them to give what little they had to the church. He guessed his charisma did the trick since he'd long ago shit-canned his beliefs of eternal salvation. These days, it was all about his high from manipulating his minions.

With still some concern about his visit to the Whidbey outpost, he decided to make the trip alone. If he pushed it, it was a two-day drive, and he'd rather not have to interact with anyone along the way.

It was late afternoon on the second day, and the drive through Snoqualmie Pass was brutal. At three thousand feet above sea level, the rain that constantly pelted the Puget Sound region in the winter fell as snow through the mountain pass. And, on this day, there was plenty of it. The forecast was for one to two feet of the stuff in the Cascades, and Driggs began questioning his decision to make the trip in two days. With daylight gone at four o'clock and the heavy white snow falling at four inches per hour, visibility was reduced to only seeing the taillights of the car in front of him.

The Cayenne was four-wheel drive, which helped, but Driggs was from the Southwest, where snow was only something from the movies. Speeds had disintegrated to twenty-five miles per hour, and the frequent roar of convoys of snow plows had the Prophet almost hyperventilating. If the climb to the summit was tedious, the downhill portion leading to the greater Seattle Region was downright death-defying. Speeds increased while spacing between vehicles decreased. More than once, he overcorrected a skid, leading to blasts of horns from nearby cars and trucks.

The snow then unexpectedly turned to sleet and then rain. When he saw the North Bend sign, the pavement was bare and wet. All that was left was to retrace his journey from two years ago and take the 405 north to the Mukilteo Speedway and then the ferry terminal. If the traffic cooperated, he'd make the seven o'clock sailing.

***

Maggie and Nancy took Francis's truck. The dogs took up all the space in the crew cab, and thankfully, the cargo cover protected everything they had to pick up. It was always iffy taking the ferry, especially over the holidays, but it couldn't be helped. They first stopped at the rental place to collect the glassware and dinnerware and then went to Costco.

The store was teeming with customers picking up platters of food, and the booze department was elbow to elbow. It appeared other folks might also be entertaining over the next few days.

"Remind me never to come here again," Maggie shouted to Nancy to be heard among the clamor.

Nancy laughed and continued pushing the gigantic grocery cart against the flow of customers. "Just a couple more things, and then we're outta here, Mags."

They skated by the receipt checker in record time, Maggie thinking the hubbub was even getting to them. Then, they began the journey through the cold drizzle across acres of parking, finally arriving at the pickup truck with the steamed-up cab.

"Looks like the boys were enjoying themselves," Maggie said, lowering the windows to dispel the musky odor from the frisky shepherds despite the rain. "Let's let the cab air out for a minute."

After loading everything into the bed and pulling the cover closed, they parked the cart and made their way to the Mukilteo Speedway. It was seven o'clock.

***

We left for Bellevue, taking the nine a.m. boat. Traffic was light going to the mainland, while the lines coming to the island were already long. Even though a number of those living on the island left during the winter, many returned for the Christmas holidays, bringing close and not-so-close relatives with them. I was afraid the wait for the ferry on our return trip would be lengthy.

We arrived at the Bellevue Club Hotel a little after ten, told the front desk attendant our names, and asked to see the manager. A slender man in his forties came around the corner almost immediately, carrying a small brown package.

"You must be Deputy Wilkie."

"I am, and this is my wife, Andie."

"Nice to meet you both. I apologize that it's taken this long to get this to you, but we only just came across it."

I accepted the package and said, "Not your fault, certainly. We will do our best to get this to Ms. Stucki's next of kin. The person responsible for her death has disappeared, and, as of now, there are no leads as to his whereabouts. If it's any consolation, I doubt whether getting this sooner would have made any difference."

"Thank you; it relieves a little of the guilt."

We said goodbye and wished him well in the new year. The center of the shopping universe was only a few blocks away, but once we were seated in the car, Andie said, "Aren't you going to open it?"

"It's evidence."

"Of what? Driggs is gone, Hannah is dead, and if anyone deserves what's in there, it's her mother if she's still around."

I thought back to our Zoom session with Sparks and his sister, who had raised Hannah. "Okay...let's take a look."

The package was barely big enough to write the hotel address on, but enough tape secured it to make opening it difficult. Finally, resorting to an X-Acto knife from my console, I cut away enough of the packing tape to expose a tiny cloth pouch, no bigger than a teabag. I could feel the stones before I poured them into my hand. There had to be more than a dozen of them, all about the size of a pencil eraser.

Andie gasped, "Holy shit Roger. They're diamonds...and they're huge."

I only nodded my agreement. It was as I expected. "For some reason, Hannah Stucki sent herself two packages. She probably wondered where the second one was, but with Driggs and Mullins on her trail, she took what they gave her and went to find Francis."

"She must have been scared to death at the end."

"Yeah...I'm sure she was, Andie." I reached over and squeezed her hand. "We'll do our best to get these to her mother if she's still around. I'll have Francis get in touch with Sparks."

I started the ignition, and we drove to Bellevue Square to hopefully brighten our spirits.

***

Terri Millar was raised in Dallas, Texas, the second of three daughters born to a radiologist father and a stay-at-home mom. She did all the things that children of privileged families do--until the ninth grade.

On her way home from school, she took a different route than usual and passed a dilapidated residence with all manner of refuse scattered about the chain-linked yard. Not used to seeing displays of poverty, she couldn't avert her eyes. Then she heard something like a child's cry.

Behind a stack of worn tires, the roof of a plywood doghouse peeked out. It was where the cry came from. She glanced around, seeing an empty driveway and no sign of anyone. Backtracking to the small gate that served as the entrance to the yard, she cautiously pushed it open. The squeak from the rusted hinges startled her, and she paused, but only briefly.

She walked quietly to the doghouse, where a scruffy mutt, some Pitbull mix, lay in the dirt, a heavy chain around his neck. He tried to stand and bark, but all that came out was a loud croak. The animal's ribs were showing, and it was clear he was malnourished. There were no food or water bowls anywhere.

She'd been told how vicious these dogs could be, but looking at this poor thing, it was hard to imagine. She walked closer and spoke in comforting tones, extending her hand. The dog shied away, probably fearing punishment, she thought.

Getting as close as she dared, she managed to pet his head, and he allowed it. Still talking soothingly, she unclipped the thick steel collar that had worn away the fur at his neck. He stood, moved closer to her, and leaned against her. She couldn't stop her tears.

She found a length of rope in one of the trash piles and tied it loosely around his neck. "C'mon, buddy, we're getting out of here, and you're coming home with me." It was her first experience seeing the damage a human could do to a defenseless animal and her first rescue. It wouldn't be her last.

It took threats of leaving home for her parents to allow the dog to stay with them. She later found out that the house she rescued Rodney from —his new name—was abandoned, and the former owner was now incarcerated somewhere. Because of his mistreatment, it took months of working daily with him before he would trust anyone but Terri. But, eventually, he became a friendly, well-mannered companion. It wasn't until ten years later that he passed away.

By then, Terri was an intern at Best Friends, and she'd found her calling. And now, she was going to a party celebrating a couple who owned one of her favorites.

Thinking she'd stay on the island for a few days to see the sights, she rented a car at Paine Field and was now parked on the hill, waiting almost three-quarters of a mile from the terminal. She was glad Francis had insisted she stay at Jake's when he heard she was coming. She'd call to let him know she'd be a little late.

Forty-Five

The 405 north was a slog with holiday traffic. Driggs's relief after making it through the snow-covered pass was replaced by impatience at the stop-and-go traffic. He settled down when he finally reached the 525 leading to the terminal. That was until he got to the backup ferry line on the hill. He couldn't believe this many people could be going to this stupid little island.

He dutifully got in the single file line and waited. His frustration only mounted as the line moved only sporadically. He'd wait with the engine running for several minutes with no forward progress, then finally shut it off, only to have to start it again to move another hundred feet. *How did people do this*, he wondered.

It was seven forty-five by the time he reached the toll booths where the attendant said he'd likely make the eight-thirty boat, the *Tokitae*. He ended up being the first vehicle in lane number one. After shutting the Cayenne down, he reclined his seat and planned to snooze until it was time to load.

***

"We should have done this earlier; now we have to wait in line with all the amateurs." The "amateurs" Maggie referred to were those travelers who rarely took the ferry and often were out of their comfort zone when following the peculiar signs and protocols necessary for herding over three thousand vehicles a day across the Saratoga Passage. The confusion of these infrequent ferry riders often contributed to the long waits, especially over the holidays.

"I'm calling Francis to let him know we'll be late." His line was busy, so she disconnected. He'd see her number.

Sure enough, a few minutes later, he returned the call. "Hey, Mags, what's up?"

"The goddamn ferry line, that's what's up."

"Yeah...well, holidays. Hey, where are you?"

"We're in line just before the bridge. I'm guessing we'll make the eight-thirty." They were close to the overpass that spanned the train tracks alongside the ferry terminal.

"I just spoke to Terri. She's gotta be somewhere near you. She called to say she'd be late."

"Let me have her number, Francis. We can hook up once we're in the holding lot if she's nearby. I know she'd love to see Henry, and I'll bet Bruno, too."

Maggie called as soon as she signed off and discovered Terri was only a few cars ahead of them in line. "We're in Francis's truck, Terri. Once we're parked in the lot, come on over."

Maggie's truck and Terri's rental ended up midway in lane number one, separated by only a few cars. It was only minutes until she knocked on the window, startling the two German Shepherds. As expected, fierce barking ensued, and then Henry noticed who the visitor was. Maggie climbed down from the truck amidst Bruno's continued barking and hugged Terri.

"Great to see you, Terri; Francis is thrilled you could make it. That's Nancy in shotgun, and I think you know this big boy." Henry began climbing over the driver's seat to get to his former pack leader while Bruno quieted, finally aware that the intruder was known by his pal.

"Who's this handsome fellow with you?" Terri asked, opening the rear door and letting Henry jump on her.

"That's Bruno," Nancy answered, "He's my neighbor's dog, but they're gone a lot, so I take care of him."

"He's a beauty," Terry said, reaching across and ruffling Bruno's fur.

While they waited for the arriving *Tokitae* to disembark, the three women stood in the drizzle with the rear door open, petting the two GSDs and catching up on each other's lives. Maggie could see that Nancy and Terri had taken an instant liking to each other.

The announcement was made for all passengers to return to their vehicles to prepare for boarding, and the three women said they'd see each other at Jake's place.

***

The slap on his hood startled him. Driggs had crashed, and the terminal attendant wanted him to get his ass moving. They were loading.

He was first in line for this because he had barely missed the eight o'clock sailing. Hurriedly starting the vehicle, he followed the loading attendant's instructions until he reached the cavernous lower deck. Another orange-vested ferry employee sternly pointed to the center aisle and aggressively waved him to the front of the boat. He pulled ahead toward yet another deckhand who impatiently motioned for him to pull forward, almost to the point of hitting him. He quickly held up both hands in a stopping motion, threw a heavy wooden chock under his right tire, and moved behind him to guide the next vehicle.

He turned the engine off and sat there, the drizzle rapidly obscuring his vision of the pitch-dark waters of the Saratoga Passage.

***

The seasoned lot attendants easily loaded 144 vehicles in less than fifteen minutes. It might have been the busy holiday season, but keeping the trips on schedule was critical.

Terri's car ended up on the lower deck in the right lane, and Maggie and Nancy were parked on the left, almost even with her. In between, in the center, was an Amazon van packed with goodies for the next morning's delivery.

Once the truck's engine was turned off, the only sound in the cab was the rapid panting of two dogs, the humidity instantly steaming up the windows.

"Let's get these two out to stretch their legs once we get underway," Nancy suggested.

"Good idea. We can walk over to Terri's car, and maybe the dog breath will dissipate a little." They both chuckled at this and waited until the *Tokitae* started moving.

***

I wasn't prepared for how bad holiday traffic could be in the Seattle area. Years on the island had insulated me from the increased number of cars on the road. By the time we finally got on the freeway in Bellevue, it was seven o'clock, and we still had to drive to Mukilteo.

Rather than take the police cruiser, we were driving my three-year-old Explorer. I began to regret the choice because, at least in the cruiser, most drivers would see the police vehicle and move aside, lights and sirens or not. It was eight-fifteen when we crested the hill at the top of the speedway and saw the red backup lights of the long line ahead of us.

"Is this one of those times, Roger?" Andie asked.

I felt guilty as hell, but I nodded and said, "You bet it is."

I swung out to the left of the line, drove down the hill, and turned right to the toll booths, cutting a dozen cars off. As soon as one of the booths was empty, I drove to the window and flashed my deputy's badge, saying to the attendant, "Sorry, but I've got to get back to the island in a hurry."

The young woman nodded knowingly, raised the boom gate, and said, "No problem, Deputy; I've heard about Roger Wilkie, and we owe you at least this much."

I drove to the head of the now vacant lane one, where the orange vest waved me to the left and onto the *Tokitae*, the last vehicle on. I turned the engine off and glanced at my smiling wife.

"What?" I asked.

"Just thinking how many more people appreciate your work than you know. I know you felt guilty about using the badge, but maybe they like doing it for you."

I leaned over and kissed her, thankful I was so lucky.

***

The thundering diesels ratcheted up a notch, and the four-thousand-ton marvel of marine engineering lumbered away from the dock, beginning the fifteen-minute crossing to Clinton on Whidbey Island.

As soon as the ferry moved, Maggie and Nancy leashed the two dogs and weaved their way through the lanes to Terri's car. She hopped out when she saw them. The wind howling through the gigantic lower deck was strong enough for them to tighten their neck scarves and tug down their hats as they turned toward the front end of the boat.

***

Still shaken by the lot attendant's abrupt thump on his hood, Driggs realized he needed to use the restroom badly. He'd been in his car for six hours straight and was exhausted.

Because he was the first car in the center lane, he was forward of every other vehicle on the boat, and until he tried to open the door, he hadn't realized the force of the oncoming wind. After his first attempt failed, he zipped up his puffy jacket and, this time, put his shoulder into forcing the door open.

With the wind howling, he climbed out, holding the door, which slammed shut behind him. After the stagnant air in his car, the salty, cold, drizzly thirty-knot wind was refreshing. He breathed in several gulps of the sea air.

***

Bruno suddenly stopped as the three women moved toward the front end of the *Tokitae*. Henry and the women were forced to stop as well, all wondering what was happening. He held his nose high and sniffed nonstop while turning his head from side to side.

He stood instantly at attention, and a low guttural growl emerged from deep in his lungs. Nancy was shocked at the reaction, "I've never seen him like this she said."

Henry mimicked Bruno's reaction, and he, too, seemed to recognize something. Now, both dogs were laser-focused on movement near the front of the car deck. Without warning, Bruno jerked the leash from Nancy and bolted forward.

Stunned by both dogs, Maggie began to wrap Henry's leash tighter, but it was too late. He, too, broke away and raced behind Bruno. All three women shouted, imploring the dogs to stop, but they weren't listening.

***

Facing the wind, the FLDS leader thought he heard someone yelling, but he paid no attention. It was only when he heard a low growl and the sound of strong claws clacking on the steel deck that he turned around.

Bruno attacked first, grabbing Driggs's calf in a ferocious grip, his teeth instantly slicing through the pant leg, through the soft flesh, and into bone. *This was the one with the gun who had scared him and killed his friend. His smell was the same; he would not get away.*

Driggs tumbled to the deck just as Henry arrived. *This man's smell was always mixed with the man who fell off the bridge and tried to hurt his pack leaders. He was in the car, by the bridge.* He chomped into his shoulder with as much force as he could. Blood was everywhere, and people were screaming. Driggs flailed wildly, punching Henry in the stomach and head while shaking his wounded leg to get it away from Bruno.

One of the punches stunned Henry, who let go to catch his breath. Driggs pulled himself up and moved in front of his beautiful silver Cayenne with Bruno still attached to his leg. He slipped on the bloody deck and crawled through the lashing straps toward the front of the boat, where the waves splashed over the deck.

Driggs kicked Bruno solidly in the head with his good leg, forcing him to release his jaws. Now, he stood only feet from the edge of the deck, with both dogs glaring at him, their teeth bared and their growling fearsome. He saw three women running toward him, hoping they might call off the savage animals.

Then, the *Tokitae* slammed into a three-foot-diameter fir log that the Passage had reclaimed during high tide. The heavy boats were used to encountering such floating debris, and while they rarely caused any serious damage, one this massive caused the front end to dip a few feet. The boat now tipped slightly to the front, and the combination of salt water and blood from his wounds caused The Prophet to slip into the freezing waters of Puget Sound.

By the time he had traveled three hundred seventy feet under the ferry and passed through two enormous Rolls-Royce Controllable-Pitch four-blade propellers, the polygamous leader was fish-food.

Forty-Six

From my position on the aft end of the *Tokitae*, I could hear voices coming from somewhere forward. A huge shudder went through the ferry like we crashed into something. I told Andie to wait in the car while I took a look.

I hustled forward, dodging other folks getting out of their vehicles to see what all the fuss was about. Several deckhands began yelling, "Man overboard," and by the time I'd arrived at the scene, the ferry had begun the Williamson turn.

It took a few seconds because of the shouting and confusion at the front of the lower deck, but I finally recognized Maggie, Nancy, and the two German Shepherds standing by with a third woman. They waved me over.

"What happened?" I shouted to be heard above the engines.

They told me the two dogs unexpectedly attacked a passenger, and he fell off the boat. It was clear the three of them were in shock. I suggested they return the dogs to the truck, and we go upstairs to discuss it.

By the time we arrived at the passenger deck, the ferry had completed the turn and was now using searchlights to attempt to locate the unfortunate passenger. I was surprised to see only Nancy and the third woman seated.

"Where's Maggie?"

"She said she had to do something; it would only take a minute. This is Terri Millar, by the way, a friend of Francis and Maggie's from Best Friends."

I'd heard of the sanctuary from Francis; we shook hands.

Maggie arrived just as Danny Collins hurriedly walked past, surely on his way to investigate conditions on the lower deck personally.

Seeing us, he stopped abruptly. "What is it?" Was all he said.

I told him we were just now going over it and asked if he'd like to sit and listen. He said his first mate could handle things briefly as he sat.

Maggie began: "Both dogs went after this poor man. I never saw anything like it. We were getting some fresh air and first Bruno, then Henry seemed to catch a scent. They bolted so fast we couldn't hold them. By the time we got there, he had already slipped off the front of the deck."

"That's it?" I said, "The dogs attacked the guy for no reason?"

The women looked at each other, and all three nodded. I looked at Terri and asked, "How about you, Terri? Ever see something like this at your organization?"

"No...not really. Sure, we get some dogs that have been mistreated and are fearful of everything, but an unprovoked attack like this? Never that I can recall."

We were interrupted by a squawk on Danny's Radio. He walked away a few feet and held up a finger, telling us to wait. He returned after a few seconds and a couple of grunts on the radio . "We're getting back underway. We marked the area for the Coast Guard, but they're not gonna get anything. Jeff thought he saw part of an arm, but then it went back under. If this guy traveled under the boat and through the props, there wouldn't be much left of him.

"Rog, will you take over the investigation? I mean, you're right here and all."

I told him I would and then told the women to return to their vehicles. When Terri left first, I spoke with Maggie and Nancy: "When we get to the island, we'll have to quarantine Bruno and Henry until we can figure this out. The state has some strict laws about when a dog causes a person's death. I think WAIF is your best bet for the next few days."

They looked at each other, both close to tears, then nodded they understood, and left for their truck. I called Andie and told her what was happening and that disembarking might take some time. Then, I had a second thought and walked by Maggie's truck on the way to the scene.

The two women sat in front, lost in their thoughts, while the dogs lay peacefully in the back. Maggie lowered the window when she saw me.

"I know this is a bad time, Mags, but can you give me a hand?"

"Of course," she said, ever the trooper.

The sea spray had washed whatever blood was on the deck away, and there was little we could do but try to identify who the unfortunate passenger was. The

Cayenne was unlocked, so we slipped on gloves and looked for anything to help us.

Maggie found it in the glove compartment. "The car is registered to an Adam Swanson in Arizona," she announced.

I thought it a little strange that a single man from Arizona would visit the island over the holidays, but he might have relatives. Then, I had a tiny, fleeting sense of recognizing the name, but it disappeared.

I called Wally and told him what had happened. I said we needed a tow truck ready to get the car to Coupeville as soon as we docked and to check out who this guy was. He said he'd get it done, and I knew he would.

Maggie returned to the pickup. She said she had to call Francis to fill him in and was dreading it. I felt for her.

Forty-Seven

T he next day should have been one of joy and happiness for the celebration of Francis and Maggie's marriage, but the Early household was far from it. Even though she was too close to things, Maggie was in Coupeville for the morning to help process the car.

Nancy, crushed by the fact Bruno acted while he was her responsibility, took up Francis's offer to spend the night at their place. She and Terri sat at the kitchen table, picking at scones and drinking coffee.

The dogs were at WAIF in Coupeville, and nobody could understand what had triggered the attack. For their part, Bruno and Henry, even though the smells at the agency were overwhelming, picked up a faint scent of the man from the boat yesterday. They missed their people but were confident they'd see them again. At least they had each other.

***

I had just walked into the station when Wally accosted me: "What?" I asked. "What's so important it can't wait until I have my first cup?"

"The guy who was killed," he said. "You know who he was?"

"No...that's why I told you to find out. Did you?"

"Yup, and if you're gonna be snotty about it, I won't tell you."

"Not the time, Buddy.... not the time."

"Okay...okay, listen up. This guy, Adam Swanson, is the goddamn leader of the FLDS in Colorado City."

Holy shit, that's where I'd heard the name. "Everything seems to lead back to that group, Wally...everything."

"Yup...I only wish it were Driggs."

"Me too, but it seems, other than being the Grand Poobah of that group, this was just a guy."

When the phone rang, it startled both of us. Bruce was out, so I picked it up. It was Maggie. "Hey, Mags, shouldn't you be getting ready for the big bash?"

"I couldn't. I came into work to check out the Swanson's car and do some other stuff."

"I'm not surprised...by the way, guess who the guy was."

"Tell me."

I told her, but when she wasn't surprised, I suspected she knew something I didn't. "You knew he was the head dude at the FLDS?"

"No...but we found out some other stuff."

"Tell me."

"We checked the car for fingerprints, you know...just for the hell of it."

"Um...yeah, so?"

"There weren't any...none, zero, zip...nada."

"What? How's that possible?"

"Only if the guy didn't have any."

"Is that a thing?" I asked.

"I've never come across it, but I've heard that one can get skin grafts from some other place on the body for a price."

"The only reason anyone would do that is if they had something to hide...right?"

"Right. You know what else?"

"C'mon...just tell me."

"While you met Nancy and Terri on the passenger deck, I grabbed a baggie and scraped up some of the blood from the deck, where the dogs attacked the guy."

I didn't say a word; I just let her talk.

"And...I ran a DNA screen on it."

"How does that help? I mean, it's only good if there's something to compare it to, Right?"

"Right…and I do. You remember the crime scene where Barnett was killed?"

"Yes."

"Cora bagged some blood from the garden shed that was nowhere near Barnett's body. It matched the blood on some paper towels in the Tomlinson house. The DNA from those samples matches the blood from the deck of the *Tokitae*."

I tried to grasp what it all meant.

"You there?"

"Are you telling me this was either Driggs or Mullins?"

"It's Driggs, you idiot, Mullins is dead. And now so is that goddamn sonofabitch who caused all this. Bruno and Henry knew who it was…*that's* why they went after him."

Still struggling to align all the pieces, I forgot to say anything.

"Rog…you got all that, right?"

"Yeah…yeah, it's finally dawning on me that we can put this whole episode to bed, thanks to you, Maggie."

"Not just me. You, Cora, Francis, Nancy, Wally, Terri, and Bruce…but mostly Bruno and Henry. They're the real heroes. If not for their sniffers, that asshole would still be living the high life."

"Have you told Francis all this?"

"Of course."

"Before your hard-working Deputy Investigator?"

"He's my hubby…what do *you* think? What I didn't tell him, though, was that I talked to Tom Davis about the dogs, and he's lifted the quarantine. I'm bringing them to the party. See you at three."

After she hung up on me, I sat there, still absorbing the news. I'd forgotten about Wally, who, although he only heard my side of the conversation, had put most of it together.

"Swanson was Driggs, right?"

"He was, yes," I told him all the parts he'd missed, and when I was through, he sat there shaking his head."

"So, the dogs are the stars."

"Yup…without them, Driggs would have gotten away with everything."

"He did all that work to change his appearance, erased his fingerprints, and, in the end, a couple of German Shepherds saw through the whole thing. Makes you wish you could smell like that...almost."

I could tell we were done with the important stuff, so I said goodbye, and I'd see him at the party.

"Okay, Boss. There are a few things here I'd like to clean up. I'll see you there."

Forty-Eight

By four-thirty, all the guests had arrived. News of who was killed on the *Tokitae* the previous evening had spread as only things *can* spread on Whidbey Island—like wildfire.

Maggie was late, but most attributed that to her duties as ME and the disposition of her current case. Although still subdued over the dogs quarantined at WAIF, Francis told me he felt they'd be freed in due course. I kept quiet.

After a few cocktails, most guests were cheerful as they congratulated Francis, but everyone wanted to know where Maggie was. Jake, whom I had given a heads-up, finally heard the doorbell amidst the laughter and tinkling of glassware.

As soon as he swung the massive door open, two rambunctious and happy German Shepherds crashed the party. Maggie trailed them, allowing them their moment of glory. Amongst the cheers and handclapping, I saw Francis tear up at the sight of Henry, then lose it completely when his bride entered the room. They embraced while the guests clapped even louder, and the two dogs danced around them.

Things eventually settled down. While the food was served and the dogs fed, the cacophony subsided somewhat, and I saw Wally slip into the room. I'd seen and chatted with Kate earlier but completely forgotten about him. Now, I wondered what he'd been up to.

While Kate gave him a peck on the cheek, he motioned me over to a quiet corner. He also got Maggie and Francis's attention, and I could tell he was bursting at the seams to tell us something.

"Guess what?"

"TELL US, Wally," the four of us said in unison.

"Okay...okay. I wondered about that no fingerprint thing with Driggs and how, for two years, no one ever recognized him."

Nobody said anything, so he continued: "So I thought he had to have plastic surgery...right? Anyway...so where do most people get facelifts and stuff?"

We knew he'd eventually get to it if we didn't talk.

"Okay...Palm Springs, right?"

I couldn't take it anymore, "Wally...would you please get to the point?"

"Sure...okay. So I thought if he had all this work done, he'd have to stay somewhere for a while, you know, to recuperate. Anyway...I checked all the big hotels there, you know, cuz he'd want to keep a low profile for a Swanson, and guess what?"

"Wally..."

"The Ritz-Carleton had an Adam Swanson stay with them for over a month back when Driggs disappeared. I checked with Sparks—Francis's buddy—and he told me he'd heard of a clinic there that could give a guy a whole new look. I passed the info on to the FBI office, who told me they knew of the clinic and had it under observation for a while. Something about offshore accounts or something. There you have it! Case closed, my friends!"

We all clapped and patted Wally on the back. Kate followed up with a big hug and a kiss, then held him apart and said, "My Hero," loud enough for all to hear.

I was a lucky guy. I had great friends, a wonderful wife, and a superb partner, and I lived on Whidbey Island.

☐

<u>**Author's Notes**</u>

Ferry Tails is a work of fiction. While there are factual elements about some of the places in this story, the characters are fictional, and any similarities to anyone, living or dead, are purely coincidental. Since there are only a finite number of names in the world, it's likely that some I've used might have been used for real people.

The Washington State Ferry System is a lifeline for those in the Pacific Northwest who are lucky enough to live on one of the islands they serve. They are also a mandatory stop for tourists visiting the area. Most of the facts about the system in this story are accurate, although I may have fudged a few. The employees who operate the boats and terminals and mostly keep things on schedule, despite passengers and vehicles not always being where they should be, are dedicated, well-trained, and as courteous as possible given the difficult circumstances they occasionally find themselves in.

The FLDS splintered from the Church of Jesus Christ of Latter-day Saints in the early 20th century after the LDS outlawed polygamy. To this day, there are still settlements scattered throughout the country, most notably in Colorado City, AZ. It is said Warren Jeffs, from his prison cell, still runs the faction. The YFZ Ranch in Texas was one of the more well-known settlements.

The depiction of Best Friends Animal Society in Kanab is accurate. They are the largest and best at what they do. It's worth a visit if you're ever near the area.

The Williamson Turn is a maneuver ships use to return to a previous position when a person has fallen overboard. It is named after John Williamson, who first used it in 1943, and is a widely accepted tactic in the maritime community.

The GSDs in this story are, of course, made up. What is not fictional, however, is their uncanny sense of smell, their loyalty to their pack, and their incredible intuitiveness.

About the Author

Ted's observations and stories are formed by his stint in the Army, his sales, marketing, and entrepreneurial activities, and his life growing up as one of nine siblings in a typical Irish Catholic family.

Starting in New England he managed to find his way to the Pacific Northwest where he has lived for over three decades. He now lives on an island in the middle of Puget Sound with his wife and trusted GSD, Emma.

Feel free to reach out with any questions or comments.
ted@tedmulcahey.com

Also by Ted Mulcahey

Bearied Treasure
Teed Up for Terror
Little Dirt Road
Juiced
Punch Down
Tanks
Lone Lake Road